DREAM LOVER

Faced with the inexplicable change in Mr. MacCairn's behavior, Anne wasn't certain how to respond. This was a side of her host she'd never seen before, but instead of relieving her, it filled her with a mounting sense of alarm. Perhaps it would be wisest to go.

"If Father is safe, then I believe I shall return to my room," she said, inching cautiously back from him. "Good night, Mr. MacCairn, I—"

"Ruairdh," he interrupted, his lips curving in a smile. "It is my given name, and as we are alone I see no reason why you shouldn't make use of it. Indeed, it would please me if you did so."

The odd sense of intuition Anne had come to rely upon sounded a clarion warning. "I do not believe that would be proper, sir," she prevaricated, aware again of their isolation.

His smile deepened. "And are you always proper, then, *leannan?*" he asked, his voice a husky purr.

Anne felt the color leave her face. "W-what did you say?"

"Leannan," he repeated, clearly amused by her reaction. "'Tis a Gaelic word, and not so scandalous as you seem to think. Shall I tell you what it means?" He reached out a powerful hand for her. Anne stumbled back, disbelief making her shake. *Leannan* was the word her dream lover whispered to her; a word she'd dismissed as imaginary. But if it was real, what else might be real?

The Shadowing

Joan Overfield

LOVE SPELL NEW YORK CITY

This book is dedicated to Trudy Doolittle,
A grand pal and an even grander lady.

A LOVE SPELL BOOK®

February 2002

Published by

Dorchester Publishing Co., Inc.
276 Fifth Avenue
New York, NY 10001

ISBN 0-505-52458-9

Printed in the United States of America.

Visit us on the web at www.dorchesterpub.com.

The Shadowing

Prologue

Castle MacCairn, Scotland, 1425

It was a day for death. Even though it was late spring, the sky was so dark a gray as to be nearly black, and the sullen rain burned with the fierce sting of sleet and ice. In the courtyard of the castle a bitter wind wailed amongst the stone buildings, sounding like the howl of a wolf. Already nervous men paused in their grisly task to glance furtively about them, and several made the sign of the cross.

" 'Tis an omen," one of the men muttered, pulling his plaid tighter about him. "It means we kill an innocent man."

"Or 'tis the work of the devil trying to save one of his own," another shot back, tying the bundle of dry wood with an angry yank. "You were no' there to hear the charges read, nor to mark the answers that were given. The priest freely admits his guilt. He bragged of his deeds, taunting us with his power and daring us to do our worst. He is a witch, and so must burn. 'Tis God's will."

There was no more talk after that, only a grim silence as the pyre was built ever higher. The witch-hunters from faraway York who'd come to hear the case against the priest instructed that only the greenest wood be used, but the laird had stood against them. For all his fierce reputation as a warrior, Aonghas MacCairn was a compassionate man, and he'd not allow even a witch to suffer needlessly. The flames would do their work, but with the pyre constructed as it was, they would do that work quickly.

At the appointed time the heretic was led out from his cell. Other men might have stumbled with fear when faced with the spectacle of the stake, but the priest walked so calmly he might have been walking to the vespers he'd mocked with his foul ceremonies. He remained silent as the charges of blasphemy, sorcery, and murder were read against him, his proud, cruel face showing no emotion. When offered a final chance to renounce his black arts and embrace the true faith, he laughed, mocking the other priests even as he was lashed to the stake.

The moment had come, and the executioner lifted the torch high. It was only then that the priest began struggling, screaming and cursing like the demon many thought him. He vilified the other priests, shouting his blasphemous words with contemptuous glee. Then his gaze fell upon the laird, and it wasn't madness that made his eyes burn with an unholy brightness, but a cold, black hatred.

"You might think yourself the victor, laird, but the true victory is mine!" he jeered, straining against the ropes binding him to the stake. "I have cast my spell, and you and all who come after you will suffer as you have made me suffer!"

"He's mad," Aonghas said, folding his arms across his chest and meeting the witch's malevolent glare implacably. "Do what must be done, and let it be ended."

"It will never be ended!" the priest screamed, fighting wildly. "So long as a MacCairn lives, it will never be ended! You call me mad, but madness will be your destiny. In madness I will come to you, and in madness you shall die! Do you hear me, laird? I curse you! In mighty Satan's name, I curse you! The prize is mine! The prize is mine!"

At that moment the torch was tossed on the pyre, and the seasoned wood caught fire with a deafening roar. The pyre was instantly engulfed in flames, and the sound of it was dreadful to hear. More dreadful still was the sound coming from the heart of the blaze, a sound that rose with the foul smoke to fill the courtyard—not the screams of agony and death one might have expected, nor even more curses from the doomed witch. It was laughter that rang across the cobblestones—laughter filled with malice and triumph, echoing louder and louder until it drowned out even the roar of the consuming inferno.

Chapter One

Castle MacCairn, Scotland, 1851

She knew this place. She knew every turret, every chamber. She knew the feel of the sharp stones in the courtyard beneath her feet, and the ghostly smell of old fires hanging in the air of the great chamber. She even knew the view from the north tower, when the moon was full and its milky white light washed over the moors. She knew this place. And she was seeing it for the first time today.

Anne Garthwicke sat in the opulent carriage, her soft gray eyes troubled as she gazed up at the moss-covered stones of the ancient castle. This wasn't the first time she'd experienced this disquieting sense of recognition, but never had she experienced it so strongly. It was as if she'd been waiting her whole life to gaze upon this keep, or as if the castle itself had somehow been waiting for her. The thought had her shivering, and she drew the folds of her traveling cloak closer about her.

"Anne?" From the seat opposite her, her father turned his head, the thick lenses of his spectacles flashing in the watery sunlight. "What are you seeing? Has the castle come into view?"

"Only just, Papa," she said, shaking off her foolish fancies. "And it's just as Mr. MacCairn's solicitor said it would be. Norman, for the better part, with several towers and battlements—"

"Yes, yes, that is all very good," her father interrupted with an irritated wave of his hand. "But you know what I mean. What does the castle *look* like? Describe it to me."

Anne felt a stab of pain at the petulant demand. Prior to his sight having failed him, her father had been the most loving of parents, patiently teaching her all he knew of ancient armaments. Now he was often brooding and critical, his moods increasingly mercurial. That was why she was so anxious. This would be his last position, and if all went well his reputation as England's premier expert on antiquities would be secured. They'd retire at last to the country, where he would be free to complete the book he had always talked of writing.

"Anne! Answer me!"

Anne tensed at his sharp tones, clenching her jaw to hold back an impatient remark of her own. She truly loved her father, and it grieved her to see him struggling so with his limited abilities, but she was finding it more and more difficult to deal with his bouts of temper. She gave herself a few moments to compose herself, and glanced once more out the window of the carriage.

As they climbed farther up the steep hill, the castle grew larger and even more ominous. She shivered again, wondering if she might have taken a chill. "The castle is round, with crenellated walls and towers," she began in the cool, concise tones she knew he demanded. "Two of the towers look to be replacements, and there are faint burn marks to the right of the portcullis."

Her father nodded, committing her description to memory. "What else? What impression does the castle give as one approaches it?"

Evil. The word flashed unbidden in Anne's mind, but she held her tongue, imagining her father's response to such a description. He'd likely scold her for being a silly female, and even though she knew he'd later regret the harsh words, she wasn't certain she could bear hearing them.

"It gives the impression of great age and power," she said instead, deciding it was also the truth. "Mr. MacCairn should have no trouble selling it, if that is his intention."

"He hasn't said, but why else should he send for me?" her father asked with an indifferent shrug. "He wants us to examine and catalog the castle's contents. I doubt he'd do so without cause."

A ripple of unease shivered through Anne at the observation. Most of the men who employed her father's services were dilettante lords driven by their excesses to sell off what possessions they could. Doubtlessly Mr. MacCairn found himself in similar circumstances, and was doing what was necessary to survive. It was understandable, even acceptable, and yet it seemed wrong that the castle should pass from the care of a MacCairn and into the hands of a stranger.

Even as the thought was forming, the carriage was rumbling through the narrow gateway and into the cobblestone courtyard. Servants in rough-spun wool came dashing up to them, and knowing what was expected, Anne turned once more to her father.

"There are several people in the courtyard, but I don't see anyone who might be Mr. MacCairn," she said, gathering up the gloves and bonnet she'd discarded earlier. "An older man is approaching. I believe he is the butler."

She scarcely had time to settle the bonnet on her dark gold hair before the carriage door was flung open, and an older man dressed in somber tones of black and white was helping her from the carriage.

"I am Mr. Angley, the laird's steward," he said, greeting them with a low bow. "I bid you welcome to Castle MacCairn."

"Thank you, Mr. Angley." Her father folded his fingers around Anne's gloved hand and carried it to the crook of his arm. The gesture looked like one of protection, but in truth it was so Anne could guide him with no one being the wiser.

"Please be so good as to show us to our rooms," he continued, his voice assuming an unmistakable air of superiority. "The journey was a long one, and I fear my daughter is quite fatigued."

An uneasy expression stole across the steward's weathered features. "Your pardon, Mr. Garthwicke, but as there was no mention that your daughter would be accompanying you, I fear we've no rooms prepared for her—only those you ordered for yourself and your assistant."

"My daughter *is* my assistant," her father replied imperiously. "Whatever arrangements you have made are quite acceptable."

"But sir"—Mr. Angley shot Anne a horrified look—" 'tis naught but a valet's room located off of your chamber! 'Tis hardly a proper room for a lady!"

"I said it will do!" her father exclaimed with marked impatience. "Anne is well aware she is here to work, and not play at being lady of the manor. Is that not so, my dear?" He turned to Anne.

Anne managed a polite nod. "Yes, Papa," she said in resignation. She'd been hoping for the luxury of a warm bath and a few moments of privacy. Now she'd have to make do with a quick splash from a jug.

While Mr. Angley led them across the wide courtyard, Anne took the opportunity to discreetly study her surroundings. She knew enough of castles and their construction to recognize what was original and what had been added on through the centuries, and she was pleased to see that so much had been left intact. They'd almost reached the steps of the keep when something caused her to glance up at the east tower. She thought she saw someone at the window, but when she looked closer, no one was there. It was only then that she noticed the window was barred.

"What is that?" she asked, moved by curiosity to stop and peer up at the tower.

"What is what, miss?" Mr. Angley inquired, his tone wary.

"There." She indicated the window with a wave of her hand. "It appears to be barred. May I ask why?"

"As to that, miss, I cannot say," came the stilted reply. "It has always been thus."

Anne's brows knitted at that. Barred windows weren't so odd a feature in a castle built to deter invaders, she brooded, but it did seem odd that only one window was barred, and in so high and remote a tower. Then her brow cleared. The tower's remoteness must account for the bars' presence, she decided as they resumed their walk. Obviously no one had the time or the inclination to bother removing them.

They continued across the courtyard to the front entrance of the keep. Anne noted the new wide marble steps and high, arched windows, and her lips pursed in disapproval. Such improvements might make the castle more palatable to prospective buyers, but she considered them a shocking desecration. How foolish to sacrifice history for fashion, she thought with mounting indignation. A heavy iron-studded door with thick, rough planks would have fit the design of the castle far better than this silly bit of—

"Anne?" Her father was frowning at her. "Is something wrong?"

Anne had been so caught up in her irritation that she hadn't realized she had stopped walking. "No, Papa," she said, forcing herself to resume climbing the steps. "I was only noticing the entrance. The Palladian windows and Italianate door are hardly in keeping with the rest of the castle, wouldn't you say? You must be certain to take Mr. MacCairn to task for replacing the original with this monstrosity."

"I shall mention it, certainly," her father agreed, picking up on the information she had dropped. "But likely it is his father who is to blame. I recall Mr. MacCairn mentioning that his father made several improvements to the castle prior to his death."

"That is so," Mr. Angley agreed, nodding his head. "The old laird went down to London when the fourth George was crowned, and he came back determined to make the castle like the fine homes he'd visited. He even spoke of installing the new gaslight that 'twas all the rage, but he was taken before he could do it."

"He died, do you mean?" Anne asked, thinking it quite sad. She knew the present laird to be thirty-five, which meant he'd have been little more than a toddler when his father had passed away. She'd lost her own mother when she was eighteen, and she knew of the terrible hole such a loss left in a child's life.

There was a pause, and then the older man nodded. "Aye, miss. He died. This way, if you please."

In keeping with the period of the castle's construction, the principal rooms were located on the upper floor, above the great chamber. Climbing the curving stairs, Anne was saddened to see that the same "improvements" that marred the entrance had been applied here with an enthusiastic and indiscriminate hand. Little of what the keep must have originally looked like was in evidence, and it made her wonder what other indignities the rest of the castle had suffered.

After pausing to change into the clothing her father deemed appropriate for their work, Anne hurried back downstairs to find the armory. Her father was resting, but when he rose she knew he would be eager to begin on their various tasks. Mr. MacCairn had indicated that he wanted them to catalog the weapons first, which must mean he already had a buyer in mind. That thought shouldn't have bothered her, and yet it did. Why would a Scotsman sell his clan's castle—a castle that had belonged to them for hundreds of years? Didn't he have any respect for his heritage? The strength of Anne's indignation surprised her; why did she care what the laird did? Her strong emotions only added to the feeling of foreboding that had settled over her since their arrival.

The footman who acted as her escort was young and talkative, for which Anne was thankful. Caught as she was between the servants' world and the master's, Anne had learned to tread with a wary step. She found servants' gossip to be the quickest and most reliable method of gathering information, and after less than five minutes in the boy's company, she'd gained a fair idea how the household was run.

"Mrs. Doughal says if you're wanting tea, you'll have to fetch it yourself," he said, guiding her down the twisting, uneven steps leading to the armory. "She'll not send a maid over here. Not that she could get one to come, even did she order it," he added, casting her a cheeky grin over his shoulder. " 'Tis haunted."

Anne said nothing. She'd worked in enough ancestral homes to have heard a dozen such claims, and she seldom gave them any credence. But there was something about this place that made it difficult for her to be so sanguine. There was an aura of deadly menace stamped into the ancient stones, and she found it uncomfortably easy to believe restless spirits walked here.

Her silence didn't seem to bother the footman, and he continued chatting as he led her to a door located to the left of the stairs.

"Mr. Angley says to mind you lock up when you're finished," he said, handing her a large key. "Will you be able to find your way back on your own, or shall I come fetch you?"

"No, I should be fine, James, thank you," she said, ignoring the sudden uneasiness stealing over her at the thought of being alone. "When my father awakens, will you please have someone come and tell me? I'll bring him here myself."

If the footman thought her request odd, he was too well trained to show it. After indicating the candles and other tools set out for her use, he scurried off, his desire to be gone plain. Closing the door behind him, Anne couldn't fault him for his haste. If ever a room resembled a scene from a Gothic horror novel, it was this place.

Unlike the rest of the castle, which had been softened by centuries of habitation, the armory was a potent reminder of the castle's true purpose. It was a room designed for war, and the implements of death were proudly displayed. Broadswords, their honed edges gleaming in the candlelight, hung on the stone walls beside crossed maces and a pair of deadly-looking battle-axes. There were several claymores as well, and the thought of facing one of the huge swords in a battle sent a shiver of fear racing through her.

The room was unabashedly masculine, and being in

it made her aware of her own femininity in a way she'd never experienced. She also had the sudden sense of being watched, and she wondered if the room had a peephole. Shaking off the troubling sensation, she turned back to the table and began rearranging the tools they would need. With her father's failing eyesight it was imperative everything be organized just so, lest he accidentally harm himself.

The next hour was spent selecting and laying out the weapons they would examine. She'd just picked up a magnifying glass to study an intricately carved blade when the door was suddenly flung open, and a tall man with black hair and piercing green eyes appeared in the doorway. For a long moment they stood looking at one another, and then he was moving toward her, his lean face cold with displeasure.

"Who the devil are you, and what the blazes are you doing here?" he demanded, his deep voice rough with the sounds of the Highlands.

The apology Anne had been about to utter withered on her lips at the arrogant demand. "I am Miss Anne Garthwicke," she said, carefully laying the blade on the table and rising to her feet to face him. "Mr. MacCairn has hired me to catalog his collection."

The stranger continued advancing toward her, his gaze even more hostile as it swept over her. "I am MacCairn," he told her shortly. "And I did no such thing. 'Twas a *Mr.* Garthwicke I engaged, and a Mr. Garthwicke I gave leave to be here. You have no such leave, and I expect you to be gone by morning."

Anne struggled to control her temper. She'd suspected the man was her employer from the first, but even now that she knew for certain she refused to let the knowledge cow her. "As it happens, sir, I am my father's assistant," she began, stalling for time while she tried to decide how best to handle the situation. "You did say he could have his assistant with him, did you not?" she added, hoping the gentle reminder would do something to soothe what looked to be a filthy temper.

"An assistant, aye, but not a female." He all but spat the words at her, as if the mere fact of her sex were somehow a grievous sin. "Pack your bags and be gone. I'll not tell you again." And with that he turned and stalked from the room, leaving Anne to gape after him in furious astonishment.

Mallachadh! Ruairdh MacCairn slammed the door of his study shut, fury boiling hot and potent in his blood. The devil take that fool of an Englishman and his wretched daughter with him, he cursed, his black hair flying about his face as he paced the confines of his study. Of all the disasters of which he might have conceived, this was by far the worst, and it was all he could do not to howl like a trapped beast.

What could the scholar have been thinking, to bring his daughter to this place? he wondered, anger giving way to frustration. Had he not heard of the legend, then? Or did he think it no more than a foolish superstition, to be believed only by half-wild and ignorant Scots? The thought had Ruairdh's lips twisting into a sneer. If Garthwicke believed that, then it was he who was the fool. For there were times when legends were real, and the truth of them more horrifying than anyone could ever imagine.

Ruairdh tensed in sudden awareness, sensing the presence of another even before he heard the hesitant tap on the door.

"Come in, Angley," he said, schooling his features to show no emotion as the elderly steward peeked cautiously around the door.

"You may enter," he said, relieved he could still feel amusement at the wariness on his old retainer's face. "And you may be at ease. 'Twas not the Shadowing that told me 'twas you out there, but plain common sense. Who else but my faithful steward would come to tell me what I already know?"

"You've no cause to be making me sound like some bloody hound licking at your boots," Angley grumbled, moving forward to join Ruairdh. "And I'd have been here sooner, had that pest of a *Sasunnach* not been forever settling in. You'll not credit it, but the fool thinks to put his daughter in the valet's room as if she were no more than a servant." He uttered a heartfelt curse in Gaelic that had the edges of Ruairdh's mouth curving into a reluctant smile.

"I've no wish to disappoint you, but I am sure Garthwicke will go straight to heaven, as befits a proper Englishman," he said wryly. "But I share your hope that it would be otherwise. He deserves eternal damnation and more for bringing his daughter to MacCairn."

There was a charged silence, and Angley shot him a searching look. " 'Tis time, then?" he asked, his tone anguished. "I prayed you were wrong. You seem so much better since you've been back amongst us."

Ruairdh turned from the pity edged with fear he could see in the steward's eyes. He wondered bleakly what Angley would say if he heard the truth: that every day, every hour, was a battle against the shadows that drew ever nearer. He could feel the demons in him straining at their leashes to be free, and he knew the day was coming when they would slip their bonds and devour him. With a terrible sense of the inevitable he knew he had precious little time left—months if he was lucky, a handful of weeks if he was not.

"I'm the better for being here," he said, deciding to spare the older man what he could. "The better for being in the hills and amongst the clan once again. But you know as well as I what must be. That is why Miss Garthwicke cannot remain. I want her gone, Angley. See to it."

"And if her father should insist she stay, what then?" Angley pressed after a moment's pause. "She is his assistant, or so they both claim, and for all that he treats her no better than a scullery maid, he seems to depend upon her."

The beast inside Ruairdh snarled and bared its fangs, and he beat it back with painful determination. "Garthwicke is here at my orders," he said, choosing coolness over the gloating rage building in his head. " 'Tis not his place to insist upon anything. I've paid him a generous advance; if he wants the rest he'll send his daughter back to England where she belongs."

She belongs here; take her. The silky voice whispering in his ear sounded so real, Ruairdh thought it was Angley speaking. His head snapped up in astonished indignation, and he was about to issue a sharp reprimand when he realized the truth: he was hearing voices.

"No," he said aloud, balling his hands into fists. "No."

"Laird?" Angley was looking at him in concern. "Are you ill? Shall I send for the doctor?"

Had the situation not been so grim, Ruairdh would have laughed. He felt like reminding the steward that the MacCairns' bodies were disgustingly fit; it was their minds that were diseased beyond any medicine's ability to cure. Instead he drew a deep and cleansing breath, and it was only when he was certain he had himself once more under control that he allowed himself to speak.

"I am fine, Angley," he said, his green eyes level as he met the other man's gaze. "Just do as I order. Miss Garthwicke is to be gone on the afternoon train. I trust you to do this for me."

Angley's mouth trembled, and his faded eyes shone with tears as he understood what Ruairdh was telling him. In a gesture dating back to the oldest times, he placed his fist above his heart and bowed his head.

"Aye, *mo tighearna*," he said, using the Gaelic word in Ruairdh's honor. "I will do as you wish."

Ruairdh thought of the woman he'd glimpsed. She'd been young, no more than twenty-three, with rich gold hair bundled back in a prim chignon and soft gray eyes the color of smoke. He had taken her for a maid at first, for she'd been dressed in a plain black gown covered by a crisp white apron. He'd been about to demand an explanation for her presence, when she told him her name. The sound of her soft, musical voice threw him into sudden, vicious arousal, and the shame of his lustful thoughts only added to his fury. That was why he was so determined she leave. It was the only way to be certain she would be safe from him.

"Not as I would wish it, Angley," he said, feeling as ancient and as doomed as the walls of his castle. "Not as I would wish."

Chapter Two

The door had scarcely closed behind Mr. MacCairn before Anne gave vent to her indignation. It wasn't often she allowed herself the luxury of emotion, but then, it wasn't often she was offered such deliberate provocation.

"Of all the ill-mannered, overbearing, arrogant beasts!" she fumed, her eyes snapping in fury. "How dare he treat me so! Does he think me a parlor maid to be sent packing with a snap of his fingers? For a pence I'd bash a battle-ax over his head; that ought to knock some manners into his thick Scots skull!"

But as quickly as it flared, her temper cooled, and her sense of hard practicality rose to the fore. Women in her position couldn't afford pride, and over the years she'd learned to swallow many an insult. The laird's imperious command that she leave presented a serious dilemma, but all was not yet lost. With care and consideration, she could still manage to prevail.

The first order of business was to break the news to her father, and upon reflection she decided that the sooner she did this, the better. She finished arranging their tools, taking care to set aside the blade she hoped to study more carefully. As she locked the door she made a mental note to ask the housekeeper for extra wood for the fire. The armory was dreadfully cold, and she didn't want her papa taking a chill.

The journey back to her room seemed longer than Anne remembered. She was certain she was following the same route she and the footman had taken earlier, but nothing about her looked familiar. Convinced she'd find her way if she only persevered, she continued walking. After several minutes of wandering, however, she came to a halt, forced to face the truth: she was well and truly lost.

It was all Mr. MacCairn's doing, she decided with a scowl. With her odd affinity for older places she'd never lost her way in even the greatest of country houses, and that she'd done so now was clearly his fault. If he hadn't distracted her, she'd never have become disoriented. The question was, what could she do to rectify the matter? Trying to retrace her steps made no sense, but going forward when she hadn't a clue as to her direction seemed equally foolish. She was about to give up and turn around, when she heard the sound of a door clanging shut. She glanced up, and it was then that she saw the staircase.

Fashioned from sturdy wrought iron and bolted into the thick stones, the narrow stairs twisted upward in a dizzying spiral. Intrigued, she trod closer, peering up into the stygian darkness. To her amazement the steps led to an ancient, wide-planked wooden door held closed with a thick metal bar. Her fingers trembled as she reached out to grasp the handrail.

"No, miss, no! You mustn't!"

The horrified gasp behind her jolted Anne out of her reverie, and she spun around to find the footman staring at her as if she'd taken leave of her senses.

"What are ye about?" he cried, his accent thickening with distress. "Away from there, away, before the *spiorad* snatches you and drags you off!"

Anne gazed at him in confusion. "I beg your pardon?"

"Ye're no' to be here; no one is," he continued, although Anne noted he made no move to come closer. "This area is forbidden to all by orders of the laird! Come with me now, else he'll be in a great thundering temper and curse at us all."

Since the laird was already in a thundering temper, Anne wasn't overly concerned, but at least she now knew what a *spiorad* was. He must be a constable of sorts, and one very likely in the pay of the laird. She cast the staircase a final wistful look, wondering if she'd ever have the opportunity to explore what lay beyond the barred door. Accepting that that was highly unlikely, she turned and followed the scolding footman to the inhabited part of the castle.

Her father was awake and enjoying his tea and bread when she entered the room. When she greeted him, he set down his cup with a sharp clatter.

"Surely you haven't finished your work already?" he

protested, withdrawing his watch from his pocket and studying it with a frown. "You could not have been at your duties above an hour."

Anne didn't bother pointing out that in truth it had been closer to two hours since she'd left him. Instead she gave a brief account of her confrontation with Mr. MacCairn, taking pains to make his actions seem even more outrageous than they were. She knew her father's first instinct would be to blame her, and she wanted it plain who was truly at fault.

"He scarce gave me time to introduce myself before telling me to be gone," she concluded, her mouth thinning in remembered indignation. "I know the Scots have a reputation for eccentricity, but this is too much even for one of them!"

To her surprise a troubled expression flickered over her father's drawn features. "That is so," he murmured, drumming his fingers as he often did when he was in deep thought. "I've heard the rumors, of course, but I thought them no more than idle gossip. This is most disturbing. Most disturbing indeed."

The remark puzzled Anne, but she had other considerations at the moment. "I thought you might speak with him, Papa," she said, sitting beside him and tentatively covering his hand with her own. "You can tell him I am your assistant, and that I am more than qualified to catalog his precious collection. Perhaps that will reassure him, and he will allow me to stay."

"Perhaps," her father agreed, his voice sounding distant. Without warning his fingers closed around hers, his eyes burning with some unnamed emotion as his gaze locked with hers.

"Anne, I want to ask you something," he said, his voice surprisingly stern, "and I want you to answer truthfully."

"Of course, Papa," Anne replied, alarmed at the sudden change in his behavior. "What is it?"

"Does the laird strike you as mad?"

Anne stared at him in horrified astonishment. "*What?*"

Her father's grip tightened. "Answer me!" he ordered. "Do you think Mr. MacCairn to be insane?"

"Of course not!" Anne replied, shaken by his question. "There is nothing ailing the man but an appalling temper and even worse manners. I think him sorely in need of a lecture on hospitality, but mad?" She shook her head. "Never."

Her father's fingers remained clenched over hers. "You're certain?"

Concerned, but not wishing to show it, she leaned forward to press a gentle kiss on his cheek. "Yes, I'm certain."

He gazed at her for several seconds before releasing her hand. "Then it's all right," he said, his breath easing out of him as he closed his eyes. "It's only a rumor, after all. I was beginning to wonder, I must admit. If it had been the truth . . ." His voice trailed off as he gazed into space.

"If what had been the truth?" she asked, curious despite herself. As a rule she had little interest in gossip, but given her father's confusing behavior she couldn't help but be intrigued.

He gave a jerk, and sent her an impatient frown.

"It is nothing," he said, dismissing her question with

a wave of his hand. "At the moment it's more important that I speak with Mr. MacCairn. I'm sure once he knows I will be in command he'll see his way clear to letting you remain. He surely can't expect me to undertake a commission of this magnitude without some assistance."

Anne remembered the furious glitter in the laird's eyes, and was less certain. The hard-faced man she'd met might well be the ill-mannered lout she'd named him, but it was obvious he was also a man who meant what he said. There would be no convincing him to do anything other than precisely what he pleased.

"Papa," she began, choosing each word with the utmost care, "I have been thinking, and perhaps it might be best if we were to tell Mr. MacCairn the truth. If we explain about your eyesight he would understand—"

"No!" her father interrupted, his face tight with fury. "Not a word to the man, do you hear? Not a word!"

"But Papa—"

"Enough!" He brought his fist down on the table, sending the delicate cups skittering. A tense silence followed, and he drew a ragged breath.

"You will not mention this again," he ordered, his tone as icy as his expression. "In the meanwhile, I want you to guide me to the laird's study, and then wait outside while I speak with him. Is that understood?"

Anne felt tears prick her eyes at the harshness in his voice. At times her love for her father was like a shackle about her throat, and she wondered bleakly if she would ever be free to follow her own course.

"Yes, Papa," she said, swallowing her unhappiness as she walked forward to take his arm. "I understand."

* * *

Fate, Ruairdh brooded several hours later, was a vicious, unprincipled whore. There was no foul trick she wouldn't attempt, no depth to which she would hesitate to sink, if it meant accomplishing her goal. And that goal, as nearly as he could tell, was to hasten his descent into madness. Why else would she throw up every barrier she could to prevent him from doing what he must? As if mocking his dark thoughts, a jagged bolt of lightning exploded across the blackening skies, and a boom of thunder rattled the leaded panes of glass in their frames.

"You must see there is no sending the lass away this night," Angley said, studying Ruairdh with a scowl. "It's not even that demon Cumberland I would be sending out into such a storm."

Ruairdh gave a half smile at his steward's observation. A hundred years or more it might have been since the clans were slaughtered at Culloden, but Scots' memories ran as deep as their hatreds. And to his sorrow, he had learned there was nothing so powerful as old hatreds.

"I am well aware of that, Angley," he said, bitterly accepting that there was nothing to be done. "Where are the Garthwickes now?"

"In their rooms dressing for dinner," Angley replied, shaking a gnarled finger at him. "And if you're thinking of hiding away, you may think again. It's still the laird you are, and you'll not disgrace the clan with your poor manners. You'll sup with them and play the proper host, or I shall know the reason why."

Ruairdh's jaw clenched at the reprimand. "Will I?"

he asked, anger coiling like a serpent deep in his soul.

"Aye, you will." Angley gave a decisive nod. "And since she'll not be going anywhere until this squall has blown itself out, I've moved the young miss into a proper set of rooms. Something you ought to have ordered yourself, laird."

That the rebuke was deserved only added to Ruairdh's temper, but he still maintained enough control to keep that temper in check. During his interview with Garthwicke, more than once he'd come perilously close to giving in to his black anger and breaking the old fool in half.

"But my daughter must remain, sir," the older man had argued, ignoring Ruairdh's objections with a determination that bordered on insolence. "She is my assistant, the only one trained in my precise methods. Without her I cannot complete this commission."

He'd continued in that vein for well over an hour, as adamant to keep his daughter with him as Ruairdh was to send her safely away. They had been no closer to resolving the matter when the summer storm descended upon the castle without warning. Such storms were not uncommon, and Ruairdh had learned to respect their deadly power. Only last year he'd lost several sheep and a young shepherd to such natural elements, and he would not risk Miss Garthwicke.

"When is dinner?" he asked, turning his thoughts back to the present.

"Seven of the clock," Angley answered. "And sherry in the library first, half an hour before. Mind you're there."

It was resentment that had Ruairdh's brows meeting

in a black scowl. "Have you any other orders?" he queried with a low growl.

"I have." The older man's weathered face split in a wicked grin. "Wear your kilt."

Ruairdh's jaw dropped in astonishment. "My kilt?"

"Aye." Angley gave a delighted chuckle. "It will do the lass good to see a real Scotsman, and it will do you good as well to wear the plaid of your clan."

Ruairdh started to protest, then closed his mouth. He supposed there was some truth to Angley's words. It had been years since he'd last worn his kilt, and who knew when or if he would ever wear it again? This one last time he would don his clan's colors and do honor to the part of his heritage he could claim with pride. It need be only a few hours, he assured himself. He could keep his beasts leashed for so short a period as that.

Two hours later he was questioning the wisdom of his decision as he sat across the candlelit table from Miss Garthwicke, his gaze hooded as he studied her. Her hair was still tucked back in that damnable bun, although she had softened its stern effect by allowing a few locks to curl about her dainty ears and forehead. The coiffure had been quite the fashion when he'd last been in London some two years ago, as, he noted with a connoisseur's eye, had been her simple evening dress of crimson velvet trimmed at the wide sleeves with bands of black lace.

The bodice of the gown was all that was proper, but above it he could see the soft swell of her breasts. They were a delectable ivory against the blood-colored velvet, and he could smell her sweet scent even across the table. It wasn't her perfume he detected, but the enticing scent of a female who'd yet to lie with a man. She was innocent, he gloated triumphantly, and she was here. If he chose to take her, who was there to stop him?

"An excellent meal, Mr. MacCairn, excellent indeed," Mr. Garthwicke said, acting every inch the agreeable guest. "Nothing in the world can compare to good Scottish venison, eh, Anne?" He gave his daughter's hand an indulgent pat.

"Yes, Papa," she answered dutifully, before turning those cool gray eyes upon Ruairdh. "Did it come from your woods, sir?"

"It did," Ruairdh replied curtly, mortified by his own dark thoughts and the unmistakable hardening of his body. He wanted to believe his was the normal response of a man to a woman, but he dared not. He knew his improper feelings toward Anne stemmed from his unbalanced mind. To cover his reaction he took another sip of the icy champagne he'd ordered served with the last course, his hand trembling as he raised the glass to his lips.

"Will you be coming to London for the Exhibition, sir?" the scholar continued, not seeming to notice Ruairdh's terse response. "If so, you'll be pleased to learn there is a special section dedicated to your charming country. It is the queen's doing, you know, for she is mad for all things Scottish." He gestured expansively, almost upsetting the glass of wine he'd set aside a few minutes earlier.

"There is also an excellent selection of ancient armory," Miss Garthwicke added, carefully moving the glass out of harm's way. "I'm sure you'll find it most interesting."

Her solicitous caretaking caught Ruairdh's notice, and his eyes narrowed in displeasure. He'd spent the past hour watching her cater to her father, and he'd had a bellyful of it. He noted the way she handed him each glass of wine, and even placed the cutlery within easy reach for him. He couldn't say why it bothered him, but it did.

"And you, Miss Garthwicke?" he asked, taking another sip of champagne and leaning back in his chair. "Do you find such things of interest as well?"

As if sensing the challenge behind the question, her chin came up another notch.

"Yes," she replied, her gaze meeting his. "I do."

He smiled mockingly, savoring her response. "An odd preoccupation for a female. The sword you were examining when I walked into the armory—tell me about it."

She blinked as if taken aback by his directness, but she didn't hesitate before responding.

"It is quite old, fifteenth century, I would say, perhaps even older." Her gray eyes took on a faraway expression. "The style is much like that favored by the later Crusaders, and judging from its weight and the sharpness of the blade, I would say it was designed for war, not show." She frowned.

"There were some odd markings engraved on the hilt. They were quite faint, but I would swear they were Templar. . . ."

The word had Ruairdh jerking forward in alarm. "Templar!" he exclaimed, a ball of ice forming in his gut. "You're mistaken, Miss Garthwicke. We've no Templar relics at Castle MacCairn!"

The vehemence in his voice cleared the mistiness from her eyes. She stared at him for a few seconds before inclining her head in what could only be termed regal condescension.

"I am sure you would know best, Mr. MacCairn," she replied in a prim tone that in no way deceived Ruairdh. "But in my own defense I should like to add that I'd scarce had time to pick up the sword before . . . making your acquaintance."

The mocking words reminded Ruairdh of his earlier behavior. He supposed he should apologize—his honor and duty to his clan demanded no less—but upon reflection he decided against it. Since ordering her from the castle hadn't worked, perhaps giving her a reason to wish to be gone might better serve his needs. His lips curved in a wolfish grin at the thought.

"You're a comely lass, Miss Garthwicke." He all but purred the compliment, his voice pitched to its most seductive tone. "I wonder that you should be so enamored of so dry and dusty a thing as history. Have you no desire for a husband, for the children the two of you would make together?"

As he expected, a soft blush of color washed over her cheeks at the outrageous observation.

"My life is with my father, Mr. MacCairn," she told him in repressive tones, meant, he supposed, to silence him. "I have no need for such things."

"Have you not?" He leaned forward to let his gaze slide over her in bold, shocking appraisal. "Then it's a cold, lonely life you have laid out before you."

"Not for Anne." The scholar seemed to have found his voice at last. "She is far too intellectual for such foolishness as love and marriage."

Ruairdh shot him a disgusted look. What sort of father could take pride in turning his daughter into an old maid? he wondered with a flash of fierce anger. Could the selfish dolt not see that Anne was a woman meant for passion, for warming a man's bed and firing his blood? It would serve him right to lose her.

The thought shimmered into existence in Ruairdh's mind, tempting him as much as it unnerved him. He shook his head in distraction, trying to think of something else to say, but it was already too late. Miss Garthwicke had risen to her feet, and was helping her father to his.

"If you will pardon us, Mr. MacCairn, Father and I shall retire," she said, the polite words in no way diminishing the challenging glitter in her crystal-colored eyes. "Good evening."

He rose with insolent grace, of a mind to match her challenge. "I was hoping, Mr. Garthwicke, to have a word with you," he said, directing a friendly smile at the older man. "We've much to discuss before you begin your task."

To his surprise the scholar hesitated. "If you wish to discuss your collection, it might be best if Anne is present," he said, seeming to cling to his daughter's arm. "As she's my assistant, I rely upon her to make certain notations and observations."

Ruairdh's senses sharpened in sudden awareness. Like a predator sensing prey he could smell the old man's uncertainty and all but taste his fear. Something was amiss here, he realized, even as he moved in with lethal skill for the kill.

"I am afraid we must do without your charming daughter's presence," he said, savoring the powerful rush of triumph in his veins. " 'Tis an old Scottish custom, you see, for the men to share a glass of whiskey before retiring. You understand, do you not, Miss Garthwicke?" He sliced her with a sharp smile.

The flash of awareness he saw in her eyes the second before she lowered them gave Ruairdh all the answer he needed.

"Of course, sir," she said, releasing her father's arm and taking a step back. "With your permission, then, I believe I will return to the library. I saw several volumes I found intriguing, and I should like to examine them. I will wait for you there, Papa."

Ruairdh watched her walk away, his sense of victory giving way to the dark, endless hunger he'd been holding at bay since first glimpsing Anne. It had been months since he'd last savored the sweetness of a woman, and he ached for release. Under ordinary circumstances he'd have availed himself of one of his former mistresses, or even one of the village prostitutes. But he'd not subject even the most common of whores to his uncertain control. The danger was simply too great.

He knows. Anne gazed into the glowing coals of the dying flames. She didn't know how he knew, but she would wager any amount of money their reluctant host had somehow ferreted out the truth. She wondered if her father was aware that their carefully constructed ruse had been discovered, and how he would react when he did know. She also wondered what Mr. MacCairn would do. From what she'd observed of him, she wouldn't be in the least surprised if he tossed them out of the castle, storm or no storm.

He was such an odd man, she mused, listening to the increasing violence raging outside. Rude and angry one moment, provocative and teasing the next; and underlying it all was the almost visible battle for control she could sense raging inside him. It was as if he was comprised of two halves of the same whole, each at war with the other. Her eyes drifted closed as exhaustion slid over her. She decided he was like Janus, the two-faced god of Roman mythology. One face split in a grin of happiness and joy, the other a mask of frozen horror, the features twisted in madness . . .

He is cursed.

Anne heard the words whisper in her mind seconds before she felt the icy brush of fingers against her cheek. She jerked awake, the heavy volume she'd been holding on her lap tumbling to the floor. She struggled up from the chair, glancing wildly about her before she realized she'd been dreaming. Feeling somewhat foolish, she bent and retrieved the book, and was straightening when the door opened and Mr. MacCairn stood in the doorway. It was so like their first meeting that her heart began hammering in response.

"Where is my father?" she asked, taking care to hide her uneasiness. She knew without questioning it that he would be merciless if he sensed the slightest weakness.

"Your father has gone up to his rooms," he informed her, closing the door behind him. "I had the footman escort him, as he seemed unsure of the way."

"I see," Anne said, hope stirring within her breast. Perhaps the laird wasn't as formidable as she feared. "That was very kind of you." She ventured a wary smile. "But there was really no need. I am accustomed to helping Papa."

"I wished a word with you," came the unhelpful reply as he continued watching her, his cold, handsome face betraying none of his thoughts.

Anne's cautious sense of optimism died a quick death. "I am afraid that's not possible, Mr. MacCairn," she said finally, seeking refuge in a sudden awareness of propriety. "It is rather late, and as we are unchaperoned, I fear it would be most improper. I shall speak with you tomorrow morning." Then, deciding she had no other choice but to brazen it out, she made to brush past him. As she expected, he moved to block her path.

She tilted her head back, her knees shaking even as she met his gaze with what equanimity she could muster. "You are in my way."

In response he smiled, a harsh, menacing smile that only emphasized the danger emanating from him like a physical force.

"I wonder," he began, his narrowed eyes dancing with emerald fire as he gazed down at her, "how long did you and your father think you could keep the truth from me? Do you think yourselves so clever or me so foolish that I would not ken the truth? Or perhaps you believed the stories you'd heard, and decided you had nothing to lose by gulling a madman. Is that it?"

This was the second time in the short space of a few hours that she'd heard mention of the laird's being unbalanced. With her father it had been easy to laugh his concerns aside, but alone in the heart of a storm with a very large and very furious male, she was far less certain.

"I don't know what you're talking about," she blustered, trying once more to move past him. His hand shot out immediately, closing about her upper arm. She glared up at him and attempted to pull free. "Sir, you are hurting me!"

His grip tightened, and he pulled her closer. "You know full well what I mean," he accused coldly. "Your father let slip that he made mention to you of the rumors, so don't play the innocent with me! You know, don't you? Don't you?" He gave her arm a small shake.

"Know what?" Anne demanded, too incensed to be afraid.

"Know that I am said to be mad."

At the quiet admission she stopped struggling, her gaze searching his tormented features for the slightest sign that he was making sport of her. "And are you?" she asked, her breath catching as she awaited his reply.

His lips twisted in a bitter sneer, and he released her so abruptly she staggered back.

"Aye, Miss Garthwicke," he told her, closing his eyes and giving a humorless laugh. "I am."

Chapter Three

Anne stood in stunned silence.

"You're lying," she managed, her voice trembling despite her best efforts.

"Am I?" He gave her a scornful smile. "And why would I do that, Miss Garthwicke?"

Refusing to be intimidated, Anne forced herself to consider the matter with the cool dispassion she used to examine a new weapon or artifact. A true madman, she reasoned, was unlikely to freely admit his affliction. Also, his discourse was far too rational to indicate any serious disorder of the mind. That left only one explanation for Mr. MacCairn's outrageous behavior.

"To frighten me," she said, relaxing as understanding dawned. "You're trying to frighten me."

Now it was he who seemed to be examining her words. "And are you frightened?" he asked softly, his jewel-colored eyes searching her face with an intensity that was almost as unnerving as his earlier words.

Such arrogance couldn't be tolerated, and she raised her head, meeting his watchful gaze with pride. "No," she lied. "I'm not."

He lifted his hand as if to touch her, and then he turned away and strode across the room to stand before the window.

"You should be," he said, his voice sounding infinitely weary as he gazed out into the blackness. "If you were half so clever as you think yourself to be, you'd be frightened for your very life."

Anne felt another shiver of unease, but she firmly ignored it. Now that Mr. MacCairn was no longer blocking her path, she was free to leave. Instead she found herself walking over to join him. He glanced down at her, surprise showing on his handsome features.

"Are you so brave, then?" he wondered aloud. "Or are you so foolish? Go." He turned back to the window. "You don't know what you risk by remaining."

Anne said nothing. She sensed he was genuinely concerned for her safety, and given that, the prudent thing would be to do as he commanded. But if she left now, she knew she might never have such a chance to plead her case. It was now or never.

"I understand you are angry," she began, "and perhaps you have cause. But I don't deserve the contempt you've shown me, any more than I deserve to be dismissed when I've done nothing wrong."

He brought his head up, the bleakness in his eyes giving way to a familiar arrogance.

"That is a matter open for debate," he said, turning to face her. "Some would say both you and your father deserve to be given the boot and worse for the game you are playing. How long has he been blind?"

With the matter put to her so bluntly, Anne could be no less than honest. "He's not blind," she replied. "At least not entirely. He can see well enough close up; it's just that he has difficulty seeing things at a distance."

"And at what distance might that be?" he challenged, folding his arms across his chest and regarding her with an unmistakable air of command. "Six feet? Seven?"

"Closer to two, I would suppose," she admitted, resentment edging her voice. "I really don't know.

"But it doesn't matter, can't you see?" she added, determined to make him understand. "I can do the cataloging of the collection, and anything else that requires normal sight. He can do the examination of the weapons and other artifacts. And in the end, isn't that what's most important?"

He continued studying her, his expression unyielding. "You should have been honest with me," he said, his words all the more cutting for their lack of heat. "The decision should have been mine to make."

Anne's anger dissolved as she was forced to admit he was right. "I know, and I am sorry. But my father has his pride, and he insisted no one know the truth."

There was a long silence. Anne watched him closely, searching his face for any hint of what he might be thinking. He was one of the most enigmatic men she'd ever encountered, and she wondered if she would ever truly know what he felt.

"You have placed me in an awkward position," he said after several seconds. "Time grows short, and I must have the collection verified. Your father's reputation is the reason I engaged his services. If he can't do the work—"

"He *can!*" Anne interrupted. "With my help, he can. Please, Mr. MacCairn, give us a chance. Is it so much to ask?" she added, frustrated by his continued silence.

"Under ordinary circumstances, I would say no, but as things are . . ." He gave a heavy sigh, and then fixed her with a stern gaze.

"If I let you stay," he began carefully, "there are certain conditions I must insist you follow."

"And what conditions might those be?" Anne asked, feeling hope for the first time in hours.

He hesitated a moment before speaking. "To begin, you're to stay out of the east wing," he told her, his harsh tone making it plain he would brook no opposition. "There are areas where the walls and floors have collapsed, and you're not to go there for any reason. It is too dangerous."

The demand had Anne blinking her eyes in confusion. "But that is the oldest part of the castle!" she protested, thinking immediately of the twisting staircase and the mysterious door. "Surely you'll want it authenticated!"

His eyes flashed with pride. "Castle MacCairn has stood guard over this valley for five centuries," he informed her, every inch the Highland laird. "That is all any *outdwellar* needs to know."

Anne wanted to disagree, but common sense prevailed. She and her father had been granted a reprieve, and that was enough for now.

"Very well," she conceded, willing to be compliant for the moment. "What are the other conditions?"

"The next condition is that you remember I am laird here," he answered after another silence. "In the castle and in the village my word is law, and I'll not tolerate any argument. You've a proud and willful nature, I've noted, and you are prone to defiance. If I decide you will remain, you will accept my command."

Anne clenched her fists, her temper all but choking her. In the five years she'd worked as her father's assistant, Mr. MacCairn's edict was one she had heard many times before. Most of her father's employers considered her little more than a servant, and she was accustomed to being treated as such. But she was hardly accustomed to having that edict stated so bluntly, her lowly position in the household all but flung in her face. It was almost as if he wanted her to refuse, she brooded, her eyes narrowing in sudden suspicion. If that was his plan, then he was as mad as he claimed to be. She would never be deceived by so obvious a ploy.

"Yes, laird," she replied, inclining her head with what she told herself was no more than cool civility.

An expression of surprise flashed in his emerald eyes, but his tone was as arrogant as ever as he continued. "The last condition is simple enough. You are to stay well away from me. I've seen you stealing glances at me, and while I am flattered, I've no intention of being trapped by your girlish infatuation. I may bed you, but I'll never wed you. Remember that."

For a moment Anne feared she would lose the struggle to keep her temper in check. Only the knowledge that that was precisely what he wanted kept her from giving in to her emotions and slapping him across the face as she longed to. Instead she took a steadying breath, making certain of her control before answering.

"I am certain I shall have no difficulty in fulfilling your conditions, Mr. MacCairn," she said, fixing her gaze at some point over his shoulder. "Indeed, the last of your conditions will prove almost a pleasure to me. Good night, sir. I am sure we shan't be speaking again." And she brushed past him, her head held high and her slender body trembling with fury.

God, what was he to do? Ruairdh stood before the French doors in his bedchamber, staring out into the darkness with a soul as black and storm-swept as the night itself. It was long past midnight, and the rest of the castle lay fast asleep about him. With the sharpened senses the Shadowing brought him, he could feel their dreams, hear the softness of their deepened breathing, and knew them to be defenseless and at his mercy. If he tried he could see them as well, but as yet he'd managed to resist the temptation. How much longer he could resist he knew not, but he prayed he would be dead long before losing that particular battle.

The sweetness of a woman's perfume and the even sweeter scent of her flesh came to him, and his body responded with instant arousal. He knew without considering the matter that it was Anne, and he cursed the Fates that had brought her to him. During their encounter in the library the scent of her had almost driven him mad, and he thanked the God he still believed in that he had not given in to the wild desire clawing at him. Damned he might be, but not so damned as to take an innocent woman into hell with him.

Why hadn't he sent her away? Sweat beaded on his forehead as he fought the raging urges of his traitorous body. Aye, he needed her pest of a father to appraise and authenticate all that would be sold, and it had become abundantly clear that the antiquarian needed Anne to complete the cataloging. Still, there had to be some other way. He had several lads in his employ clever enough to be of service. Garthwicke had taught his daughter his ways; could he not also train one of the footmen in the same skills?

Or he could send to Edinburgh for someone to aid the scholar, he thought, shifting restlessly as the sudden thought occurred to him. The ancient city with its grand university was certain to be filled with young men eager for such an opportunity. Once Garthwicke had taken such a student under his wing and taught him what he needed to know, Ruairdh could send the troublesome older man back to England on the next train.

But as quickly as these faint hopes stirred to life, Ruairdh rejected them. Not only was there not enough time to find and then train such a person, but from what he had observed of the cautious scholar, it was unlikely he would be willing to share his specialized knowledge with anyone. And however much he might wish it otherwise, Ruairdh accepted that he could hardly compel Garthwicke to reveal his secrets against his will. More was the pity.

Sighing heavily, Ruairdh turned toward the large tester bed set opposite the fireplace. Exhaustion tugged at him, but he was still reluctant to sleep. Since the Shadowing had begun, sleep and his dreams had become a dubious sanctuary, and his rest was often disrupted by horrific visions. Perhaps tonight would be different, he thought, peeling off his robe and climbing into bed.

He fell asleep almost at once, and his dreams started soon after. Images and emotions flitted through his tortured mind, surrounded by a swirl of wild noise that had him tossing and turning in vague torment. He felt both a participant and an observer of the chaotic scenes flashing before him, and he struggled fiercely for control. The voices filling his head rang out with malicious laughter, and then lowered to sibilant, seductive whispers. He tried closing his ears to the taunting, but he could not. The words became louder, more insistent, urging him further toward madness.

Then everything changed; the voices grew silent, and the bright, garish colors blended into soft, soothing shades of cream and gold. He was in a bedchamber, walking toward a bed draped in cream-colored silk. A woman lay on the bed, her blond hair curling about her in shimmering waves of burnished gold and her slender body glowing in the dancing candlelight. When she saw him her gray eyes grew warm, and her arms opened in silent welcome. Feeling as if he were coming home, he slid into her arms, lowering his body to cover her even as his lips sought the sweet taste of her lips.

The kiss was both comforting and carnal, stirring him to wild hunger. He slid his mouth down her neck, pressing urgent, openmouthed kisses to her shoulders even as his hands cupped the full glory of her breasts.

Her flesh responded instantly to his touch, and she gave a soft cry of delight.

"*Mo cridhe.*" He whispered the endearment hoarsely, his tongue teasing the delicate pink nipple to hardness. "I want you."

The woman arched beneath him, her beautiful eyes closing as an expression of exquisite desire stole across her flushed features.

"Ruairdh!" She sighed his name, her fingers digging into the thickness of his hair as she pressed him closer.

He accepted greedily her unspoken surrender and intensified his lovemaking. He drew her breast into his mouth, suckling at it like a babe until she was writhing beneath him and he was half-mad with desire. At her wanton urging his caresses grew bolder, his fingers sliding lower to tease the moistness of her feminine flesh. Finding her more than ready for what was to come, he moved over her with passionate purpose.

"Let me have you, *leannan,*" he urged, parting her legs with his and pressing intimately against her. "Anne, let me love you."

"No!"

The word was torn from his throat as Ruairdh shot straight up in bed, his heart hammering and his breath coming in heaving gasps. His body was hard, screaming for the release it had been denied when he'd ripped himself out of the dream. Even now he was shaking, desire so intense and demanding it consumed him like the fires of the stake. He gulped in the cold air of the bedchamber, holding it in his lungs before slowly releasing it in a heavy sigh.

My God, he thought, resting his head on his bent

knees and bleakly closing his eyes. What in heaven's name ailed him? How could he have so vivid a dream about a woman he scarcely knew, and one who was an innocent as well? Had the madness progressed so far so quickly? The possibility brought a cold sweat to his forehead. Then he thought of something that had him raising his head in cautious hope.

His ancestors had meticulously chronicled the progression of the Shadowing in painful detail, but he couldn't recall any mention of lascivious dreams. The nightmares and the sharpening of the senses were all part of the fate awaiting the MacCairns, and he had been experiencing them for the past several months. If such dreams were also part of the curse, would he not have had them before this?

Perhaps it had naught to do with the Shadowing, he thought, his heart beginning to race again. The nightmares and the heightened senses carried with them a sense of malevolent power, and he hadn't felt that in his dream. Indeed, his only emotion had been an overwhelming urge for sexual release. Not so surprising, he decided; it had been many months since he'd last trusted himself with a woman. Miss Garthwicke was the first female other than his servants whom he'd seen since returning to the castle, and however uncomfortable he might find the admission, she was also very beautiful and very desirable. Was it any wonder he should dream of her?

Feeling marginally reassured, he lay back down again. He'd done well to give Miss Garthwicke a thorough dislike of him, he mused, tugging the bedclothes over his bare shoulders. The Shadowing made his control uncertain enough; if the sexual desire he'd felt for her in his dream carried over into real life, then he was well and truly damned. The bleak thought nibbled at his already troubled conscience, following him into an uneasy sleep.

"Anne!" Her father glared at her through the thick lenses of his spectacles, the sharpness of his voice making it plain that it wasn't the first time he had attempted to capture her attention.

Anne jolted guiltily, her cheeks pinkening with embarrassment. She and her father had been hard at work since breakfast, and she was drooping with exhaustion. Shaking off her weariness, she sent him a strained smile.

"I beg pardon, Father," she said, her fingers tightening about her magnifying glass. "What did you say?"

"Well, you have given very poor service this morning, I must say!" he snapped, obviously not pleased. "What is wrong with you?"

Her weakened state left her fighting both tears and temper, and it was a moment before she trusted herself to speak.

"I am tired, Father," she answered, struggling to remain detached. "I didn't sleep at all well last night."

"That is hardly any reason to sit and dream away the day!" he retorted, his features pinched with fury. "You must know Mr. MacCairn is tolerating your presence only because I assured him you would be useful. If you cannot do better than this, then I greatly fear he would be well within his rights to demand that you leave."

And for a ha' penny she would go, Anne thought,

remembering the unpleasant encounter in the library. Unfortunately she couldn't tell her father about that, and so she kept the words to herself.

"I will do better, sir," she promised, although the apology all but choked her. "I give you my word."

He gave a curt nod. "See that you do," he said, picking up his quill and bending over the record book. "Now, kindly answer my question. What is your decision on the sword?"

Swallowing her temper once more, she turned her attention back to the weapon she had been examining. "It is certainly from the fourteenth century; perhaps even earlier that that," she answered, picking up the heavy sword and holding it between her gloved hands. "The blade is very finely honed, and the double sides are still quite sharp. It is heavy but perfectly balanced, which means it would be easy to wield in battle. This was fashioned for war; it's not some pretty piece for tourney or show."

"And the markings you mentioned?" her father asked, frowning over her observations. "Have you identified them yet?"

Anne glanced back down at the sword. "No, not yet," she admitted, running her thumb lightly over one of the engraved figures. "I've never seen their like before."

"Then why did you think them Templar?" he demanded crossly. "The Templars weren't known for engraving their weapons, you know."

"I am aware of that," she said, stung by his criticism. "But this is clearly the mark of their order; two knights on one horse."

"A forgery then," he said with a dismissive wave of

his hand. "You will have to learn the difference if you have any hopes of carrying on my work."

"The sword is genuine," she replied, unwilling to continue accepting his insults in meek silence. "There is no doubt."

He made an impatient sound. "The sword may be genuine, but it doesn't mean the engravings are. They were obviously made at a later date, to give the weapon more value, perhaps, or merely as a fancy. When I was a youth, Scott's foolish novels had everyone running mad for anything touching on the Templars and the Crusades. Obviously one of MacCairn's relations thought to add to their consequence by possessing such a relic."

Because it was a possibility that couldn't be dismissed without further study, Anne held her tongue. "What of the other engravings?" she asked. "Shall I describe them to you?"

"To what purpose?" her father asked, shrugging his shoulders. "I have already told you they are not authentic, and therefore have no effect on the evaluation. You may list the sword as genuine if you are so convinced, and place it with the other pieces to ship to London. It will fetch a fine price, I've no doubt, given the renewed interest in the Age of Chivalry. Just make certain to include all notations of it you can find. We must take care to verify its authenticity."

"Yes, Father," she said, not bothering to tell him she was well aware of what was expected of her. She was about to set the sword on the table when something made her hesitate. The first consignments bound for London weren't scheduled to be shipped for another week. What harm could there be in her conducting her own study? Mr. MacCairn needn't know, and if she was correct and the sword *was* Templar, then it would be that much more valuable. How could Mr. MacCairn possibly object to that?

The possibility of flaunting the proof of her expertise in the laird's arrogant face was too tantalizing to ignore, and she made an abrupt decision. A furtive glance at her father showed him to be lost once more in his own work, and she quickly set the weapon to one side. Later, when there was time, she would take it up to her rooms and examine it at her leisure. Her father might not think the engravings worth further investigation, but she did. The mysteries of the past had always intrigued her, and the Knights Templar had always been of particular interest to her.

She and her father worked quietly until it was time for luncheon. As had become his habit, he retired to his rooms after the meal, leaving Anne to work on her own. Usually she looked forward to her solitude, but as she made her way back to the armory, Anne found the prospect growing less appealing. Although she wasn't the sort given to fancy, the feeling that she wasn't alone wouldn't leave her, and the farther she moved away from the inhabited portions of the castle, the uneasier she became.

Even though she knew it was foolish, she could feel unseen eyes watching her from the shadows, and she sensed an unseen presence stalking her like a wolf stalking a lamb. The image had her increasing her pace, and the sound of her footsteps echoed eerily about her as she hurried along the deserted corridor toward the uncertain sanctuary of the armory. She'd almost reached the twisting staircase leading down to the armory when she heard the distinctive clank of metal on stone. The sound brought her to an abrupt halt and she spun around, determined to confront whoever had been following her.

"Who is it?" she called out, her voice firm despite the terror that had her heart racing in her chest.

The hallway was empty.

Anne stared down the deserted corridor in disbelief, wanting to doubt the evidence of her own eyes. Someone had to be there, she told herself, shivering as she gathered her shawl tighter about her. She might have imagined the sensation of being followed, but she *knew* she hadn't imagined that sound. It had been too real, too distinctive, to be mere imagination, and the realization had her shoulders slumping in relief.

Of course it was real, she told herself, turning back toward the staircase. Doubtless it was one of the footmen thinking to make sport of her. Now that he knew she wasn't so easily frightened, he would find something else to occupy his time. If not, she would simply have to have a word with his fearsome employer. However much he might resent her presence, she was fairly certain Mr. MacCairn wasn't the sort to tolerate such foolish behavior from his servants.

Shaking off what she now dismissed as boyish games, she flung herself into her work. She spent the next two hours examining and cataloguing the various weapons her father had set out, making careful notes that would aid in authenticating the collection. It surprised her to discover that the weapons were in such excellent condition, the blades of the swords dangerously sharp and ready for use. She wondered if Mr. MacCairn was expecting someone to lay siege to the castle, and the thought made her smile. If so, he should have no trouble holding them off. There were arms enough to hold off a battalion.

Unbidden, a sudden image of Mr. MacCairn flashed in her mind. She could see him bent over a sword with a whetting stone in his hand as he carefully honed the edge of the blade to a deadly sharpness. He worked with cold purpose, and she could sense that his intense concentration centered on his task. His black hair hung about his face, and as she watched he tucked an errant strand behind his ear. He muttered a Gaelic imprecation and then glanced up without warning, his green gaze narrowing as he surged powerfully to his feet.

"You were warned, *mo ceile*," he said, raising the sword high over his head and advancing slowly toward her. "You were warned. Now you will die."

Anne leaped to her feet with a sharp cry, stumbling back from the table with her arm raised in self-defense. Sensing someone behind her for the second time that day, she whirled around, and this time she found one of the footmen gazing at her in wide-eyed horror.

"Your . . . your pardon, Miss Garthwicke," he stammered, looking as if he might swoon. "I didna mean to frighten you."

Anne lowered her arm, her face coloring in embarrassment. "It is all right, James," she replied, struggling to regain what she could of her equanimity. "I didn't hear you knocking, that is all. Is there something you wish?"

The footman drew himself upright. "Mrs. Doughal begs your pardon, and asks if you will please join her in her sitting room," he said, delivering the message with commendable precision. "She would like to speak with you."

Anne almost sighed in relief. Usually she resented any interruption of her work, but she was suddenly anxious to put some distance between herself and the armory. The ancient room with its menacing air of violence and death was beginning to have a troubling effect upon her.

"I should be delighted," she said, managing a hasty smile. "Just let me lock up, and I shall follow you."

After making certain the room was safely secured, Anne followed the footman back up the stairs. Walking at the footman's side, Anne recalled what had happened earlier, and decided that now was as good a time as any to learn whether her suspicions had any foundation.

"This corridor seems rather deserted," she observed, keeping her voice carefully controlled. "Is it much used?"

"Oh, no, miss," the lad denied with a vigorous shake of his head. "The laird doesna like people down here, and allows only himself and Mr. Angley to come this way. And now you and your father, of course," he added in diffident tones.

Anne digested that in thoughtful silence. Try as she might she had a difficult time imagining the cold and autocratic Mr. MacCairn creeping down the hallway like some character out of a Gothic horror novel. It was even more difficult imaging the ancient butler indulging in similar sport, and she decided there had to be some other explanation for what she had experienced. Then it came to her.

"But how are you to move from one room to the other?" she asked, feigning polite curiosity. "Are there secret passages?"

"Oh, aye, the place is a rabbit warren of such things," he assured her with considerable enthusiasm. "Not that they are much used, mind. But for the armory, there are no other rooms in this wing that are opened. And a good thing too," he added, giving her a solemn look. "It is haunted."

His words confirmed Anne's suspicions that she'd been made a game of, and her jaw clenched in temper. "I see," she said, sounding bored. "How interesting."

Her ploy worked, and he gazed at her in astonishment. "You're no' afraid of ghosts, miss?"

"Of course not," she replied, happy to rob him of whatever pleasure he might have derived from his little charade. "There are no such things. I've worked in several ancient houses, all reputed to be haunted, and I've never so much as caught a glimpse of a single ghost. Stuff and nonsense, James, that is all it is."

To her surprise he didn't follow up her challenge with heated denials and grim stories of the castle's grizzly past. Instead he maintained a strained silence, depositing her at Mrs. Doughal's door before taking his leave with what could only be termed undue haste.

The plump housekeeper was much like the other housekeepers Anne had grown accustomed to dealing with, possessing a comfortable and decidedly matronly air. After settling Anne in the chair facing hers, Mrs.

Doughal poured her a cup of tea and then settled back in her own chair with a contented sigh.

"Are you finding all to your liking, Miss Garthwicke?" she asked, her dark eyes bright as she studied Anne over the rim of her cup. "The laird is most interested that you and your father are comfortably settled. He gave most strict orders that you were to have anything that you require."

"That is very good of Mr. MacCairn," Anne replied, not really surprised by the laird's command. However vexing she found him, he struck her as a man who could be counted upon to do his duty. "But we lack for nothing, I assure you. The castle is quite comfortable, despite its great age."

"Aye, and old it is," the housekeeper agreed with obvious pride. "Five hundred years this castle has stood, and not once in all that time has it been taken. Not even that English dog Cromwell could storm it, try as he would. No offense, miss," she added, as if belatedly recalling Anne's nationality.

Anne smiled to show that no offense had been taken. "Yes, I can believe this place would prove a tempting target," she said, taking a polite sip of tea. "I noted the burn marks by the portcullis: a memento of a siege, I take it?"

"And so it is," Mrs. Doughal confirmed. "But that was from another time, when Clan MacTeaugh sought to take advantage of the Shadowing and stormed the castle. They soon learned the error of their ways, mind, though it cost them a hundred or more dead in the learning. But that's a MacTeaugh for you." She tapped her forehead with her finger. "Thick as planks, the lot of them."

Not having met any MacTeaughs, Anne was willing to bow to the housekeeper's knowledge of the species. Then she thought of the odd expression the housekeeper used, and frowned thoughtfully.

"The Shadowing?" she repeated, leaning forward in interest. "What is that?"

A look of horror flashed across the housekeeper's face—and was just as quickly gone. "Oh, 'tis nothing, Miss Garthwicke," she assured her quickly. "An old Highland expression, that is all." She took a hasty gulp of tea and then flashed Anne a strained smile.

"But tell me how goes your work," she said, her tone as falsely cheerful as her smile. "A clever lass you must be, to know so much of old guns and the like."

Anne hesitated briefly before replying. But even as she answered Mrs. Doughal's questions, part of her was keeping wary watch. She had no idea what "the Shadowing" might be, but she was fairly certain it was far from "nothing." The housekeeper's response was yet another of the mysteries to confront her since she'd come to the castle, and like the other mysteries, it was something she was determined to solve.

She had told James she had no belief in such things as spirits, and for the most part that was true. But however much she might wish to dismiss the preternatural, there was no denying something untoward was happening within the ancient walls of the old castle. Was it truly ghosts, or something more sinister, something involving the handsome and enigmatic laird of Castle

MacCairn? Anne didn't know, but she did know that the answers to those questions were rapidly becoming of greater and greater importance to her. One way or another, she would have the truth.

Chapter Four

The first three days the Garthwickes were in residence passed slowly for Ruairdh. During the sunlight hours it was easy to cling to his decision to keep his distance from Miss Garthwicke, for she was as anxious to avoid his presence as he was anxious to avoid hers. The few times he encountered her she was distant, her manner no more than polite. Once or twice he thought he caught her looking at him with some curiosity, but she never spoke about anything not connected with her work.

Even the time he was forced to spend with her over dinner proved no problem, as her father dominated the conversation. The old fool never seemed to tire of the sound of his own voice, and prattled on and on about his progress in the armory. He never mentioned Anne's hard work, Ruairdh noted, and he had to bite his tongue more than once to keep from pointing out this fact.

But if Ruairdh was successful in keeping thoughts of the alluring blonde from his mind during the day, the nights were another matter. Erotic dreams of her plagued his sleep, the sensual images causing him no end of torment and delight. He'd taught himself to awaken before the dreams went as far as they had that first night, and for that he was grateful. Still, his desires haunted him, making his temper more uncertain than ever.

That afternoon Ruairdh was in his study going over Miss Garthwicke's latest report when Angley entered the room, his lined features set in a dour scowl.

"You're wanted downstairs," he informed Ruairdh with a grumble of disapproval. "Your fine solicitor is come from London, and he'll no' leave, he says, until he's spoken with you."

Ruairdh glanced up at his steward, his eyebrows arching in surprise. He hadn't been expecting the solicitor for several weeks yet, and wondered what had brought the rather studious young man from the city. Then he thought of something that had him paling.

"Did he say what he wanted?" he asked, fearing he might have sent for the man without realizing what he was doing. Such things were possible, he knew, recalling stories of how his father had behaved before being taken at last. He would say and do things one day, and then claim to have no memory of them the next.

"Matters pertaining to the estate, he said, as if it had naught to do with me," Angley's indignant sniff went a long way toward setting Ruairdh's mind at ease.

"Whatever were you thinking, hiring a *Sasunnach* to see to the clan's business? What does one of them know of us and our ways?"

"Enough to keep the clan intact when I am taken," Ruairdh replied bluntly, feeling his relief give way to the terrifying black temper that was growing increasingly difficult to control. "See to his needs, Angley, and tell him I shall be with him shortly. Do not argue with me."

"As you wish, laird," Angley said, too lost in his own anger to note the change stealing over Ruairdh. "But I still say—"

"Be silent, old man!" Ruairdh roared, but it wasn't his mind that formed the words, nor his voice that spoke them. "Do not presume to question my authority again, or, by the devil, I will break you in half!"

As if from a distance Ruairdh could hear the deep voice speaking, and then he was himself again, gazing at his stunned steward in sick horror.

"Angley," he managed to say, nearly collapsing with relief at the reassuring sound of his own voice emerging from his lips. "Angley, I am so sorry. I—"

"Do no' worry yourself, *tighearna*," the older man said, his faded eyes filling with tears. " 'Twas no' you. And your pardon for plaguing you when you are so tired. I'll see to the young gentleman, as you bade me." And he quietly walked from the room, his back stooped with the weight of his years.

Ruairdh watched him leave, fury and despair rising up in him in a swirling tide. Swearing softly, he turned to his desk, opening the secret compartment and taking out the pistol he had hidden there. It was small and almost delicately made, but its elegant appearance belied its true power. He'd had it designed for himself in Edinburgh and knew that it was every bit as effective as any of the weapons hanging in the armory. Indeed, he was counting upon it. When the time came, it would be his only salvation.

Ruairdh paused to change his clothes before going down to meet his guest. He also took a few moments to calm himself. The incident with Angley had left him shaken, and he wanted to be certain of his control before meeting an outsider. Not that George Hughes, the young solicitor he'd engaged before leaving London, would dare say a word no matter how madly he behaved. The lad was as affable as a puppy, and every bit as eager to please, which was why Ruairdh had hired him. A solicitor with his own opinions was likely to ask questions, and that he would not tolerate.

The solicitor was pacing nervously in front of the fireplace when Ruairdh walked into the parlor. At the sound of the door opening he jumped like a startled doe, whirling around to confront Ruairdh with an expression of fear on his face.

"Good day to you, Mr. Hughes," Ruairdh said, wondering what ailed the lad. "Welcome to Castle MacCairn."

"Thank you, M-Mr. MacCairn," the younger man stammered, his cheeks going from deathly white to bright pink as he flushed. "I hope you don't mind my coming without being summoned, but I have important news to discuss with you, and didn't wish to wait. I-I trust I haven't given offense?" Wide blue eyes regarded him with vague alarm.

So he hadn't sent for the lad, Ruairdh thought, relaxing with a sigh. "Not at all, Mr. Hughes," he said formally. "Good news is always a welcome guest, as are you. Pray be seated, and tell me what has brought you all the way from London."

Mr. Hughes glanced at the pair of massive chairs sitting before the fire Ruairdh had indicated, and swallowed visibly. "Oh, yes, of course, Mr. MacCairn," he said, sounding as if he'd been offered the hangman's rope instead. "Thank you."

Ruairdh raised an eyebrow as he took his own seat. He'd known the other man to be a wee bit timid, but he hadn't taken him for such a coward. The darker part of him sneered in derision, but Ruairdh closed his mind to those whispers.

"Very well, then," he said, settling in the chair facing Hughes and arrogantly folding his arms across his chest. "This news you bring, it is good, I take it?"

The question had the other man preening like a delighted schoolboy. "Oh, yes, Mr. MacCairn, indeed it is!" he exclaimed, all but squirming in pleasure. "The very best news, in fact." He leaned forward in the manner of a friend passing on a confidence. "I believe I have found a buyer!"

Something in Ruairdh screamed out a howl of outrage. "For the castle, do you mean?" he asked cautiously, tightening the reins of his control.

"For everything!"

"Everything?" Ruairdh repeated, frowning over the other man's gleeful response.

"The paintings, the furnishings, the antiquities, all of it!" Mr. Hughes was all but giddy with joy. "And for the very price you named! Mr. Pelham didn't quibble by so much as a farthing."

Ruairdh clenched his jaw to hold back a wail of anguish. He felt as if Hughes had taken one of the broadswords from the armory and gutted him with it. The pain was agonizing, and it was several seconds before he managed to speak.

"I see," he said, forcing himself to remain emotionless. "That is good news."

His words must have been even less convincing than his flat tone, as the pleasure slowly faded from Mr. Hughes's face and was replaced by an expression of bewildered uncertainty.

"Do . . . do you wish me to proceed, Mr. MacCairn?" he asked diffidently, regarding Ruairdh askance. "You do not seem overly pleased, if you do not mind my saying so."

"I am selling land and property my clan has bled and died for," Ruairdh retorted curtly, his nerves too raw for him to prevaricate. "You cannot think I do so with any great joy."

Mr. Hughes's boyish cheeks suffused with color. "Of course, Mr. MacCairn," he said, lowering his eyes. "Forgive me. I-I didn't think."

Ruairdh gave an uncomfortable shrug. "It is not important," he replied, thinking only of what must be done. "Thank you for bringing me the information so quickly. As for the sale, you may begin drawing up the necessary papers. Although I'll want it made plain that the actual sale is to take place only upon my death."

Mr. Hughes looked so horrified Ruairdh wondered if he would swoon. "Your death, sir?" he repeated in patent astonishment. "You'll forgive me, I am sure, but you are a young man yet, in the very best of health. With God's blessing you could live a good fifty years, if not more. Mr. Pelham is hardly likely to wait so long as that to take possession."

The sudden desire to grab the young fool by the throat and snap his damned neck rose up in Ruairdh, but he beat it down with grim determination. Instead he surged out of his chair and began impatiently pacing the length of the parlor, coming to a halt in front of the French doors overlooking the back of the castle. The idea of explaining himself was both humiliating and infuriating, but he knew he would have to bear it. What other choice did he have?

"I do not have fifty years left to me," he said at last, his hands clenched behind his back as he gazed out at the stark and beautiful Highlands he loved with all his heart. "It is likely I'll not even see out the end of this one." He swung around to face the solicitor, who was regarding him in stunned horror.

"Why do you think I am so determined to sell all that I have, all that I am?" he demanded, making no attempt now to hide his pain and his anger. "I want the clan looked after once I am taken, and this is the only way to see it done."

Mr. Hughes grew even paler, his discomfort plain as he met Ruairdh's defiant gaze. "I do not know what to say," he said quietly, his eyes soft with compassion. "Pray accept my deepest condolences, sir. I didn't know you were ill."

Ruairdh's shoulders slumped, his temper easing out of him like a sigh. "There is no reason that you should have," he said, dismissing the younger man's pity with an impatient wave of his hand. "It is not something that is common knowledge."

He returned to his chair and sat down, once more in firm control of his emotions. "Now, as to the offer," he began, his manner brisk, "return to London and tell Mr. Pelham of my conditions. If he is agreeable to them and will still pay the price I ask, we'll have a bargain."

Mr. Hughes all but leaped out of his chair in his eagerness to be away. "Yes, sir, as you wish," he said, already inching toward the door and escape. "I shall leave on the train first thing tomorrow. Now, if you'll excuse me, I must return to the village and seek a room at the inn. I saw one just as I was getting off the train. Good day to you." And he bolted for the door.

Ruairdh watched him with resignation. God knew he had no desire for the dolt's company, but that didn't mean he could abandon his responsibilities. "You needn't seek lodgings at an inn, Mr. Hughes," he said, just as the other man was reaching for the latch. "We've rooms enough here in the castle to put you up."

The solicitor spun around, an expression of almost comic dismay on his face. "Oh, no!" he cried, and then as if realizing what he'd just said, he added, "That is to say, it's very kind of you, but I've no wish to impose. I shall do quite well at the inn, I assure you."

The polite smile Ruairdh had pinned to his lips disappeared at this. The offer had been made more out of form than anything else, and he didn't care to have it thrown back in his face.

"Ah, but I am afraid I must insist, Mr. Hughes," he

said, taking cold delight in watching the other man squirm. "Here in the Highlands hospitality to a guest is a matter of great importance. I would not think to dishonor my name and my clan by sending a guest out into the dark. You will remain with us."

Mr. Hughes looked as if he might dissolve into tears, and then he drew himself up with commendable fortitude.

"Thank you, Mr. MacCairn," he said, his hands rigidly clenched at his sides as he resolutely met Ruairdh's gaze. "It is very kind of you."

Ruairdh's lips curved in a smile he neither felt nor instigated. "Is it?" he asked, his voice sly and deep. "We shall see, lad. We shall see."

The news that a guest would be joining them for dinner had the little maid assigned to Anne twittering in anticipation. She insisted Anne wear her best evening gown and set of jewels in the gentleman's honor, and then set about doing Anne's toilette with an astonishing degree of enthusiasm. Anne did her best to remain silent, but when the younger woman began twisting her hair into a tortuous arrangement of curls, she felt the time had come to put a halt to the nonsense before it was too late.

"Really, Jennie, there is no need for you to make such a fuss," she said, her voice softly chiding as the maid patted another curl into place. "My usual style will more than suit, I am sure."

"Indeed, miss, it will not!" the maid shot back, looking horrified. "The gentleman's a solicitor come all the way from London, Molly says, and as handsome as can be in the bargain. Who is to say he'll not take one look at you and fall madly in love? That would be a fine thing, wouldn't it?"

To Anne's dismay, she could feel herself growing warm. "Nonsense, Jennie," she said, glancing at her reflection and doing her best to look aloof. "I am far too practical to think of such things. Besides," she added, holding back a sigh, "I have my father to think of."

"If you say so, miss." Jennie gave a loud sniff. "But if you're wanting my opinion of it, this terrible, dark place could do with a bit of romance. And it would do the laird's heart good, I think, to see some happiness about him. God knows the poor man will know none of his own, doomed as he is."

The word had Anne starting in surprise. "Doomed?" she repeated, turning on the bench to gaze up at the loquacious maid. "Jennie, whatever do you mean?"

The maid began snatching up pins and ribbons and stuffing them into Anne's dressing kit. "Nothing, Miss Garthwicke," she said, her eyes carefully avoiding Anne's. "Listen to me, kimmering away like a magpie when I ought to be about my chores! Mrs. Doughal will have my head and more if she hears of it. Ring for me when you've need, miss. Good night."

After the girl had fled, Anne sat in front of her mirror frowning at her reflection. What the devil was going on? she wondered, picking up the bottle of lilac-scented toilet water and dabbing the crystal stopper against her neck. First Mrs. Doughal's odd remark about "the Shadowing," and now Jennie's careless comment about Mr. MacCairn being doomed. Both women had quickly tried to brush the matter aside as nothing, and yet she couldn't help but be troubled. If it was nothing, why did they not speak of it? What were they hiding, and more important, why did they feel compelled to hide it? Anne shook her head.

What foolishness, she decided, the silk skirts of her blue gown rustling as she rose to her feet. Of course there was nothing wrong; she was being overimaginative and emotional, that was all. Her father was forever warning her against such behavior, and it would seem he had the right of it. Servants were often given to speculation and gossip about their employers, and the less credence she gave their tattle, the better.

But even as she was reading herself this bracing lecture, she was shaking her head in denial. Something *was* wrong, and it had been wrong almost from the first moment she'd set eyes upon the castle and its brooding laird. Perhaps James was right and the castle was haunted, she thought, rubbing arms that were suddenly pimpling with the cold. Certainly only a ghost or some other spiritual phenomenon could account for the disquieting events that had befallen her since her arrival.

"Anne?" Her father tapped on the door and then stepped inside, blinking at her in his owlish way. "Are you ready, my dear? We cannot keep our host waiting, you know."

"Yes, Papa," Anne said, picking up her shawl and hurrying over to join him. He was growing quite absentminded of late—moving things about and then forgetting where he had put them—and she was increasingly concerned. She couldn't bear to think his mind was beginning to fail him as well as his sight.

The laird and his guest were seated in the drawing

room when she and her father made their entrance, and she was somewhat taken aback to see that Mr. MacCairn was once again wearing his Highland dress. He'd worn it on the night they'd first arrived, and she recalled thinking how very regal he'd looked sitting beneath the battle flags and pennants of his clan.

"I see you are wearing your plaid, Mr. MacCairn," she said, hoping her father would pick up on the none-too-subtle hint. "You honor us, it would seem."

"It is kind of you to say so, Miss Garthwicke," he said, bowing with the aloof politeness he usually afforded her. "Although I would say 'tis you who honors us with your beauty. Would you not say so, Mr. Hughes?" And he turned to the brown-haired young man standing at his left, who was regarding Anne with obvious appreciation gleaming in his light blue eyes.

"Indeed I would, Mr. MacCairn," he agreed, bowing as well. "It is a pleasure to meet you, Miss Garthwicke."

There was an uncomfortable silence, and then Mr. MacCairn was performing the more formal introductions. The young solicitor was also a great admirer of her father, and the two men fell into an animated conversation about the exhibition being held in London.

"I have gone several times already," Mr. Hughes said, taking care to include Anne in the conversation. "What of you?"

"A few times only, I fear," Anne replied, smiling at the memory. "There were so many fascinating things, but the crowds were quite dreadful. One could scarce get a proper look at anything without having to peer around a bonnet or over the top of one of the gentlemen's hats."

"To be sure," Mr. Hughes agreed with a happy nod. "What is your favorite exhibit? I must own to a partiality for the rugs and furnishings from India. I have always longed to go there."

"Oh, the elephant," Anne said at once, her dark thoughts forgotten for the moment. "It was so enormous, one could scarce credit it had ever been alive! And the display of ancient weaponry was interesting, of course. Papa acted as an adviser for it, didn't you, Papa?" she added, turning to her father.

"Indeed," he agreed, brightening with pleasure. "His Royal Highness had read one of my articles in an antiquarian journal and insisted I be consulted. Naturally I was more than delighted to offer him whatever assistance I could."

"And you, Mr. MacCairn?" Mr. Hughes asked, glancing hopefully at the other man. "Were you able to see the Exhibition before leaving London?"

"No." Mr. MacCairn's reply was as cool as his expression. "I was not."

The awkward pause that followed this curt response was relieved by the announcement that dinner was being served, and they rose to their feet. Anne turned to assist her father, only to find their host blocking her path.

"Miss Garthwicke," he said, holding his arm out to her in obvious command.

Anne hesitated for a moment, but it was long enough to have him raising his eyebrows in silent challenge. Tempting as it was to spurn the autocratic offer, Anne knew she dared not, and laid her hand on his arm. To her surprise the muscled flesh beneath her gloved fingers was as unyielding as stone, and she realized he wasn't as sanguine as he appeared. She shot him a worried glance from beneath her lashes, but as usual his harsh features revealed nothing of his inner thoughts. Deeply troubled but not knowing why, she remained silent as he escorted her into the dining room.

In honor of Mr. Hughes dinner was an elaborate affair, and course followed course as they dined leisurely into the night. A variety of wines accompanied the dishes, and Anne watched uneasily as her father drank far more than was his custom. Mr. Hughes also seemed to be enjoying the castle's excellent cellars, and Anne noted that his wineglass seldom remained full for very long. She also noted that while the wine made her father more animated, it appeared to be having decidedly the opposite effect upon the solicitor.

The younger man vacillated between periods of bright, meaningless chatter, and sudden bouts of uneasy silence during which he would cast their host nervous glances. His manner put Anne in mind of a fearful child in the presence of a strict and disapproving parent, and she wondered what ailed him. He seemed almost terrified of Mr. MacCairn, and, glancing at their mysterious host, Anne supposed she couldn't fault the poor fellow for his fears.

Sitting at the head of the massive table, his lean face illuminated by the flickering candlelight, Ruairdh MacCairn looked like a demon sprung straight from hell itself. His coal black hair was brushed straight back from his forehead, and was long enough to touch the top of his broad shoulders. His green eyes glittered like the most expensive of jewels, but however bright their color, they reflected neither light nor life. It was like looking at a well-wrought painting, a beautiful work of art that captured the image of a man, but lacked that man's heart and soul. The thought had her shivering.

"Are you cold, Miss Garthwicke?"

The deep, hypnotic voice broke through Anne's musings. She blinked her eyes, only to find the subject of her thoughts regarding her with sharp-eyed concern. To cover her sudden uneasiness she reached for her wineglass, taking a deep sip before answering.

"Only a trifle, Mr. MacCairn," she said, refusing to let him know he had discomfited her. "But in a castle so old as this, drafts are to be expected. It adds to the charm."

His green eyes sparked with emerald fire as he gave her an impersonal smile. "So that is what you think it is?" he asked, his deep voice taking on a mocking drawl. "A draft?"

"Of course," she replied crisply. "What else could it be?"

He leaned back in his chair, his expression shifting from concern to sly amusement. "Many things, Miss Garthwicke, many things. This castle is said to be haunted. Perhaps it was a *spiorad* you felt. A ghost," he added, at her frown.

"Ghosts, is it?" Her father gave a low chuckle, the wine having loosened his tongue. "You'll have to do better than that, Mr. MacCairn, if you wish to frighten Anne. My daughter is far too sensible to believe in such things."

The look the laird aimed at her father was one of cold dislike. "You dismiss rather quickly powers which you cannot hope to understand," he said, his hand balling into a fist. "Are you God, then, to declare with such certainty what does or does not exist?"

Her father's indulgent smile wavered and was gone. "Indeed not, sir," he answered cautiously. "I am a man of science and reason. Everyone knows ghosts are nonsense. No one in these enlightened times believes in them."

Mr. MacCairn brought his fist crashing to the table. "Science?" He all but roared the word. "Reason? What have those to do with anything? Look about you, scholar. Do you think 'twas reason that built all of this, or science that kept it in MacCairn hands against all who would take it?"

Her father paled, his hands fluttering up to straighten his elegant cravat. "I . . . That is to say, I meant no offense," he stammered, sounding like a bewildered child. "I merely spoke in jest, I assure you."

Anne placed her hand on her father's arm in a protective gesture. "Mr. MacCairn knows that, Papa," she soothed, meeting that icy green gaze with simmering anger. "Now it is he who jests with us. Is that not so, sir?" She raised an eyebrow in deliberate challenge.

There was a brief hesitation when she feared he would throw her challenge back in her teeth; then he was dipping his head to her in silent acquiescence. "Perhaps," he agreed, his tone thawing slightly. "We Scots take great pride in our ghosts and we do not care to have them slighted, especially by learned *Sasunnachs*. Who knows what the *bogles* might do to punish us?" he added, with a flash of boyish charm that had both her father and Mr. Hughes relaxing with visible relief.

The rest of the meal passed in relative tranquillity. Mr. Hughes seemed to have lost his initial uneasiness and spoke to her with increasing animation. His bright, friendly chatter made a pleasant change from the oppressive silences she had grown accustomed to, and she found it easy to respond in kind. Although he was older he seemed no more than a boy to her, and she treated him with the same gentle encouragement and kindness as she did the young men her father occasionally took on as pupils.

Finally the meal was at an end, and they rose from the table. There would be sherry served in the library, and Mr. Hughes and her father started in that direction, lost in their discussion of the latest scientific developments. Anne made to follow, only to find her way blocked by Mr. MacCairn.

"A moment, Miss Garthwicke, if you please," he said, gazing down at her with dark, unreadable eyes.

Anne's heart immediately increased its pounding—a reaction she had learned to keep carefully hidden behind a cool, social mask. "Of course, sir," she said, managing a polite smile. "What is it?"

He remained silent several seconds before responding. "Our guest seems to find you most charming," he said at last, his manner chilly with disapproval. "I should take care if I were you to mind he doesn't find you *too* charming."

She froze at the audacious words. "I beg your pardon?"

His expression remained aloof. "I spoke clearly enough." His voice held little inflection. " 'Tis plain Hughes is smitten with you, and would take you to his bed did you offer him the smallest encouragement. I am telling you not to offer that encouragement."

Anne's cheeks warmed with color. "How dare you!" she exclaimed furiously. "Mr. Hughes is a gentleman!"

"He is a man," Mr. MacCairn returned, moving closer, until she could feel the raw power emanating from him. "And I dare because I am the laird here. I'll not have you making a scandal with that tame puppy."

Anne was too outraged to exercise caution. "I would hardly call a polite conversation conducted in the presence of my father making a scandal," she retorted. "And if it were, it is hardly your place to take me to task for it. You may be laird of Castle MacCairn, but that doesn't give you any power over me!"

His expression of stern disapproval shifted into one of powerful sensuality. "Do not be so sure of that," he said, reaching out to stroke her cheek with his finger. "Under my roof I own all. I could take you, if such were my wish, and there would be no one to stop me. Remember that, *boidheach*. I'll not warn you again."

Something in his words sent a shiver of apprehension shuddering through Anne. She stared up into a face she had studied much over the last few days, and yet saw someone she didn't recognize. The thought had her jerking free, and she hurried out of the dining room, aware of his heated gaze following her.

Chapter Five

Her lover's hands caressed her with breathtaking sensuality, his clever fingers making her shiver and burn by turns. His lips and tongue teased her breasts, and when he drew the throbbing nipples into his mouth, the wild pleasure she felt had her crying out. Her hands fisted in the thickness of his hair, her body arching as she offered herself to him in shameless abandon.

"More, leannan.*" Her lover groaned, pressing his weight against her and making her intimately aware of his desire. "Give me more. Open your legs for me and let me inside."*

The shocking words should have horrified; her instead they filled her with smug pleasure, and she did as he bade. His fingers skimmed down her body, playing at the soft folds of her femininity before slipping deep inside to sample the sweet dampness gathering there.

"Oh!" Anne gave a keening cry, a shudder of pleasure

shaking her as her eyes fluttered open. She gazed up at the canopy curved over her bed, gasping for air as her shattered senses took in her surroundings. It came as no surprise to find she was alone, and as she always did when awakening from one of these dreams, Anne wasn't certain if she was relieved or disappointed.

Shaking her head, she rose from the bed and padded over to stand before the window, her expression troubled as she gazed out into the blackness of the night. She knew it would take some time for her senses to return to her control, and until then attempting to sleep would be useless. The thought had her sighing as she pressed her fevered brow to the cool glass. God in heaven, what was happening to her?

The dreams had started that first night, and with each succeeding night they grew increasingly graphic. In those dreams she knew what a man's most intimate touch felt like, and how his breathing changed as his lovemaking intensified. She was a virgin who'd never shared more than a chaste kiss with a man; such things should be beyond her experience. Indeed, the very thought of them should have her swooning in maidenly horror. But it wasn't horror she felt; it was pleasure—pleasure made all the more confusing because even in the most intimate of embraces, she never saw the face of the man who made such ardent love to her.

He came to her out of the darkness, a formless shadow as raw and elemental as the night itself. She knew his touch, the burning feel of his flesh beneath her hands, but his features remained a blur in her mind. At first she feared it was Mr. MacCairn she dreamed of, and the thought had her writhing in mortification even as she accepted the logic of it. The powerful and enigmatic laird occupied so much of her mind during the day, it was understandable that thoughts of him should follow her into her dreams at night.

Yet if it was Mr. MacCairn she dreamed of, she wondered, confusion giving way to intellectual curiosity, why didn't she see his face? Feminine modesty was one thing, but it seemed ridiculous to her that she could dream of him touching her in so intimate a manner and yet draw the line at seeing features that were as familiar to her as her own. It made no sense, and she was getting heartily tired of things not making any sense.

Perhaps they should leave, she thought, and was surprised at the pain the admission brought her. They'd been in Scotland for over a week, and despite the unease she often felt, she had come to love the ancient castle. And it was more than her unusual affinity for such places, she admitted uneasily. It even had very little to do with the reluctant fascination she felt for the castle's brooding owner. Instead it was as if the very stones of the castle were calling to her, whispering to her to remain with them forever.

The fanciful notion had her shaking her head a second time, and she was about to return to bed when something caught her attention. Frowning, she leaned closer, peering through the glass for the faint flicker of light she'd glimpsed out of the corner of her eye. At first she didn't see anything and was almost convinced she'd been imagining things; then she saw the light again. It was coming from the barred window she'd noticed upon arriving, and the shock of that sent all thoughts of her heated dreams fleeing from her mind.

The tower was kept locked on the laird's orders; entrance forbidden on the grounds that the decrepit building was too dangerous to be explored. The servants seemed as terrified of their employer as they were devoted to him, and she couldn't imagine one of them defying him over so grave a matter. She also recalled hearing whispers that the tower was haunted, and she recalled the genuine terror on the young footman's face as he'd warned her away from the staircase. Then she thought of something that had the very blood freezing in her veins.

Her father hadn't been pleased when he'd learned of Mr. MacCairn's edict that no one was to enter the abandoned tower. He'd become quite furious over the matter, accusing her of carrying tales to the laird behind his back. He'd even threatened to enter the forbidden wing in defiance of their host's orders, vowing to prove he was still capable of carrying out his duties. He wasn't, of course, and Anne had been near tears before she'd managed to dissuade him.

But what if she hadn't dissuaded him? she wondered, sliding an uneasy glance toward the light flickering through the barred window. Her father had always been proud of his accomplishments, and she knew how his infirmity and growing dependency upon her grated on that pride. What if all the wine he'd so foolishly drunk had filled him with enough false courage to defy Mr. MacCairn and enter the forbidden tower? His eyesight was poor under the best of circumstances; in the dark of night, in a dangerous, crumbling tower, death was but a misstep away. The thought galvanized Anne into action, and she dashed over to the wardrobe to retrieve her cloak from its cavernous depths.

Pausing only long enough to slip on her sturdiest shoes and pick up a brace of candles, she slipped out of her room and into the dark and deserted corridor. This part of the castle had been redecorated along with the front of the house, and modern gaslight flickered softly from the sconces on the wall. Usually she disdained their garish brightness, but tonight she was grateful for their light as she hurried down the wide staircase and back toward the oldest parts of the castle. The thought of exploring the ancient building in darkness didn't bear considering.

Anne left the inhabited part of the castle behind her, and was soon in the hall just above the armory. The east wing lay to her right, and she was trying to gather enough courage to enter the dark and foreboding hallway when she heard a footfall behind her. The sound had her heart leaping into her throat, before she remembered the same thing had happened once during her first days in the castle. She'd been terrified then too, convinced someone was following her, but when she'd turned to look there had been nothing there. The memory reassured her and she turned around, certain she'd find nothing but darkness and shadows behind her.

The sight of a tall figure emerging out of the half darkness of the hallway froze the cry of terror rising in her throat. Sheer instinct had her clinging to the candles rather than dropping them, but the fragile flames flickered and almost died before she was able to control her wild trembling. The footsteps grew nearer, but before she could draw in enough breath to scream, the figure emerged fully into the light. The breath she'd gathered exploded out of her in a sigh of recognition.

"Oh, Mr. MacCairn, you frightened me nearly to death!" she said, so relieved to see him instead of some dreadful apparition that she forgot her earlier pique. "What are you doing creeping about this time of night?"

He stepped farther into the light, the flickering candles casting demonic shadows across the lean planes of his face. "What am I doing?" he repeated, his eyes furious as he studied her. "A better question might be what are you doing? Or need I ask?"

Anne's relief was replaced by wariness at the insinuating words. "What do you mean?" she demanded, uneasily aware of his masculinity and the fact that they were far from help should she have need of it.

As if sensing her thoughts he moved even closer, until he was all but looming over her. He was dressed as he had been earlier in the night, his hard, muscular body wrapped in the plaid of his clan, and she could feel the tension radiating from him. His sudden closeness brought to mind her heated dream, and she took an instinctive step back from him.

He took in her involuntary response with an expression suspiciously close to satisfaction. "I mean, Miss Garthwicke," he continued, his deep voice silky with menace, "if you are looking for your admirer's room, you have come too far. Mr. Hughes's rooms are above yours in the newer wing."

Anne flinched, but she refused to be drawn into verbal battle with him for the second time that evening. "I was about to retire for the night when I saw a light burning in the tower window," she began, deciding she had nothing to lose by telling the truth. "I thought my fath—That is," she amended hastily, "that someone may have gone exploring and become lost."

"Which tower?"

"The barred one in the east wing."

His expression hardened at the news. "You are mistaken," he told her imperiously. "No one is allowed in that part of the castle. It is too dangerous."

"I am aware of that, which is why I was so concerned," Anne answered, growing impatient. With each passing second her concern for her father grew greater, until a feeling of utmost dread had her trembling with fear. Anxious to reach her father, she tried walking around Mr. MacCairn, only to have him move more firmly into her path.

"I will see to the matter," he said, gazing down at her, his green eyes cold and remote. "Return to your bed."

Anne's worry over her father overcame her customary reticence, and she firmly stood her ground. "I should prefer to continue, if you do not mind," she said, drawing her cloak close about her and feigning a calm she did not feel. "Someone could be hurt, and I shan't be able to sleep until I am assured all is well."

A look of marked impatience flickered briefly across his face. "As it happens, I mind a great deal," he informed her curtly. "And no one is hurt. Like as not one of the footmen has managed to lure one of the maids into the tower for a bit of lovemaking, and I doubt it will be a sight for a proper little *Sasunnach* like you. For the last time, Miss Garthwicke, return to your room, else I will be forced to wonder if you've another reason for wandering my halls in your nightclothes."

Temper and chagrin overrode Anne's unease. "You may wonder what you wish, Mr. MacCairn," she replied frostily, "but I am going to the tower. If you wish to accompany me, you will be welcome; if not, please stand to one side."

Mr. MacCairn stiffened; his eyes narrowing and his lips tightening in anger, and Anne feared she'd gone too far. To her amazement his expression seemed to waver, like a reflection in a pond, and then he was smiling, lifting his hand to brush the tips of his fingers across her cheek.

"If it's your father you're worrying over, you needn't bother," he said, his deep voice as provocative as the unexpected caress. "Had you thought to look in on him, as I did, you'd know he is snoring peacefully away in his bed. All is well, I promise you."

Faced with the inexplicable change in his behavior, Anne wasn't certain how to respond. This was a side of her host she'd never seen before, but instead of relieving her, it filled her with a mounting sense of alarm. Something wasn't right, she decided, shivering slightly. Perhaps it would be wisest to go.

"If Father is safe, then I believe I shall return to my room," she said, inching cautiously back from him. "Good night, Mr. MacCairn, I—"

"Ruairdh," he interrupted, his lips curving in a smile. "It is my given name, and as we are alone I see no reason why you shouldn't make use of it. Indeed, it would please me if you did so."

The odd sense of intuition Anne had come to rely

upon sounded a clarion warning. "I do not believe that would be proper, sir," she prevaricated, aware again of their isolation.

His smile deepened, and the eyes she'd thought the color of emeralds gleamed like jet in the wavering light of the candles. "And are you always proper, then, *leannan?*" he asked, his voice a husky purr.

Anne felt the color leave her face. "W-what did you say?"

"*Leannan*," he repeated, clearly amused by her reaction. " 'Tis a Gaelic word, and not so scandalous as you seem to think. Shall I tell you what it means?" He reached out a powerful hand for her.

Anne stumbled back, disbelief making her shake. *Leannan* was the word her dream lover had whispered to her—a word she'd dismissed as imaginary. But if it was real, what else might be real as well?

"I-I must go," she stammered, her mind racing with possibilities, each more horrifying than the last. And it wasn't just the word that was frightening her, she realized, desperation wrapping its vicious fingers about her throat. There was something about Mr. MacCairn, something that made her think that if he touched her again, she'd never survive. Unwilling to remain in his company a moment longer she turned and fled, the sound of his mocking laughter following her as she raced through the empty stone corridor.

Ruairdh woke the following morning with a heavy head and a heavier heart. He remembered encountering Miss Garthwicke in the hall and hearing her speak of the tower; after that there was only the teasing ghosts of memories. He had asked her to call him by his name, or at least—he frowned—he thought he had. It was all very hazy, like images wreathed in smoke, and his inability to clearly recall the night's events was troubling. It meant the Shadowing was closer than he had feared.

There was no sign of either the Garthwickes or Mr. Hughes when he came down for breakfast, and Ruairdh breathed a silent sigh of relief. Until he was more certain of himself and his control, he preferred not facing the others just now. He dined in solitary splendor before going to his study to begin his day's work, and wasn't in the least surprised to find Angley waiting for him.

"You're late," the steward snapped disapprovingly. "You're becoming indolent, lying in your bed until nearly noon."

Ruairdh accepted the scolding without comment, despite the fact that it was scarcely ten in the morning. Instead he settled into the chair behind his desk, his expression shuttered as he studied his steward.

"It is probably nothing," he began cautiously, "but I found Miss Garthwicke wandering about last evening, and she claimed she'd seen a light in the tower."

Angley gave a horrified gasp. "The tower? You didna go near that terrible place, did you?"

Ruairdh's lips twisted in a smile of bitter acceptance. "No. I've no desire to tempt fate just yet. I told her she was mistaken, and she returned to her rooms and I to mine. But I thought we should check, just in case. See to it, Angley." He didn't see any reason to share the rest of the night's events—especially since he couldn't be certain what was real and what was not.

"I will, laird," the older man replied with a nod. "But in truth I cannot think who would dare defy your orders."

"It is probably nothing, as I said," Ruairdh said, anxious to change the conversation. "In the meanwhile I need to speak with Hughes before he leaves. Is he awake yet?"

Angley gave a derisive snort. "He's awake. Green as a frog and moaning like a bogey, but awake. The scholar's not much better, I'm hearing, and will likely keep to his bed for the day." He shook his head. "These English, they've no' the head for spirits as we Highlanders. I'll just go and rouse the lad, else we'll never be shed of him."

Knowing how ruthlessly efficient his steward could be, Ruairdh quickly removed the letter he kept locked in the drawer of his desk. He'd written it shortly after returning to the castle, and however much he might wish it otherwise, he knew the time had come to make certain the document was placed in the proper hands. He was sealing the letter when there was a hesitant tap on the door, and Mr. Hughes crept inside.

"You . . . you wished to see me, Mr. MacCairn?" he asked diffidently.

Ruairdh glanced up, amusement stirring at the sight of the younger man cowering in the door. He inhaled deeply, his heightened senses savoring the reek of fear and weakness he could smell wafting from the boy. The lad thought him a demon, he realized, reading the other man's mind with dark satisfaction. It might be amusing to prove him right. The thought had scarcely formed before Ruairdh was forcing it from his mind.

"Come in, Mr. Hughes," he said, hiding his clenched fists beneath his desk. "You slept well, I trust?"

The stunned look on his guest's face made it plain he wasn't certain what to make of the prosaic words. "Quite well, thank you," he said, his eyes cautious as he inched closer. "Your home is very lovely."

"Be sure you tell Mr. Pelham as much," Ruairdh said with a bitter laugh. "We wouldn't want him thinking he's made a bad bargain and changing his mind, would we?"

"Oh, there is no chance of that, I am certain," Mr. Hughes assured him as he took his seat. "I spoke with both Mr. Garthwicke and his charming daughter, and from what they have said, I daresay Mr. Pelham will be even more eager to buy Castle MacCairn. It is precisely what he was looking for."

Anger, black and vicious, erupted inside of Ruairdh, but he fought it back. What did it matter who lived in the castle after he was gone? he asked himself. The clan would be provided for, and that was all that should concern him.

"Miss Garthwicke has told me about the work she and her father are doing in your armory," Hughes continued, oblivious to Ruairdh's tense silence. "It sounds fascinating, although I don't approve of her handling such dangerous weapons. The sword she was describing sounds especially deadly. What if she should cut herself?"

Ruairdh stirred uneasily, an image forming in his mind of Anne holding a sword balanced in her delicate hands. She was wearing a pair of white cotton gloves, and he could read enough of her mind to know the gloves were more to protect the ancient steel than to save her fingers from a nick. Her dark blond eyebrows were knitted in a small frown, and her smoky gray eyes were narrowed in fierce concentration as she examined the weapon. She did indeed seem captivated, he mused, and wondered if she would bring the same intensity to a man's bed. Another vision began forming in his mind, and when he realized its direction, he banished it with an impatient shake of his head.

"As we are speaking of Miss Garthwicke, sir"—Mr. Hughes was regarding Ruairdh cautiously—"I wonder if I might have your permission to write her? A-about the work she is doing, that is," he added, when Ruairdh's expression hardened. "I shall need to be kept abreast of the restoration and cataloging, you know."

The beasts Ruairdh kept tightly leashed began to snap and growl at the thought of the younger man sniffing about Anne. "Shouldn't you be addressing your question to Mr. Garthwicke?" he asked, hiding his fury behind a mask of icy indifference. "He is her father."

"That is so," Hughes agreed in prim tones, "but as she is in your employ, I thought it wisest to seek your permission first."

Because both parts of him wanted to kick the useless piece of *caac* out on his ear, Ruairdh saw no reason to be civil.

"Write whomever you wish," he snapped impatiently. "It has nothing to do with me." To distract Hughes as much as himself, he picked up the letter and handed it to him.

"This is to be opened upon my death," he said, keeping his voice devoid of any emotion. "It contains precise instructions on what is to be done, and I expect you to follow them."

Mr. Hughes paled as he stared down at the sealed envelope. "Of course, Mr. MacCairn. I shall be honored to do whatever is necessary. I only wish there were something else I might do to be of service." He raised his eyes to meet Ruairdh's gaze.

"You will forgive me for presuming, sir," he began, his expression filled with quiet regret, "but are you quite certain there is nothing to be done? The recent advances in medicine are really quite extraordinary. There must be something."

Ruairdh felt a flash of pain at the younger man's words. Since boyhood he'd accepted his fate, and he'd learned that hope was an enemy deadlier than the most cunning of foes. It made one wish and then believe, and that was the surest way to the madness that awaited him.

"No," he replied, anguish making his voice rougher than he intended. "There is nothing."

Mr. Hughes was gone by luncheon, a fact Ruairdh found much to his liking. He knew the other man had sought Anne out for a private audience, and he would have paid greatly to know what was said between the two of them. With his awakening senses it would have been easy for him to learn whatever he wished, but he still retained enough conscience to keep from doing just that. He mightn't be able to control the Shadowing, but he was determined to control all that he could for whatever piece of time he had left to him.

Because Mr. Garthwicke was still ailing, Ruairdh

wasn't surprised to find himself taking his midday meal alone. Anne was too aware of propriety to risk her reputation by dining with him, and he supposed he couldn't fault her for her caution. Still, he couldn't help but feel her absence, and the thought added to his bitterness. With the end so near he couldn't afford the luxury of emotion, and the last thing he needed was this growing fascination he felt for Anne. Whatever it took, he would conquer his feelings.

He was repeating this vow an hour later, standing outside the door of the armory. He hadn't meant to come, but the compulsion to see her was too strong. From Mrs. Doughal he'd learned she'd not dined with the upper servants, nor had she requested that a tray be brought to her, and the thought of her going hungry troubled him. Under his roof she was his responsibility, and a MacCairn never neglected his responsibilities so long as he was able. He would just check to make certain she was well and then be on his way, he told himself, knowing it was a lie even as he pushed open the heavy wooden door.

As he'd seen in his vision she was sitting at the table, her blond head bent attentively over the sword she was examining. She glanced up at his entrance, her gray eyes going wide with wariness as she rose gracefully to her feet.

"Mr. MacCairn," she said, bobbing a polite curtsy. "How may I help you?"

He gazed at her for a long moment, drinking in the sight of her as a thirsty man gulped down precious, life-giving water. She was so delicate, so beautiful, and he longed for her in ways that went beyond the hungering of his body. As he had since the first moment he'd seen her, he found himself thinking the forbidden words, *if only* . . .

To hide his discomfiture he gestured at the weapon lying on the table. "What is it you've there?" he asked, closing the door behind him and stepping closer.

She turned back to her work, carefully picking up the heavy sword and offering it to him with gloved hands. "A broadsword," she replied, her tone formal and polite. "Spanish steel from the seventeenth century, perhaps later. From its markings I would say it is Flemish in origin, and would assume it is booty won in battle. What do you know of it?"

Ruairdh took the sword from her, feeling a jolt of power surge through him as his fingers wrapped about the padded hilt. " 'Tis a good weapon," he said, extending the sword and squinting down its length. "Well-balanced and sharp. It would be effective in close combat. And you're right about it being spoils. It was won by a younger brother, who fell later in another battle. He was the fortunate one."

His oblique comment had her brows gathering in confusion. "Fortunate to be killed?"

"Fortunate to die for something, rather than for nothing," he replied, laying the sword on the table. "Is this what you have been working on all this long morning?"

Her creamy cheeks suffused with pink, and the soft lips he longed to taste firmed in displeasure. "No, sir, it is not," she said, her tone filled with ruffled pride. "I have been cataloging and cleaning several weapons, and—"

"It wasn't criticism I was offering, Anne," he interrupted, his lips curving in a smile, "but concern that you've missed your meal. Have you not eaten since breakfast?"

The blush staining her cheeks deepened as she turned away. "I wasn't hungry," she said, stripping off the gloves and laying them on the table beside the stack of books she'd been consulting. "And I often miss meals when I am working. I tend to lose myself." The words were accompanied by a shy smile as she looked back at him over a slender shoulder.

Another man might have accepted her humble explanation, but he was not another man, and he sensed easily the true reason she had avoided joining him for luncheon, the reason she had turned from him just now. Surprised at the pain caused by her rejection, he walked around the table to confront her.

"So nervous, *mo cailin*," he murmured, cupping her chin in his hand and tilting her face up until he could gaze into her mist-colored eyes. "Have I given you cause to so distrust me, then?"

The sight of her tongue anxiously licking her upper lip was nearly his undoing. Fearing his control, he released her, his hands clenched at his sides as he took a careful step back.

"What is it about me that frightens you, Anne?" he asked, praying he'd done nothing to warrant the caution he sensed in her. "Answer me."

Her response was to glance down at the toes of her shoes peeking out from the hem of her serviceable blue gown. "I didn't give you permission to address me by my given name," she said, her gaze still avoiding his. "It is unseemly."

Even though he knew this to be an evasion, Ruairdh decided not to press the issue. "Aye," he agreed, "it is. But who is here to object?" His impatient gesture encompassed the vast chamber. "The stones, perhaps? Or the swords? Or is it you who object, Anne?" he added, resting his hands on her shoulders and holding his breath as he waited for her answer.

Much to his relief she didn't pull away, but her manner was as evasive as ever as she spoke. "Not precisely," she admitted with a slight shrug, "although as I said it is most improper, and a woman in my position must be cautious. The slightest bit of gossip attached to my name could be my ruin, and that of my father. I cannot allow it."

"Nor would I allow it," he replied, softening because he had already considered her objections and could see the sense of them. Hoping to reassure her, he offered her another smile.

"All who work here are of my clan, and they know better than to speak of what happens in the castle. They'll not wag their tongues about you; I give you my word.

"However," he added, when it looked as if she would protest, "if it will ease your mind, I'll call you Anne only in private, as we are now. Is that agreed?" He tipped his head to one side and studied her, hope fluttering in his breast.

"I suppose that would be acceptable," she agreed at last.

"And you will call me Ruairdh," he said, eager to win

another victory. There was a heavy silence and he feared he'd pushed her too far; then her smile slowly bloomed.

"Ruairdh," she repeated, raising her eyes to meet his with a hint of boldness he found enchanting.

"Very good," he said, wisely hiding his amusement at the way she mangled his name in her clipped English accent. "You'll have to practice, though, to get the right of it."

A determined look flashed across Anne's face. "Ruairdh," she said, struggling to say it just as he had. "Is that better?"

"Indeed it is," he congratulated her with a laugh. "We'll make a proper Scot of you yet, lass."

She gave him another smile, and Ruairdh felt his chest swell with a warm burst of emotion. It wasn't desire or even simple pleasure, he realized later, as he escorted her back to the drawing room. Instead it was an emotion he'd not known in years: happiness.

Slender white tapers flickered in the velvet darkness, their soft golden light spilling out to illuminate the entwined lovers lying on the silk-draped bed. Anne moaned softly, arching her back at the feel of her lover's lips teasing the sensitive tips of her breasts. His face remained as elusive as ever, but Anne knew it was Ruairdh who loved her with such fierce mastery.

"Yes." She sighed, twining her arms about his broad shoulders. "Love me, Ruairdh. Love me."

"Annsachd." *He pressed a burning kiss to her parted lips, his tongue thrusting deep inside to torment and tantalize.*

"My darling, say you are mine. Say you will give yourself to me."

"I will," Anne promised, trembling with delight. "Make love to me, Ruairdh. Please."

To her confusion she could feel him drawing away, and she reached up to capture him. "No!" she protested, moving fitfully on the bed. "Don't leave me! Come back!"

Her eyes fluttered as she began to awake, and then she felt the pressure of a man's body pressing intimately against her own. Thinking it was a continuation of her dream, she breathed a low sigh of relief. She began slipping back into the mists when her fingers touched the rough cloth of a cape. Instantly her eyes flew open, and she found herself meeting the black, fathomless gaze of a stranger.

For a brief moment she was caught between dream and reality, uncertain which was which. She started to speak, but before she could draw breath the man closed his fingers viciously about her upper arms.

" 'Tis too late, *siursach*," he jeered, giving her an angry shake. "I have won. The prize is mine. The prize is mine."

He began laughing, and when his hot breath struck Anne on the face she realized to her horror that she was awake, and that this man was real. His black eyes narrowed in cold amusement, and even as she began screaming he vanished, his evil laugh echoing in the night.

Chapter Six

The sound of a scream had Ruairdh leaping out of bed, his heart racing even as he was grabbing for a robe to cover his nakedness. He'd been in the middle of a sweet dream, and he didn't care to be awakened just as Anne was about to surrender to him. Feeling decidedly out of sorts he stepped into the hall, his impatience vanishing when another scream tore through the air, and he realized it was coming from Anne's rooms.

"Anne!"

Calling out her name, he dashed down the corridor, pushing his way through the group of servants standing in a knot before Anne's door. He could hear her wild sobbing and ran into the room, ready to do battle with whomever or whatever had threatened her. To his surprise she was sitting up in bed, her father and maid bent attentively over her.

"A man," she cried, her blond hair in wild disarray as she clung to her father for support. "He was here in my room! I saw him!"

"Nonsense, child." Her father was briskly patting her back and scowling down at her in mild disapproval. "It was a dream, that was all. Merely a dream."

"No!" She shook her head, and Ruairdh could see the tears on her cheeks as she tilted her face up to her father. "Before, it was a dream. But this was real. He said—" She broke off when she saw Ruairdh standing in the doorway, and her pale cheeks suffused with embarrassed color.

"Are you all right, Miss Garthwicke? What is this about a man?" he asked, forcing himself to speak calmly even as his temper flared with possessive rage. He knew it was only proper that Anne turn to her father for reassurance, but that did little to soothe the dark beast stirring inside of him. He was the only man who had the right to touch Anne, and it was all he could do not to knock the old fool aside.

"It is nothing, Mr. MacCairn," Mr. Garthwicke answered, rising to his feet and laying a warning hand on Anne's shoulder. "I fear my daughter was having a nightmare. That is all."

Ruairdh ignored him, turning his gaze on Anne. "Miss Garthwicke?" he pressed gently, willing her to look at him so that he could study her face.

"I-it is as my father has said, sir," she stammered, pleating the bedsheets between her fingers and studiously avoiding his gaze. "It was a bad dream only. I am sorry for having disturbed you."

Ruairdh's lips thinned in displeasure. He knew

damned well it was far more than a dream troubling Anne, and had she not been so pale and shaken he would have demanded the truth and not stopped until he had it. As it was there was little he could do, and the realization left him feeling impotent and furious by turns. Glancing at the maid standing beside the bed, he rapped out an impatient order.

"Remain here until the morning," he said, his voice rough with command. "And take care to leave a candle burning."

"That is very good of you," her father began in his pompous manner. "But I do not think it is necessary. Anne will be fine, won't you, my dear?" He gave Anne a stern look.

"I don't recall asking you for your opinion, Mr. Garthwicke," Ruairdh said coldly, before Anne could respond. "If I may remind you, you are under my roof, and under my roof it is as *I* wish it. Mind that you remember that."

"I say!" Mr. Garthwicke began sputtering, but Ruairdh paid him no mind. He turned to the group of footmen huddled by the door.

"You two," he said in Gaelic, "take some pistols from the gun room and stand guard in the hall for the rest of the night. The rest of you rouse the others and begin searching the castle. If you find anyone you don't know, bring him to me."

The first two servants went dashing off to carry out his orders, but the others remained, studying him with wary diffidence.

"The entire castle, laird?" one of the older footmen asked carefully, his voice quavering with fear. "Are you certain? It could take the whole of the night and well into tomorrow as well."

"I don't care if it takes an eternity!" Ruairdh snapped, furious that his commands should be questioned. "Do as I say, or I'll have you thrown from the castle!"

The rest of the servants needed no further convincing, and Ruairdh waited until they'd gone before glancing back at Anne. He could see the fear and confusion darkening her eyes, and his heart twisted in response. He'd give all he possessed to have spared her the terror she'd known this night, but as matters stood there was little he could do to comfort her. He almost hoped someone had been in her room, he decided darkly. It would give him a great deal of pleasure to throttle the life from the bastard.

After bidding Anne and her father a curt good night, he returned to his room and hurriedly donned his clothing. When he stepped out into the hall, Angley was waiting for him.

"And where are you off to?" the steward demanded crossly, glaring at the pistol Ruairdh carried in his hand.

"To help with the searching," Ruairdh replied shortly, striding down the hall to the curving staircase. "You didn't think I'd go back to bed while the others searched, did you?"

"With your sense of duty?" Angley gave a derisive snort. "I hope I'm no' so big a fool as that. But why put them and yourself to such pains? You heard the lass. 'Twas a bad dream, and nothing more. You canna catch what's no' there."

Ruairdh's jaw hardened in annoyance. "There's

something there. Anne's not the flighty sort to be screaming at shadows. If she said there was a man in her room, there was. Her father might be comfortable brushing it aside, but I cannot. If someone's found his way into the castle, I mean to see him caught."

"And if 'tis a will-o'-the-wisp?" Angley pressed. "What then?"

"Then we'll have lost nothing more than a night's sleep," Ruairdh retorted. "And I'll know I've done my best."

That seemed to satisfy Angley, and nothing else was said as they continued down the stairs. The servants were gathered in the great hall, flaming torches and a variety of weapons in their hands as they awaited his instructions. He divided them into teams of three, sending half to begin searching the dungeons while the others were to search the attics. If there was anyone in the castle, he wouldn't be able to remain hidden for very long.

After pausing long enough to make certain his orders were being carried out, Ruairdh picked up a torch and began walking in the direction of the armory. Angley remained at his side, his expression growing increasingly alarmed.

"Where are you bound?" he demanded sourly. "And mind your pace. I'm no' a lad to go tearing about in the dead of night."

"To the East tower," Ruairdh replied, slowing his stride to accommodate the older man. "I've been thinking about the light Anne said she thought she saw in the tower room. What if she did?"

"*What?*" Angley's hand clamped down on Ruairdh's

arm, forcing him to halt. "Are you daft?" he demanded incredulously. "You canna go there! The danger is too great!"

"If 'tis dangerous, then who better than I to face it?" Ruairdh answered. "I am still the laird, Angley. I'll not play the coward and let others take risks that are more mine than theirs."

"But the risk to you is different from the risk to the others!" Angley protested. "Who is to say that you'll not be completely taken if you so much as cross the threshold of that place? We need you too much to lose you over what may not even be there!"

"Angley, I told you—"

"That the lass saw something," Angley interrupted, "and perhaps she did. Perhaps 'twas a ghost, or the remnants of a dream that seemed real to her upon wakening. Have you no' dreamed something so deeply, so vividly, it seemed the truth to you?"

Ruairdh thought of the highly erotic dreams that had become both his torment and his salvation. There'd been times they seemed so real he'd awakened on the brink of release, but that was information he'd as lief not share with anyone.

"I've no more desire to see my future prison than do you to show it to me," he said at last, hoping to reassure the older man. "But what choice is there? All in the valley know the legend; who is to say one of them isn't seeking to make use of it for his own ends?

"Think about it," he added urgently. "If you were going to infiltrate an enemy's stronghold, what better place to hide than the one place no one would dare look?"

"What enemies?" Angley demanded, clearly vexed. "This is the nineteenth century, you're forgetting, and not the seventeenth. Clan warfare is over and done with. And why should the English try to take the place when you're about to sell it to one of them? 'Tis madness you're speaking!"

A look of horror flashed across his features as he realized what he'd said. "Laird," he began shakily, his faded eyes filling with tears, "forgive me. I didna mean—"

"I know, Angley," Ruairdh said, gently covering Angley's gnarled hand with his own. "I know. And if it will ease your mind, I give you my word I won't go into the tower. Have James and Connor search, but not until tomorrow when it is light. And mind they only go in far enough to make certain the room is empty and not in use."

"I will," Angley promised, his voice quavering with sorrow. "And again, I pray you will forgive me for my foolish tongue."

Not knowing what else to say, Ruairdh continued searching, although he'd lost the heart for it. It was nearing dawn before he called a halt, reluctantly accepting that he'd done all that he could to locate the intruder. After thanking the footmen for their help, he sent them off to bed with orders they were to sleep until noon if they so desired. He went up to seek his own bed, but the thought of trying to fall back to sleep held little appeal, and after considering the matter he quickly shaved and dressed for the day. It had been more days than he could remember since he'd last ridden, and the idea of a gallop across the moor sounded sweetly appealing.

The sun was just peeking over the top of the crags as he saddled his horse and rode out into the glory of a Scottish dawn. The rolling hills were bursting with wildflowers, their blossoms tightly closed against the chill of night. In the pink-tinted sky, birds wheeled and soared, their keening cries ringing out over the rocks and heather. Ruairdh rode to the top of hill overlooking Castle MacCairn, his gloved hands clutching the reins as he gazed down at the ancient fortress that was his home.

He waited as the sun climbed over the peak of Craig Dhucairn, turning the stones of the castle first a delicate pink and then a warm gold. He could feel the tears burning in his eyes, but felt little shame in them. He loved the castle, he thought, his heart aching with despair. He loved every inch of the land his father and his father's father had bled and died for—land they had held with sometimes brutal determination, despite the terrible price that was theirs to pay. It was land that had passed from father to son in an unbroken line stretching back for over five hundred years, and selling it was almost as agonizing as what awaited him.

He was the last of the MacCairns; he had vowed that the day he knew his father to be lost to him forever. No other son would watch helplessly while his father descended into madness, knowing his own turn would come all too soon. The curse would be ended with his own death, and perhaps then his clan would be able to find some measure of peace. The thought turned his fragile contentment to bitterness, and he wheeled his mount around and thundered off, driving his horse and himself as he sought to outride the merciless fate nipping at his heels.

"What the devil were you thinking?" her father raged, glaring down at Anne. "I have never been more embarrassed in my life!"

"Papa, I—"

"Will you be silent!" he roared, his face purpling with rage. "You've already said more than enough, if you want my opinion of it. I can only hope your foolish accusations haven't given Mr. MacCairn such a horror of us he'll toss us out on our ears. I could scarce blame him if he did."

"Papa, I have already said I am sorry," Anne said quietly, although the words all but choked her. "And I mean to apologize to Mr. MacCairn as soon as he returns from his ride."

"Little good your apologies will do," he said with a sneer. "The butler informs me Mr. MacCairn and his staff were up half the night searching for this hobgoblin of yours. Needless to say," he added with a sniff, "nothing was found."

Anne continued holding her tongue, despite the resentment simmering inside her. Last night in the aftermath of her horrific encounter, she'd been more than willing to be convinced it had been part of a dream. People simply didn't vanish into nothing, and since her sensible mind rejected the notion of spirits, the only possible explanation was that she'd dreamed the entire thing. Her acceptance had made falling back to sleep easier, and she'd awakened more embarrassed than afraid. Then she had found bruises on her upper arms; bruises in the shape of a man's fingers.

At first she'd stared at them in confusion, trying to think of some explanation for the marks. The only man to touch her in recent days had been Ruairdh, but he'd never touched her in a manner that would account for the bruises. Nor had he grabbed her by the arms, now that she thought of it. He had touched her cheek, her shoulder, and in her dreams he touched her everywhere, but with hands that coaxed and pleased rather than hurt. . . . She jerked in horror, trembling in mortification at the direction of her thoughts.

"Well you may shudder," her father said, jabbing an accusatory finger at her. "Your foolishness may have cost us our reputations, and if it has, then I wash my hands of you. I am done pretending you know what you are doing."

The accusation was as brutal as a blow, and Anne flinched in pain. "I do know what I am doing," she said, struggling to remain calm. "I follow your instructions to the letter, and I have learned all you could teach. I have been your assistant for five years—"

"How dare you put on airs with me!" Her father brought his fist down on the desk, sending the pot of ink skittering. "My assistant, indeed! You are a female, suited for nothing more than gracing a man's parlor, and you've done so poor a job at that, you've not received so much as a single offer!"

The unfair insult brought Anne to her feet, her hands clenching as she faced her father. "And how could I hold any expectations of receiving an offer when I've spent every day since Mama died catering to you?" she demanded, hurling the words at him in frustration. "Since I was eighteen I have followed you from post to post, acting first as your amanuensis, and then as your assistant!"

"That is not so!"

"It is so!" she retorted, so hurt and furious she ignored the stunned expression on his face. "And since your vision began failing I've been your eyes and hands, doing your work and trying to pretend I wasn't! And not once—not once!—have you ever said thank-you to me."

Her father sat back down, his anger evaporating into childlike hurt. "Why should I thank you?" he asked, his voice shaking as he withdrew his handkerchief from his pocket to dab at his brow. "You are my daughter; it is your duty to be of help to me."

"If it is a duty, then it must be one I do quite well," she shot back, aiming her barb with deliberate intent. "You know as well as I that our last three positions have been due to my work, not yours. You haven't verified a single artifact in three years."

"That is layman's work," her father said, sounding perilously close to tears. "Why should I trouble myself with trinkets and toys? I am the most acclaimed antiquarian in the country. My reputation is above reproach."

His strained tone and the wounded expression on his face finally penetrated Anne's fury, and she made a mental grab at control. "Of course it is, Papa," she said wearily, tucking a tendril of hair back into her chignon. "I didn't mean to imply it was not."

"It's not my fault my eyes are failing," he continued, like a sulky schoolboy defending his poor behavior. "And I don't need your help. I can carry out my responsibilities without you."

Anne said nothing. She knew she should offer assurances, agree with his insecure boasting, but she was too heartsick and too angry to make the attempt. She had never spoken so bitterly to her father, and the confrontation had left her drained. Later she would manage to find the proper words, but for now she couldn't bring herself to try.

A telling silence hung between them, and after several seconds her father rose to his feet.

"Your silence is most eloquent, daughter," he said with a harsh laugh. "You don't think I can do it, do you?"

"Papa—"

"No." He held up his hand to silence her. "I find I prefer your insolence to your pity. I believe there is nothing left to be said. If you will excuse me, it is time to be about my dutics."

Anne watched him take his leave, her eyes smarting with tears. She knew how much she had hurt him, and she genuinely regretted her loss of temper. She hated acting like a shrew, and hated more the fact that she would have to go to considerable lengths to make amends. *Wonderful*, she thought glumly. Now instead of making her apologies to one impossible man, she would be making them to two.

She learned from the wide-eyed maid who brought her breakfast that the laird had returned from his ride and was in his study. The idea of bearding the lion in his den wasn't a pleasant prospect, but she didn't think there was any other choice. The sooner the matter was behind her, the sooner she could return to the armory.

There was no one about as Anne made her way to Ruairdh's study. The maid had also told her the laird had ordered the footmen to sleep late in order to make up for the sleep they'd lost searching for her intruder, and she felt another stab of guilt. Would she have to apologize to each of them as well? she wondered, sighing as she raised her hand and knocked on the closed door.

"Enter."

Anne jolted at the clipped command. She thought the voice sounded like Ruairdh's, if a trifle rough and impatient, but through the thick wood it was hard to be certain. She paused long enough to straighten her lace collar, and after drawing a breath for courage, she opened the door and stepped into the study.

The thick blue velvet drapes covering the French doors were pulled open, and sunlight poured through the diamond-paned glass to fill the room with light and warmth. Ruairdh stood in front of the doors, his back to her and his hands resting on the desk as he stared out into the gardens.

"Say what you've come to say, and be done with it," he ordered, the roughness in his voice more pronounced. "It's not all day I have to wait on the likes of you."

Anne opened her lips in automatic protest at such rudeness, and then wisely closed them. The man had been roused out of bed in the dead of night and forced to search a castle, she reminded herself. He was entitled to be churlish. Lifting her chin, she began to recite the speech she had carefully rehearsed.

"Mr. MacCairn," she began, her shoulders soldier-straight, "I wish to apologize for my behavior last evening. I realize I behaved foolishly and put you and your staff to a great deal of bother, and I want you to know I am sorry."

Her stilted apology met with stony silence, prompting her to continue. "I know I have no right to ask for your forgiveness," she said, her words tumbling over each other in her haste to get them out, "but that is what I am doing. This position is very important to my father, and I would hate to see his standing jeopardized by my idiotic behavior."

More silence. She thought she saw Ruairdh shift, as if he meant to look at her, but he remained as he was, his back firmly turned to her. If he thought such tactics would intimidate her, she decided with mounting indignation, he was sorely mistaken.

"Mr. MacCairn, it is very difficult to apologize to your back," she said, taking a brazen step forward. "Kindly do me the courtesy of looking at me while I am begging your pardon."

There was a moment's hesitation, and then he slowly turned around, his lips curving in a cold smile, and his green eyes burning black with malevolent satisfaction.

"Why so shocked, lass?" he asked, moving toward her with the slow, unsteady gait of a drunkard. "Didna I tell you the prize was mine?"

Anne stumbled back in horror, unable to believe the evidence of her own senses. The man advancing on her was Ruairdh—she *knew* he was Ruairdh—but his face was that of the man from her upsetting dream the night before. The very figment of her imagination for which she had come to apologize.

"It can't be," she repeated, shaking her head as the man continued his inexorable advance. "It can't be."

His answer was an ugly laugh, and the sound of it made her shudder. "So you would beg for your father, would you?" he asked, his harsh features twisting into another smile. "That is good. I like my lasses biddable."

Before she could react his powerful hands shot out, his fingers curving over the bruises he had put there last night. Anne cried out in pain and fought furiously, but she was no match for his brutal strength. He pulled her against his chest, and she recoiled at the icy chill emanating from him. Touching him would be like touching a corpse, and the very notion filled her with such revulsion she managed to fight her way free of his embrace.

The struggle knocked him back, and he landed awkwardly against the side of the desk. He started forward again, and then came to an abrupt halt, trembling as with a fever. He lowered his head, his chest heaving, and when he looked up at her again, Ruairdh stared at her with dazed green eyes.

"Anne?" He blinked down at her in confusion. "What are you doing here?"

Ruairdh gazed at Anne, his head reeling like a drunkard's and a distant roar, like the sea in a gale, ringing in his ears. His last clear memory was entering the study to go over his accounts, but after that things were decidedly uncertain. What this portended was enough to make his soul twist in fear, and he quickly covered his response. Without thinking he took an impulsive step toward Anne, stopping when she began backing away from him in obvious fear.

"Keep away," she warned, her hand held out in front of her. "I shall fight, I warn you!"

Ruairdh believed her; her determination was plain in her eyes and in the belligerent set to her chin. *My God,* he wondered dully, *what have I done?*

"Miss Garthwicke," he began, hoping his formal use of her name would reassure her, "there is no need for such theatrics, I promise you. If I have given offense, then naturally I apologize."

"Offense?" she repeated, her temper flaring. "Is that what you choose to call it? You assaulted me, and well you know it!"

For a moment Ruairdh feared he would become physically ill. His stomach rolled, and his knees threatened to turn to water.

"I did not," he denied hoarsely, praying it wasn't a lie.

"You most certainly did!" Anne tossed the charge back at him in defiant anger. "Would you care to see my bruises? They match the ones you put there last night while you were playing your silly little games!"

There was no reason now to feign his confusion. "What silly little games?" he demanded, his brows wrinkling in thought.

"You know perfectly well what I mean," she shot back, advancing toward him like a small fury. "A castle as old and vast as this one must be riddled with secret passages; I can't imagine why I didn't think of that sooner. How easy it must have been for you to sneak into my room and then sneak out again when I began screaming! I am sure you must have found it very amusing to come dashing into the room with the others, so concerned, so proper, and all the while you were laughing up your sleeve at me!"

The derision in her voice had Ruairdh's own temper stirring to life. "You've a right to be angry with me, if I laid hands on you as you claim," he told her with cool pride. "But you've no right to question my honesty or my honor. I was not in your room last evening until after you screamed; I give you my most solemn word."

Her head jerked back at his words. "It was you," she insisted, although he thought he could detect a slight doubt in her voice. "It had to be you."

"It was not."

She drifted closer, seeming unaware that she had moved. She stood before him, and it was the most natural thing in the world for him to slip his arms about her slender waist. In a gesture equally as natural she laid her hands on his arms, gazing up at him with a pensive expression.

"What is happening, Ruairdh?" she asked softly. "Something is going on here, something terrible. What is it? Tell me so that I may be of help to you."

Her plea touched him as nothing had since the moment he'd been old enough to fully comprehend the horror of his legacy. "There is nothing that can be done, *mo cridhe*," he said, aching to touch his lips to hers. "But I thank you for asking. It means more to me than I can ever say."

"But—"

He silenced her by laying his finger over her lips. "No more questions, Anne," he said, his voice raw with anguish. "Later. Later I promise to tell you what I can. Not all of it, mind, for I'm bound by clan law, but I promise to tell you what truth there is. Will that satisfy you?"

She continued holding his gaze, compassion and more gleaming in her silver-hued eyes. It was the tantalizing promise of the "more" that broke Ruairdh's control, and, unable to resist a moment longer, he bent his head and covered her lips with his own.

The feel of her was soft and arousingly feminine, and the taste of her even sweeter than the most erotic of his dreams. A harsh groan tore from his throat as he gathered her closer, his mouth pressing more urgently on hers. She hesitated, and then her arms were reaching up to encircle his neck. Because he was so much taller than she, she had to stand on her toes to accomplish the task, and the action brought her soft body flush against his own.

"Anne!" He tore his lips from hers, her name an urgent groan. "I adore you, *annsachd.* I need you!"

"Ruairdh." She whispered his name on a sigh, her eyes slumberous with awakening passion. "You make my head spin."

The artless confession delighted Ruairdh, and he lowered his lips to hers again. This time her mouth met his, and, encouraged by her shy response, he deepened the kiss even further. He parted his lips, tracing the curve of her upper lip with his tongue. The bold caress had her gasping, and he reluctantly withdrew his tongue, not wishing to frighten her. Later there would be time to instruct her in the many ways lovers kissed; for the moment he was content to hold her and drink his fill of her sweetness.

They lingered over the kiss, and Ruairdh was so lost in the magic of the embrace it took several seconds for him to realize the wild pounding he was hearing was coming from the hallway, and not his own heart. He lifted his head, but before he could release Anne the door was flung open and several men rushed into the room. He thrust Anne behind him, shielding her with his body before he recognized the men as being in his employ.

"What is it, Thomas?" he demanded, thinking that the lad had best have a good reason for violating his sanctuary. "Is the castle afire?"

"No, laird," the younger man said, his anguished gaze sliding past Ruairdh to rest upon Anne.

" 'Tis your father, Miss Garthwicke," he said, his eyes filling with tears. "You must come straightaway. There has been a terrible accident."

Anne fought her way past Ruairdh. "Is he all right?" she cried, her face paling.

Ruairdh jerked, the blood in his veins turning to ice as a vision exploded in his mind. He saw the old scholar, his body lying twisted and broken at the bottom of the stairs, a look of horror forever frozen on his face. Ruairdh reached for Anne instinctively, wanting to protect her, but it was already too late.

"No, miss," Thomas said gently. "He's dead."

Chapter Seven

Dead.

The word struck Anne with the viciousness of a blow. She couldn't think, couldn't speak, couldn't breathe. She could only stand gazing at the footman, struggling to accept the terrible finality of his words.

"Where?" She forced the word out, trembling with the effort it cost her.

"In the old tower, miss," the footman replied, his eyes filling with tears. "He fell down the stairs. I am sorry."

Anne flinched, remembering the narrow, winding staircase. She wouldn't think of that now, she told herself, concentrating instead on what was to be done.

"Take me to him," she said, drawing herself up with what courage she could muster.

The footman turned to Ruairdh. "I dinna think that

wise, laird," he said, clearly distressed. " 'Tis no' a sight for a lady."

"Anne." Ruairdh's tone was gentle as he laid a restraining hand on her arm. "Remain here. I will see to the matter for you."

Pride and cold anger were preferable to the wild emotions raging inside her, and Anne clung to both in grim desperation. "This isn't a 'matter,' Mr. MacCairn," she said, throwing the words back at him. "This is my father, and I want to be taken to him at once."

Ruairdh studied her for several seconds before inclining his head. "As you wish, Miss Garthwicke," he said, offering her his arm with the gravest of courtesy. "Shall we go?"

Anne laid shaking fingers on his arm, her stomach rolling and pitching as he led her from the room. A group of servants was knotted outside the door, their expressions oddly fearful when they saw Ruairdh. Without speaking they fell into step behind them, providing a silent escort as Anne and Ruairdh made their way from the central part of the castle to the abandoned east wing.

Through the interminable journey Anne's mind remained an icy blank, and it required all of her will to continue putting one foot carefully in front of the other. A sense of disembodiment stole over her, making it seem as if she were watching herself from a great distance. Only Ruairdh's solid presence beside her kept her from shattering into a thousand shards of brittle glass, and Anne was touched by his strength and compassion.

They were almost at the staircase when he drew her

to a halt, his expression solemn as he studied her. "Are you certain of this?" he asked, his deep voice softer than she had ever heard it. "No one will think less of you if you choose to return to your rooms and await us there."

Because she wanted so desperately to accept the quiet offer, Anne forced herself to reject it. "I would think less of myself," she said, raising her eyes to meet his steady green gaze. "He is my father. I will do what I must."

His expression flickered briefly, and then he carried her hand to his lips. "You're brave as a Highland lass, *mo cridhe*," he murmured, brushing his mouth over her chilled flesh. "How proud of you your father would be."

Anne didn't answer, her heart wrenching in pain as they resumed walking. She would have given all she possessed if she could believe he was right, but she knew better. Her father, angry and resentful that she wasn't the son he had craved, had never once been proud of her, and now he never would. The bitterness of that truth was nearly her undoing.

More servants were gathered at the base of the winding staircase Anne had seen that first day. The men were silent, while the women murmured amongst themselves, dabbing at their eyes with their aprons. When they became aware of Anne and Ruairdh the crying stopped, and as if possessed of one mind they moved silently to one side, giving Anne her first glimpse of her father's body.

He lay crumpled at the bottom of the staircase, his body twisted at an unnatural angle. Blood pooled beneath his head, and the eyes gazing sightlessly up at her from his gray face were wide and staring. Anne saw the accusation in them and her vision momentarily darkened. Ruairdh's arm slipped about her at once.

"Come away now," he crooned, gently tugging her back. "Come away, Anne. There is nothing you can do."

She shrugged his arm off, moving to kneel beside her father's body. It was obvious he was dead but still she forced herself to be certain, laying her hand on his chest and then against his neck. To her shock his flesh was still warm, but no pulse beat beneath her fingertips. Even as her hands registered the heat of his body she could feel it slipping away, as the icy chill of death chased out the last vestige of life. With unsteady hands she gave her father's cheek a final caress, the tears she had been fighting spilling out to flow down her face.

"Oh, Papa," she whispered, breaking at last. "What have you done?"

The next several hours were a blur. Giving in to Ruairdh's quiet insistence, Anne allowed herself to be taken back to her rooms, where a tearful Jennie was waiting for her. The usually talkative maid was subdued, her manner gentle yet determined as she bullied Anne out of her gown and into bed.

"A bit of a lie-down is what you're needing, miss," she said, ignoring Anne's protestations as she pulled the sheets over her. "Rest for a wee bit now. I'll sit right here with you."

Continuing the argument required more energy than Anne possessed, and so she simply closed her eyes, shutting out Jennie and the rest of the world. But try as she might she could not shut out the picture of her father lying bloodied at the bottom of the staircase.

The image haunted her, and she knew it was a memory she would take with her to her grave.

What had he been doing in the old wing? she wondered, tears spilling down her cheeks to dampen the pillowcase. Ruairdh had made it plain that entry to that portion of the castle was forbidden to all, and she knew her father desired their employer's goodwill too much to risk offending him without cause. But what cause could there have been to make him defy Ruairdh's edict? What could have driven him up that twisting staircase and ultimately to his death? She froze, anguish exploding inside of her as the truth came to her in a searing flash.

She was the cause. In her anger and hurt she'd lashed out against her father, hurling his failings in his face without thought for the consequences. Better than anyone she knew of the pride he took in his work and how his growing inability to do that work had gnawed away at him. For two years she'd managed to hold her tongue, doing everything within her power to maintain the fiction that he was the one in command. Then in an instant she had shattered that fiction, and the cost had been greater than anything she could have calculated: her father's life.

"No!" The word erupted from her in a howl of anguish. "No! No! No!"

After trying in vain to soothe her Jennie went scurrying off, returning a short while later with Mrs. Doughal. The no-nonsense housekeeper soon took matters into her capable hands, and between the two of them they managed to pour a dose of laudanum down Anne's throat. Anne fought the cloying effects of the drug, but in the end her struggles proved useless, and she was sucked down into the smothering darkness of unconsciousness.

A confusing kaleidoscope of images and fragmented memories haunted her uneasy sleep. She saw her parents as they'd been in her youth, her mother laughing and playing the piano while her father looked on with an indulgent smile. Gone was the bitter, unforgiving man he'd become, and, remembering them like that, she could feel the love she'd once known returning to warm her in gentle waves.

Her lover was there as well, and although his face remained as lost to her as always, she could sense him in the darkness with her and drew comfort from his presence.

" 'Tis all right, *annsachd*," he murmured, his husky voice a gentle purr as his hands stroked over her hair. "I'll bide with you a wee while. I'll not leave you alone."

But even as he spoke the reassuring words she could feel the air stirring. The soft breezes blew sharp, and a terrible blackness began filling the room like an icy fog. To her horror her father's face wavered and changed, his happy smile turning to a grimace of fear and death. His head twisted and his body contorted, and she was seeing him as he'd looked lying at the bottom of the stairs. As she watched, the pool of blood beneath his head spread out and began streaming toward her, the rivulets of brilliant red becoming clawing fingers that snatched eagerly at the hem of her dress. She stumbled back with a cry and reached for her lover's hand, but he was already moving away from her.

"No," she cried, stretching out her fingers in desperation. "Don't leave me! You promised! You promised!"

"Wake up, Anne," he said softly, his voice echoing as if from a great distance. "Wake up. 'Tis only a dream, *leannan;* it cannot hurt you. Open your eyes now and look upon me."

A warm hand settled on her shoulder and shook her gently. The feel of his flesh touching hers broke the chains of the dream holding her, and she fought her way out of sleep. At first she saw only the darkness and the single flame of the candle burning at her bedside; then a noise to her left drew her attention, and she turned her head to see Ruairdh sitting there.

"Ruairdh?" She blinked up at him in sleepy confusion, uncertain whether he was real or not.

His green eyes burned with exhaustion as he smiled down at her. "Aye," he said, covering her hand with his own. "Was it someone else you were expecting, then?"

She was too befuddled with the drug and the grogginess of sleep to mind her tongue. "I thought it was him. But that's all right, isn't it, because I thought he was you."

His only response was a gentle shake of his head. "I see I shall be needing a word with Mrs. Doughal," he said, rising to his feet. "She has too free a hand with the laudanum, I'm thinking."

There was the rattle of glass and the sound of pouring water, and then he was lifting her up gently to press a glass of water to her lips.

"Mind you drink all of it," he scolded, tipping the glass slightly. "It will help lessen the effects of that cursed potion they gave you."

Anne did as she was bidden, grateful for the cool liquid as it slid down her parched throat. With every second her wits grew stronger, and with the return of reason came a sudden awareness of her situation. One step from a servant she might be, but that didn't mean her reputation could survive if it became known she had been alone in her bedchamber with her employer. But as quickly as the thought occurred, she was dismissing it. Her father was dead, she thought glumly. What did propriety matter now?

"Are you wanting some food?" He settled her back against the cushions and was hovering over her like an anxious servant. "I can ring for something if you would like."

The thought of food made her stomach give a vicious twist. "No, thank you," she said, doing her best not to shudder. "I am not hungry."

"As you wish," he said, moving back to take his seat. There was an awkward silence, and Anne stirred uncertainly on her bed.

"Where . . . where is Jennie?" she asked, belatedly wondering what had become of the cheerful maid. For all her liveliness she was very attentive, and Anne found it difficult to believe she would be so neglectful in her duties.

"In bed," Ruairdh replied, his voice suddenly grim. "As are all the others. It's after midnight, and we've a busy day tomorrow." He paused as if searching for the right words, and then he met her gaze.

"There is to be an inquest."

Nothing he might have said could have shocked her more. "An inquest? But . . . but why?"

"Your father died suddenly and very violently," Ruairdh answered, his lips thinning in an angry line. "The circumstances are not to the magistrate's liking, and so he refuses to sign your father's death certificate until he is certain there was no crime committed. I am sorry, Anne, but until the fool is satisfied, there can be no talk of a funeral."

Anne shook her head. "But it was an accident," she said, struggling to understand what she was being told. "I do not see why there should be any mystery about it.

"And you are the laird, are you not?" she added, shooting him a confused look from beneath her lashes. "I should have thought your word would prove more than enough."

He gave a humorless laugh. "The title is an honorary one only. English law long since took away any real power I might have wielded as the head of my clan, and always they want more. That is why I am determined to see that all is settled as quickly as possible. I'll not leave those under my care to the mercy of the English when I am taken."

Something about the odd phrase struck Anne as familiar, but she had more pressing matters to consider at the moment.

"Will I be required to give testimony?" she asked, trying to imagine what would be expected of her.

"It cannot be avoided, I fear," he replied, his hard frown making his displeasure plain. "I am sorry, for I know it will distress you."

The idea of clinically discussing her father's death brought a painful lump to Anne's throat, but she forced it down. "If it will help clear matters, I shall say whatever I must," she said. Sensing the grimness in him, she added, "It was an accident, Ruairdh. I know that."

His gaze sharpened. "Do you? What was your father doing on those stairs, Anne? I thought I'd made it clear that no one was to enter that part of the castle except by my authority. Was he searching for something, do you know?"

The guilt that lay like a leaden weight upon Anne's heart made it impossible for her to continue looking at him. "No," she said, lowering her eyes to her hands. "We spoke briefly just before . . . just before it happened, but he never said anything about going into the east wing." This at least was the truth, but uttering it still made her feel like a liar.

"Are you certain?" he pressed. "The magistrate seemed most curious about why he should be there."

His words added more weight to the guilt. "I am certain," she said quietly. "Father never gave any indication of his intention to visit that part of the castle. If he had, I should have done my best to stop him."

"Och! And what is this?" An outraged gasp came from the door where the housekeeper stood, her hands on her hips and an expression of extreme disapproval on her face.

"Laird, what are you thinking?" she scolded, bustling forward. "You canna be found here! A scandal's the last thing we're needing. Away with you, now. Away!"

Ruairdh had risen to his feet. "Mrs. Doughal," he began, his tone stern, "I can assure you I—"

"Is your hearing as poor as your sense?" the older woman interrupted, brushing aside his explanation with an impatient wave of her hand. "Go! I will stay with the lass."

To Anne's astonishment Ruairdh took his dismissal with more or less good grace. He gave Anne one final look and then left the room, taking care to close the door quietly behind him. The moment he was gone, the housekeeper rounded on Anne.

"And you . . ." she said, fixing her with a fierce glare. "I've a maid bringing a bowl of broth, and you'll eat every bite of it. Is that clear?"

Anne remembered the ease with which the redoubtable woman had sent Ruairdh packing, and sank lower in the bed. "Yes, Mrs. Doughal," she said, drawing the sheets up to her chin and meekly accepting defeat.

What was he to do? Ruairdh lay in bed, his head pillowed on his arm as he gazed up at the velvet drapes hanging from his tester bed. He'd been abed for hours, and sleep remained as elusive as did peace. Angley had left a decanter of fine whiskey at his bedside, but with the Shadowing drawing near he had no desire to dull his senses with alcohol. Whatever came next, he meant to meet it with as clear a head as possible.

The magistrate was his primary concern, he decided, forcing himself to think rationally. The purse-lipped, greedy little sot had been a thorn in his side since his return to the castle. The other man clearly resented the respect those of his clan accorded him as laird, a respect that had not been accorded the magistrate. Those of the tiny village regarded him as an *outdwellar*, and took no pains to hide their opinion. An understandable reaction, Ruairdh mused with a wry twist of his lips, even if it was making his own life merry hell.

Another concern was the scholar's death. An accident, perhaps, but even accidents had their causes. After seeing that Anne had been taken away with the servants, he'd ordered Angley and the others back, and had carefully climbed the winding staircase. Being so close to the tower had been a horror beyond enduring, but he'd forced himself to endure it nonetheless. He'd ignored his fear and the sly, malevolent voice whispering in his ear, looking for anything that might have caused Mr. Garthwicke to fall. The staircase was unsteady, yes, but not so unsteady as to cause a man to lose his balance. The servants also reported hearing a scream before the scholar tumbled down the stairs. What had made him scream? The realization he was about to fall, or something else, something that had brushed Ruairdh's mind with the cold touch of death?

His ultimate concern was Anne. She knew more than she was telling of her father's death, and her reticence was troubling. His heightened abilities let him sense her guilt and confusion, but not the cause behind them. He knew she loved her father, so her unwillingness to be truthful made no sense, and he had no time for things that made no sense. Trying to solve the mystery availed him nothing, and so he closed his eyes, willing himself into the deep mists of sleep.

This time she came to him. Soft, sad, her gray eyes silver with moisture, she slid into his bed without making a sound. Her arms twined about his neck, and when she laid her cheek against his bare chest, he could feel the dampness of her tears.

"Let me stay, my love," she implored. "Hold me. I cannot be alone tonight."

Moved, he cuddled her to his heart, murmuring reassuring words as he combed his fingers through her tumbled curls. When she began touching him, stroking him, it was with a quiet desperation that tugged at his very soul. He loved her ardently, completely, and when the dream faded, as such dreams always did, it was he who had tears staining his cheeks.

The next morning he awoke hollow-eyed and grim, feeling like a knight of old about to ride into battle against the deadliest of foes. He wasn't surprised to learn that the magistrate had already sent word to expect him, but it did surprise him that the other man announced his intentions to arrive within the hour. He would have thought such a self-important *Sasunnach* wouldn't stir from his bed until well after noon. He observed as much to Angley, who gave a snort of agreement.

"Aye, the English were ever the ones for sleeping away the morning. And like as not Beechton would still be abed were it not for his glee at having you at his mercy. You'll want to watch that one. It's your head he means to have."

Ruairdh's eyes narrowed, and a deadly fury coiled in his heart. "Let him try," he challenged, surprised at the depth of his animosity, his hand dropping to his waist as if toward the magistrate. "I'd fell the man with a single blow given the slightest provocation."

Angley gave a sharp bark of laughter. "A pleasing thought, but what would that accomplish but to bring more magistrates down on our heads? Better the devil we know, eh, laird?" He cast Ruairdh a rare grin.

Ruairdh thought of the particular devil stalking him. "Aye," he agreed grimly. "Better the devil we know. Come, join me for breakfast."

Anne's absence was sorely felt as Ruairdh sat down to eat. He learned from Mrs. Doughal that she'd already awakened and had taken her morning meal in her room, and was waiting until it was time for her to speak to the magistrate. The housekeeper also made a pointed reference to Anne's lack of a chaperon, and after careful reflection he hit upon what he thought would be the perfect solution.

"Is Mr. Gordon's sister still living with him?" he asked, setting his untouched cup of tea to one side.

Angley glanced up from his porridge, his eyebrows lifting in inquiry. "That she is, and near to driving the good parson to drink, or so I am hearing. Why?"

"Send word and ask her to come to the castle," Ruairdh said, hiding his unease behind an air of decisiveness. "It need be only a night or two."

"That foolish female?" Angley's pale blue eyes bulged in horror. "You canna mean so! She has a laugh like a rusty gate, and she is forever setting her cap at the laddies and then swooning if they so much as glance in her direction."

The telling description of the unfortunate Mrs. Collier had Ruairdh fighting a smile. "It cannot be helped," he said instead. "Miss Garthwicke must remain until the magistrate is satisfied, and she cannot remain under my roof unchaperoned without risking both our reputations. See to it, Angley."

" 'See to it,' he says," Angley muttered, tossing down his napkin in disgust and rising to his feet. "Aye, and so I will, and it's soon mad we'll all be, I've no doubt. Ah, well, maybe she'll have heard the stories, and will refuse outright. There's a thought." And he stomped away still muttering to himself.

Following breakfast Ruairdh went to his study to await the magistrate's arrival. Although he'd never served in war he had the mind of a warrior, and he knew the advantage always went to the one who first held the ground. Mr. Beechton would be brought to him, he decided, rather than him going to Mr. Beechton like a wayward schoolboy being called to the headmaster's office. It was a small ploy, to be sure, but such small ploys had been known to win battles.

Mr. Beechton arrived some twenty minutes later, his displeasure at being ushered into Ruairdh's presence plain by his sour expression and sullen demeanor. With him was another man he introduced as Lord Cedricks, the chief magistrate of Edinburgh. What he thought to accomplish by bringing the man with him, Ruairdh knew not, acknowledging the introduction with a cool nod.

"But where is Miss Garthwicke?" Mr. Beechton asked, looking about the book-lined room in disapproval. "You must have known I would need to speak with her as soon as possible."

"And you must know that as she is my guest, Miss Garthwicke's well-being is my greatest concern," Ruairdh shot back, refusing to be intimidated either by the magistrate or his highborn associate. "Her father's death has affected her greatly, and I'll not have her hounded by the likes of you."

Mr. Beechton's face flushed red with fury. "Sir, I must protest—"

"To the devil with your protests, man," Lord Cedricks retorted before Ruairdh could speak. "The lad is behaving as is proper, which is more than can be said of you." He turned to Ruairdh.

"If you would so be kind as to have someone fetch the young lady, Mr. MacCairn, we should be most grateful," he said, smiling. "I daresay you must be as anxious as we to resolve this unfortunate situation."

"Indeed I am, my lord," Ruairdh agreed, his temper mollified by the older man's easy manner. "Although 'tis more for Miss Garthwicke's sake than my own. As I said, her father's death has been hardest on her." And he shot Mr. Beechton a look of undisguised dislike.

While they were waiting for Anne, Lord Cedricks chatted easily of the beauty of the valley and moors and his admiration for the castle. He was questioning Ruairdh about the castle's history when Anne entered the room, her slender body draped in black bombazine.

"Miss Garthwicke, pray accept my apologies for disturbing you at such a time," Lord Cedricks said, rising to his feet and hurrying forward to greet her.

"I understand, my lord," she replied, her tone guarded as she allowed him to guide her to her chair. "Mr. MacCairn said there were some questions you needed to ask of me. What is it you wish to know?"

"Tell me, Miss Garthwicke," Beechton began, resting his hands on the lapels of his jacket and staring down the length of his nose at her, "do you know what your father was doing in the east wing yesterday morning? It was not his habit to work there, I gather?"

"No, it was not," she replied, meeting his gaze with a dignity worthy of a queen. "Our first day here I was warned by a member of Mr. MacCairn's staff that that portion of the castle was dangerous and we were not to go there. I told my father of it, and to my knowledge he heeded the warning."

"But he didn't, did he?" The magistrate pounced eagerly on her words. "Not if he fell down the staircase. Why should he have climbed it after being warned of its dangers, can you tell me that?"

For the first time Anne faltered, and once again Ruairdh could sense that she was hiding something of importance. "In the last few years my father had become increasingly forgetful," she said at last, her gaze fixed on the handkerchief knotted in her hands. "He often wandered off on his own and later had no idea where he'd been or how he came to be there. He must have come upon the staircase and been intrigued by it, forgetting the danger in his excitement to go exploring. It is precisely the sort of thing he would do."

"But the fall, Miss Garthwicke, how do you explain that?" Lord Cedricks asked gently. "Unless your father had some sort of sickness that made him subject to sudden dizzy spells?"

She shook her head. "No, he suffered no such affliction," she said. "But he was older, and his eyesight was not what it used to be. I believe in the poor light he misjudged a step, lost his balance, and fell. It was an accident, no more."

"And you are content with that?" Mr. Beechton demanded with a derisive sniff.

Anne glanced up, tears staining her pale cheeks. "I accept it," she corrected. "That is far different from being content."

There was a charged silence, and then Lord Cedricks rose once more to his feet. "If you accept that he met his death by accident, my dear, then so shall we," he said, giving her a deep bow. "I thank you, Miss Garthwicke, and once again, pray forgive us for intruding at such a sad time." He shot Beechton an annoyed look. "Come, Beechton," he said sharply, "it is time we were on our way."

"But . . . but Lord Cedricks, surely you don't mean to let it end like this!" the other man protested, clearly distressed.

"Like what?" Cedricks demanded crossly. "The man fell; it is as plain as that. Sign the papers and be done with it. If I hurry I can catch the next train and be in Edinburgh by nightfall."

"But the rumors, my lord!" Beechton wailed. "I have explained—"

"Old wives' tales and crofters' nonsense have no bearing in this inquiry," Lord Cedricks interrupted impatiently, "and I'll have none of it. Sign the certificate and let this poor young lady bury her father. I have better things to do with my time than to go tearing about the countryside chasing after foolishness."

Faced with the naked command from his lordship, there was little Mr. Beechton could do but comply. Muttering that he would have the necessary documents delivered to the castle before the end of the day, he took his leave, pausing to give Ruairdh a final, warning glare. Ruairdh paid him little mind, his attention fully centered on Anne.

"Are you all right?" he asked, studying her worriedly. She was far too pale for his liking, and the shadows beneath her eyes were so dark they stood out like bruises against the translucency of her flesh. Perhaps he should send for the doctor, he brooded, furious with himself for not having seen to the matter sooner.

"I am fine," she replied, although he noted that she still had yet to fully meet his gaze. "There is so much to be done, I scarce know where to start."

"You'll want your father buried as soon as possible, I would presume," Ruairdh said, more than willing to be of what help he could. "I can arrange for transportation, if you'd like. Have you somewhere in mind?"

She shook her head, her troubled gray eyes briefly touching his before she glanced away again. "To be honest, I'm not certain where I should bury him," she admitted with a troubled sigh. "We spent the past few years moving from position to position, and we haven't a real home. I—I could bury him in the churchyard with my mother, I suppose," she added with an uncharacteristic hesitancy that tore at Ruairdh's heart.

He thought for a moment before answering. "We have a graveyard in the village," he offered, wishing there were more he could do. "If it is your wish, I can have him interred there."

Now she was looking at him, gratitude obvious in her expression. "He would like that," she answered, her lips lifting in a tremulous smile. "Thank you, Mr. MacCairn, that is very generous of you."

Her use of his proper name made Ruairdh's temper flare, and the beast he'd kept tightly leashed slipped its bounds. He moved around the edge of the desk to tower over her.

"Is it?" he challenged in a cold voice.

She tipped back her head to gaze up at him. "Of course it is," she said, sounding puzzled. "More than generous, in fact."

"Perhaps I merely seek to ease my guilty conscience," he said, driven by demons to tear the truth from her. "If I am to blame for his death, why shouldn't I bear the cost of burying him? 'Twould be the least I could do, some would say."

"But you aren't to blame for his death!" she protested. "It was an accident, just as I told the magistrates."

"There was much you told the magistrates," he agreed. "But even more that you did not. What is it you didn't say, Anne? What secrets do you clutch so tightly to your heart?"

The evasiveness she'd displayed since her father's death was evident in the way she tried moving away from him. "I have no notion what you mean. I answered all the magistrate's questions."

As if they possessed a will of their own, his hands reached out to grasp her about the waist. "Their questions, yes," he said, drawing her inexorably against him, "but not mine. It's answers I want from you, *mo cridhe*, and answers I mean to have."

Instead of struggling, as he half expected, she remained where she was standing, her gaze fixed firmly on the center of his chest. "What sort of answers?"

That was the first thing he meant to address, Ruairdh decided, slipping his hand under her chin and raising her head.

"Why don't you look at me when you speak to me?" he asked softly, brushing his thumb across her soft mouth. "Why do you jump like a cat when I am near you?" He paused, then forced himself to ask the question he had most been dreading: "Are you afraid of me?"

"No!" She gasped, her distress too genuine to be anything but the truth. "Oh, Ruairdh, no. Never that."

Ruairdh squeezed his eyes closed as relief shot through him. "Then what else could it be?" he persisted, opening his eyes to meet her gaze. "Do you blame me for your father's death? Is that the answer?"

"I have already told you I do not!" she exclaimed. "You are not responsible for what happened."

Something about the way she said that had Ruairdh's senses sharpening in awareness. "Then who is? Who, Anne?" he demanded when she remained stubbornly silent. The last thing he expected was the answer she gave.

"I am," she blurted out, tearing herself out of his arms and dashing from the room, ignoring his calls to come back.

Chapter Eight

Anne fled down the corridor of the castle as if the devil himself were chasing after her.

"Anne! Come back!"

Ruairdh's imperious command echoed behind her, but she was too heartsick to care. Shame and sorrow were devouring her, and the pain of the emotions was so overwhelming that the only thought in her mind was escape. Blinded by tears, she paid no mind to her direction, and would have tumbled down the staircase if not for the strong pair of arms that caught her from behind.

"Have a care where you go!" Ruairdh snapped, dragging her to safety back against his chest. "Or is it your intention to die as your father did?"

Her father. Grief welled up in Anne in a huge wave, and the power of it drove her to her knees. Her legs folded beneath her, and if Ruairdh hadn't been holding her, she would have collapsed onto the flagstones.

"It is my fault he is dead!" she choked out, unable to remain silent another moment. "I killed my father. I killed him." And she began sobbing as if her heart would break.

A soft curse sounded above her head, and then Ruairdh was sweeping her up in his arms and carrying her back the way they had come. She heard the shocked whispers of the other servants as he carried her through the great hall, but Ruairdh ordered them back in a sharp tone that made it plain he would brook no interference. He carried her up the wide staircase, but instead of taking her to her room, as she expected, he kept climbing the stairs to a part of the castle she had yet to visit. She had the impression of a vast space, and then Ruairdh was gently setting her down in a nest of soft cushions.

"You will remain here," he ordered, his jaw set in stubborn lines. "Do not think to leave, Anne; I mean this." And with that he stalked out, leaving her alone.

After regaining her composure, Anne wiped her eyes and sat up, glancing about her as she took stock of her surroundings. From the thickness of the curved stone walls and the slant of sunlight streaming through the narrow windows she realized she was in the castle keep. The realization intrigued her, but more intriguing still was the strong sense of familiarity she felt. She recognized this room, she realized, and it was more than her usual affinity for ancient castles that was to blame. The answer came to her with a jolt of astonishment.

This was where her dream lover had brought her in

many of the wild, improper dreams she'd had since coming to Castle MacCairn. He would kiss her patiently as he laid her down among the pillows, covering her naked body with his own as he made love to her. The memory had her leaping to her feet, staring down at the cushions with a horror strongly mixed with embarrassment. She'd always thought the dreams nothing more than mere imagination. But if the room was real, what else might be real as well? It reminded her of the night Ruairdh had used the same term as her dream lover.

She was mulling over the ramifications of this when Ruairdh reentered the room, a tea tray balanced in his hands.

"Now, *annsachd*," he said, setting the tray on the low table and gesturing for her to join him on the settee, "we will talk. What do you mean, you killed your father? You surely don't believe such nonsense, do you?"

Anne reluctantly sat down beside him, uncertain what to say or how to say it. Her feelings for Ruairdh were so tangled, but everything else aside, she respected him more than she had ever respected another man. The knowledge that her actions would surely repulse him cut almost as deeply as her father's death, and she wondered if she would have the courage to admit the truth.

"Anne, why do you not tell me what you mean?" he demanded, his expression cross as he studied her. "I insist that you do."

His gruff command released the tide of words inside her, and they rushed out of her in a painful torrent. In a broken voice she told him of her argument with her father, tears flowing down her cheeks as she admitted the role she had played in his death.

"I was so hateful," she concluded, unable to look at him because of her shame. "So full of pride and anger that I tossed his infirmity in his face. I all but called him a useless old man, and then I let him walk away from me without a word of apology. I should have known he would do whatever it took to prove me wrong. And now he is dead because of it."

There was a long silence as Ruairdh sat studying her. As always, his countenance gave away little of his thoughts, and she grew anxious waiting to hear his response.

"You wrong yourself, *leannan*," he said at last, reaching out to take her hand in his. "Your father is not dead because of anything you did. He is dead because of his own pride and foolishness, nothing more. You say he knew of the old staircase, and I myself warned him any number of times to stay out of the east wing. Why he chose to go there is of no importance; the fact remains that it was his choice. He did what he wished to do, and that it ended as it did was nothing more than fate. His death was none of your doing."

But it was, Anne thought bleakly, withdrawing her hand from his and picking up her teacup. Had she apologized to her father and begged his forgiveness, there was no doubt in her mind he would still be alive. The responsibility for his death lay squarely on her shoulders, and it would be for her to determine how she could set right so terrible a wrong.

"When do you wish the funeral to be held?" Ruairdh

asked after a few moments, his emerald gaze sharp as he examined her.

Anne shoved her pain to one side as she contemplated the matter. "As soon as possible, I would suppose," she said softly, trying to be as logical as her father would expect. "It needn't be a grand affair. Father didn't know very many people in this area."

"As you wish." Ruairdh inclined his head. "However, you should know I've sent word to London of his death. No doubt there will be some notice appearing in the papers, and I am certain we can anticipate that a few of your father's friends and colleagues will wish to attend his service. We must give them time to make the journey, else I fear it will cause some unpleasant talk."

Anne repressed a groan as she realized he was right. Her father was something of a legend in the small circle of antiquarians, and his sudden death would undoubtedly cause a great deal of tattle. If on top of that his funeral was whispered to be held too precipitously, she could well imagine the gossip that would follow.

"Shall we say Friday, then?" she said, doing some swift calculations. "That will give everyone three days to get here—more than enough time, I should think, considering it took Father and I less than two days to get here from Blackpool."

"Friday," he agreed. "And in the meanwhile, I want you to remain here at the castle. There will be precious few rooms to be had in the village, and none of them are proper accommodations for a lady."

Anne gave a guilty start. She'd been so lost in misery that it hadn't occurred to her she would be forced to leave the castle, but now she wondered how she could have been so lost to the reality of her situation. Staying under a bachelor's roof without a proper chaperon the night of her father's death might be considered acceptable, but to remain there three days *and* three nights was another thing altogether. The scandal would ruin her once word of it was whispered about.

"Again, sir, you are most kind," she said, her heart lurching at the thought of leaving the castle, "but I fear that wouldn't be advisable. I am unmarried, and to remain beneath your roof without a chaperon—"

"But you shall have a chaperon," he interrupted, looking oddly pleased with himself. "That is something else I wished to discuss with you. I've sent word to Mrs. Collier, the widowed sister of our village parson, and she has graciously agreed to remain here while you are in residence. Believe me, there's no one who would dare find fault with her here; that I promise you."

An image of an older woman full of starch and sharp words flashed in Anne's mind, and she didn't know if she should be thanking Ruairdh or cursing him. She chose the farmer.

"You have thought of everything, it seems," she said, offering him a tentative smile. "Thank you."

To her surprise his eyes flashed with annoyance. "Must you be eternally thanking me?" he demanded crossly. "I am only doing what is right. You've no reason to be mouthing your gratitude every cursed second."

Anne blinked, amazed to find that beneath the myriad of other emotions besetting her, she could still feel anger. The normalcy of her temper shocked her, and she was instantly ashamed.

"This is a most interesting room," she said, deciding a change of subject might be advisable. "But better seen by moonlight, I should think."

A sly expression darkened his eyes. "Aye," he all but purred, "and so it is. You'd know that well, wouldn't you, lass, considering the many times you've been here."

Something about his words, his tone of voice, struck her as odd, and a frisson of alarm shivered down her back. "I am not certain of your meaning," she said, busying herself by pouring another cup of tea. "This is my first time in this part of the castle."

"And you've no' dreamed of it?" he asked, leaning closer. "You've no' dreamed of a handsome lover who laid you upon these cushions, and loved you in all the ways a man loves a woman?" His fingers snaked out to grab hers, and this time his flesh was like ice.

She jerked back her hand, sending the delicate teapot crashing to the floor. The sound of the shattering china had him leaping to his feet and glancing about him wildly.

"You . . . how could you know?" Anne whispered, the blood draining from her face as she stared up at him. A terrible thought was occurring to her, and the very idea that it might be true was enough to momentarily push her father's death from her mind.

"Know what?" He was breathing faster than usual, his bronzed face alarmingly pale. "One moment we're speaking of Mrs. Collier, and in the next you're smashing the china like an ill-tempered hussy. Has Mrs. Doughal been dosing you again?" He glared at her suspiciously.

Anne stumbled to her feet, her legs unsteady beneath her. "My dreams," she whispered, trying to understand what was happening. "How could you know about my dreams?"

A hunted, almost desperate look stole across Ruairdh's face, but was as quickly gone. "Your dreams, Miss Garthwicke?" he asked, raising a black eyebrow in mocking challenge. "And pray, what dreams might those be? Describe them to me."

Anne's cheeks turned a bright red as she realized the impossibility of answering his question in a truthful manner. To admit to such dreams would label her the most shocking sort of female, and in the end it would avail her nothing. If what she was beginning to suspect was true, he already knew the content of those dreams, and was toying with her for dark reasons of his own. Uncertain what else to do, she pursed her lips tightly together, fixing her gaze over his shoulder and maintaining a sullen silence.

Several seconds passed before he gave a small nod. "Just so," he said, sounding pleased. "Your grief has overcome your nerves, and 'tis plain you should be abed. I will escort you to your rooms. Your new companion will have arrived by now, and you'll be wanting to meet her. Come." He held out his arm in unmistakable command.

Anne stared at him in sudden unease, remembering the iciness of his hand when he had touched her a few minutes earlier. His skin had been so cold it was like brushing against a tombstone. The thought of feeling that horrible chill again filled her with profound distaste, and yet she could see no way to refuse without making an even bigger fool of herself. Gathering her courage she laid the very tips of her fingers on his velvet-clad arm, almost jerking them back at the warm feel of living flesh beneath her own.

He shot her a concerned look. "Is something wrong?"

More confused than ever, Anne could only shake her head. "No," she replied, taking care to mask her feelings as he led her toward the staircase. "There is nothing."

He'd known what was happening.

Ruairdh paced the length of his bedchamber, remembering those few seconds in the tower room with Anne. Except for those rare times when his voice was not his own to control, always before when the Shadowing had overtaken him, there'd been no memory of what was happening. He'd be in one place in time, and then in the blink of an eye he'd be in another, with no idea how he'd gotten there or what had occurred in between. It was as if he had dozed off while watching a play, and then awakened to find himself watching quite another. The sensation was highly unsettling, and he'd learned to mask the brief period of confusion that followed. But this time there was no need for such subterfuge. This time he'd known precisely what was going on.

He stopped pacing to close his eyes, focusing his preternatural abilities to conjure up the precise moment when the Shadowing had come over him. He'd been sitting next to Anne, hurt and furious over her insistence upon thanking him, and he'd felt the sudden presence of another. Then he realized he was watching Anne through eyes that were not his own, hearing a voice coming from his lips he did not recognize. Most horrifying of all was when he'd felt Anne's hand beneath his fingertips, and knew it was not he who was touching her. The realization filled him with such fury he'd turned on the other presence, doing his best to force it out of his mind.

Never before had the madness felt so strong. It was as though the voices in his head had converged into one ominous being, a powerful creature determined to rule his body. Ruairdh surpressed a shudder. The evil mutterings and sibilant whispers had been annoying and distracting; this new presence was malevolent and powerful.

Determined not to relinquish control of his mind and body, determined to protect Anne, he'd fought with all his being against this new form the madness had taken. And he wasn't certain he would have succeeded in overcoming the evil had the sound of the teapot hitting the floor not broken the spell the madness had cast over him. The Shadowing was gaining strength.

It had been too late to take back all that had happened in those few seconds when he'd lost control, but he'd thought he'd done a rather good job of hiding the truth from Anne's too-sharp mind. Or had he? He frowned, remembering the stunned expression on her face as she'd accused him of knowing about her dreams. He froze as he remembered the words he'd spoken while under the Shadowing's evil influence.

You've no' dreamed of a handsome lover who laid you

upon these cushions, and loved you in all the ways a man loves a woman?

He sat down, his stunned mind refusing to accept what he now knew to be true. His dreams. Anne's dreams. They were one and the same. He was struggling to understand what this might portend when there was a rap at the door, and Angley came stomping in.

"And a fine place this is for the laird of MacCairn to be hiding when his guests are arriving like an invading army," he grumbled, stalking over to glare down at Ruairdh. " 'Tis below you should be, and not up here cowering like a maid. You—" He broke off in mid-sentence, his eyes widening in alarm.

"Laird, are you ill?" he asked urgently, disapproval fading to anxiety as he crowded closer. "Is it a doctor you're needing, or—"

"No, Angley," Ruairdh interrupted, resisting the urge to order the older man to leave him alone. "I am but tired. 'Tis been a long day."

"And looks to be a longer night," Angley agreed with a sigh. "Half the valley or more has come to pay Miss Garthwicke their respects, when 'tis plain the wee lass would do better to be resting than entertaining the likes of them. And you've guests from Edinburgh as well, all come for the funeral and the scandal."

Ruairdh waited, but the whispering voice remained silent. He would like to think it had been vanquished forever, but such optimism was not in his nature. Burying his impatience, he rose to his feet, again tugging on the heavy responsibilities he bore as head of his clan.

"Has Mrs. Collier come?" he asked, turning his

thoughts to Anne and how best to protect her from wagging tongues. It would be better, he knew, to have the companion safely in place before the bulk of the guests made their appearance.

Angley's nose twitched in disapproval. "Aye, she's come, with a hill of luggage and enough smelling salts to revive the dead. Twice she's fainted in the hour since she's been here, but what else can one expect of a *Sasunnach* woman?" This last was added with a shrug.

"You're forgetting Miss Garthwicke is a *Sasunnach* as well." The good breeding he still claimed compelled Ruairdh to point out the obvious to his dour steward.

"Aye, but 'tis common sense and kindness she has as well, which is more than can be said of that other one," Angley replied in his tart manner. "Still, for the lass's sake, 'tis as well you thought to have her here. The *ruddochs* would be sharpening their knives as well as their tongues on Miss Garthwicke's name were it not for her."

Hearing his steward speaking so disrespectfully of their guests gave Ruairdh a much-needed laugh. "I should mind who you call a *ruddoch*, old man," he said, giving Angley an affectionate grin, "since you're just as ancient and twice as bad-tempered as the lot of them put together."

Angley's reply to this was in sharp Gaelic, and the memory of it had Ruairdh hiding a grin as he took his place at dinner later that night. Since he had no hostess it fell to Mrs. MacGinty, the mayor's wife, to sit at the foot of his table, where she proceeded to lord it over a sour-faced Mrs. Collier with obvious relish. Anne sat between the two ladies, looking pale and lovely in her simple dress of mourning black, her burnished gold hair tucked back in a prim bun. How much rather he would have preferred to see her sitting at the place of honor, he thought, and quickly glanced away lest any of the other guests catch the direction of his gaze.

"Of course," Mrs. MacGinty was informing one of the visitors from Edinburgh in a superior tone, "I have been to the castle any number of times as a girl, and I quite agree it is a grand place. And I suppose I can see why those of a susceptible nature could be persuaded into believing it is haunted." Here a killing glance was leveled at Mrs. Collier.

"My nature is no less susceptible than that of any Christian woman." Mrs. Collier was quick to leap to her own defense. "The devil has held sway here for untold generations, and all in the valley know it as well. None of them, you will note, were brave enough to remain here past sundown." And she preened in obvious pride at her own daring.

The guests, two of Mr. Garthwicke's colleagues and their whey-faced wives, shifted uneasily on their chairs and cast uneasy glances about them. Ruairdh was trying to think of some way of assuaging their fears when Anne suddenly spoke.

"Most old places, Scottish or English, do seem to have such legends attached to them, do you not agree, Mr. Cavendish?" she asked in her soft voice, addressing her remark to the older of the two men who was sitting across from her. "I believe you wrote a paper on the subject?"

"Yes, and so I did," the older man said, brightening at the notice. "I have done thorough research on a dozen or more legends attached to some of the finest homes in our country. England, that is," he added, giving Ruairdh an apologetic look. "I fear I am not so well versed in the lore of Scotland, although I am certain it is equally as interesting."

"This place has more than a legend attached to it, I should say," the second man said, looking thoughtful. "I did a spot of research when your father mentioned he would be taking this position, and I wrote him of the curse that is said to have been placed upon the laird and his family. I also recall mentioning rumors that in the past five hundred years, not one laird of the clan MacCairn has lived out his life a sane man. I warned him it would be the death of him, but—" he stopped, his eyes widening in horror as he realized what he had just said.

"My dear Miss Garthwicke, you must forgive me," he stammered, his thin face growing red in the candlelight. "I did not think—"

"That is quite all right, Sir Lorring," Anne reassured him, albeit with a tremulous smile. "Father was most gratified by your concern, but naturally he knew that as a man of science you could not possibly believe in such nonsense as a curse."

The elderly baronet cast a furtive glance at Ruairdh. "Indeed not," he said, taking a hasty sip of wine. "Nonsense, as you say."

Liar. The old fool believes every word of it, and fairly stinks with his own fear. The voice was back, whispering evilly in Ruairdh's ear. He tried to ignore it, but there was an edgy feeling of darkness growing in him, and whether it was the demons goading him on or his own black temper, he was suddenly unwilling to drop the matter.

"So you are saying no man of my blood died sane," he asked, drawling out the words in his most insolent tones. "If so, 'tis brave of you to say so. *I* might be mad, for all you know."

There was an uneasy silence as the guests glanced uncertainly at one another, and from the dramatic way Mrs. Collier was clasping her hand to her bosom, it looked as if she would be swooning a third time. Anticipation built in Ruairdh, but before Mrs. Collier could collapse gracefully on the floor, Anne spoke again.

"Mr. MacCairn's sense of humor takes some getting used to, I fear," she said, her calm voice smoothing over the volatile moment. "Of course there is no truth in such tittle-tattle. Father would never have allowed me to accompany him had there been the slightest danger of Mr. MacCairn's not being in the most sound of mind."

"Of course he would not have," Mrs. Lorring answered bracingly. "Your father was a man of science, as is my husband." Her muddy gaze flashed back to Ruairdh.

"You mustn't let Sir Lorring's talk of curses and madness offend you, Mr. MacCairn," Mrs. Lorring said, all but simpering at him. "I can assure such Gothic matters are of passing interest to him, no more. In fact, he is almost as much an authority on antiquities and the like as was poor Mr. Garthwicke. I daresay you should be hard-pressed to find another scientist more qualified to finish authenticating the collection for you."

Such obvious jockeying for the position only recently made available because of the death of Anne's father had Ruairdh's lips curling in disdain. But even as he was resisting the urge to tell the toadying female precisely what he thought of her, he realized he had just been handed the solution to a very tricky matter. Until now he'd been so intent on how her father's death had affected Anne, he hadn't given a thought to how it had affected him. Much as it galled him to offer the position to the baronet and his encroaching wife, he feared he had no other choice.

"It would be a pleasure, sir, a pleasure," Sir Lorring assured him, nodding eagerly. "Why, next spring, when I am finished with my position at the university, I should be delighted to—"

"Next spring?" Ruairdh interrupted, seeing his chance for the clan's salvation slipping away. "That is too late. I need the collection cataloged and authenticated now."

"Of course you do not, sir," Mrs. Lorring corrected him, shaking her head. "This castle and its relics are centuries old; what difference could a few months make? And naturally you will want a renowned authority on such matters to complete the work for you." She cast a sharp look at Mrs. Cavendish, who looked as if she were ready to offer her husband's services in the baronet's stead.

"What of you, Mr. Cavendish?" Ruairdh was one step ahead of her. "Can you begin right away?"

A look of sincere regret was his answer. "I am afraid

I cannot, Mr. MacCairn," the older man said with a sigh. "I should love it above all things, but unfortunately I am accompanying Lord Bereston to Italy to authenticate a Roman ruin that has only recently been excavated. And Roman and Grecian antiquities are really more in my line, as I am sure Miss Garthwicke would be happy to tell you." He gave Anne a kind smile.

She returned it without her usual degree of warmth. "I am sure a gentleman of your accomplishments is capable of whatever he sets his mind to, Mr. Cavendish," she said, her slender fingers toying with her glass of wine. "But as you say, you are more familiar with the Spartans than you are the Templars."

"The Templars?" Both scholars spoke at the same time.

Anne blinked, seeming unaccountably uneasy. "I cannot imagine what made me mention them," she said, ducking her head as if in embarrassment. "Forgive me."

"No, do go on, Miss Garthwicke." It was Mrs. Collier who spoke, her eyes gleaming with excitement. "What of the Templars?"

Anne gave a small shrug. "It is nothing, merely that one of the artifacts I found of most particular interest was a battle sword with the most intriguing markings. I thought them remarkably like the symbols associated with the Templars, but Father reminded me that the warrior monks never engraved their weapons. We were debating the matter, but we'd come no closer to finding an answer when . . . when he died."

"As there is no record of the knights having been in this area, Miss Garthwicke, I fear I must agree with your father," Sir Lorring said with a pompous nod. "But you mustn't be embarrassed, my dear. As you are a female, you cannot expect to be knowledgeable of such things. I, on the other hand," he added, turning to Ruairdh, "am something of an expert in that area. If you like, Mr. MacCairn, I should be happy to bring the sword back to Edinburgh with me."

Rage and fear had Ruairdh snapping the stem of the wineglass he'd been holding. The sharp shards sliced into his skin, and his blood mingled with the wine spilling out onto the starched tablecloth.

"He who touches the blade will die." He issued the threat in a guttural voice, his entire body quivering with rage. "It will never leave this place, do you hear? Never."

Sir Lorring paled. "I . . . It was but a suggestion, sir," he stammered, his hands fluttering up to pull at his black-edged cravat. "I meant no offense, I assure you."

Ruairdh stared at the man, as appalled by his own response as were his guests. He was trying to think of some explanation for his behavior, when there was a low moan and a rather loud thump from the end of the table. Mrs. Collier had achieved her third swoon of the day.

It took Anne the rest of the evening to calm Mrs. Collier and the other ladies. It didn't help that the moment the other woman recovered from her faint it was to find herself in Ruairdh's arms as he was carrying her to her room. The dratted creature emitted a loud shriek and swooned again, and remained insensate until she'd been placed carefully on her bed. Anne was so disgusted with her idiotic behavior at this point that she wouldn't have blamed Ruairdh had he dropped her on her well-padded posterior. Indeed, she rather found herself hoping he would, but as usual, Ruairdh proved himself to be every inch a gentleman.

The other ladies required equal attention, and she found herself pouring increasingly larger doses of brandy to stop their tears and their babble.

"He is a devil, Miss Garthwicke, a devil," the usually shy Mrs. Cavendish insisted, clinging to her glass of brandy with obvious desperation. "Did you see his eyes, so cold and dark . . . ? I vow, they seemed almost black in the candlelight. Did you notice?"

"Indeed I did," Anne replied, thinking that it wasn't the first time she had observed the phenomenon. "But as I said, it is only Mr. MacCairn's odd sense of humor. You mustn't pay him any attention."

"Well, I for one am relieved you shall be leaving this awful place the moment your father is buried," Mrs. Lorring said when Anne went to check on her. "I would offer to take you with us, but I am certain you would never wish to impose yourself upon an elderly couple. Besides you will have to return to London and see about a future. Perhaps it is time to get married, my dear."

"I do not think Castle MacCairn so very awful," Anne replied, carefully avoiding the matter of her departure and her uncertain plans. "It has a grandness to it, don't you think?"

"I dc not!" The older woman glowered at her, jabbing a finger at Anne in emphasis. "And if you are even thinking of remaining here one second past the funeral,

I should strongly advise you against it. That half-witted woman Mr. MacCairn employs to give you countenance isn't fit to chaperon a hen, and if you want my opinion, I rather suspects she tipples. One can always tell." And she took a healthy sip of brandy, emptying the glass before handing it back to Anne in a silent demand for more.

After leaving the two women in the dubious care of their husbands, Anne returned to her companion's room, only to find the good Mrs. Collier loudly snoring away. A quick whiff of the brandy fumes emanating from the other woman made Anne think that perhaps Mrs. Lorring wasn't so very far off the mark after all, and she quietly closed the door behind her. With nothing left to do she returned to her rooms, nearly leaping out of her skin when a movement in the shadows caught her eye. Fearing what it might be, she spun around, the scream in her throat dying as she recognized Ruairdh's harsh features as he stepped closer to her.

Relief coursed through her, but so did a belated wariness as she thought of all that had happened since her arrival in the castle. Not certain of who or what she might be facing; she ventured a tentative smile. "Mr. MacCairn, I—"

"For the love of all that is holy, Anne, I beg you, do not retreat behind a wall of respectability. I do not think I could stomach it," Ruairdh said, and Anne gave a silent sigh of relief as she recognized his voice—impatient and frustrated, she decided, but still Ruairdh's voice; the thought was oddly reassuring.

"I have been too long trapped between the worlds of

servant and master to abandon all notions of propriety," she said, deciding caution mightn't be so bad a thing. After all, Ruairdh was not the person to whom she should be turning for solace, despite her natural inclination that way. "As I believe I have commented before, a female in my position needs to exercise every caution—all the more so when she returns to her rooms to find her employer waiting for her."

A look she couldn't identify flashed across his face and was gone. "I am not your employer now," he said, stopping a hairbreadth from where she was standing.

Anne decided not to argue the matter now. There was something else she wanted to discuss with Ruairdh, something so extraordinary and out of the realm of everything she knew that she had no idea how to begin. But she had to know the truth; it was the only way she could ever sleep again.

"Ruairdh," she began, resisting the urge to take that one step closer that would put her in his arms, "there is something I must ask you. Something so fantastical I almost hesitate asking you, but I must know." She gazed up at him, forcing herself to meet his intense green gaze. "Do you dream about me?"

His lips tightened and his hands balled into fists. "Yes." He ground the answer out as if it caused him the greatest pain.

"When—" Her courage dried up, forcing her to clear her throat and start again. "When did these dreams start?"

"The night of your arrival."

The blunt answer was more or less what she expected, and she waited patiently for him to enlarge upon it. When he did not, she drew another steadying breath.

"In these dreams, do I . . . do you—" She stopped, then threw caution and modesty to the four winds. "Do we make love?" she demanded.

His eyes burned into hers with emerald fire. "Yes, we do."

Anne tried to remain calm, although inside she was writhing with mortification. Still, she thought her modesty of less importance than learning the truth of what was happening. "Have you had dreams of this nature in the past?" she asked, determined to remain coolly objective.

"Aye," he admitted, and then smiled when he saw her lips tightening with disapproval. "Do not glare, *annsachd*," he said, wryly. "We men are poor, base creatures at best, and such dreams, I fear, are common for us. But," he added, before she could speak, "I cannot remember ever having dreams that were so vivid, so real. And I am fair certain I have never shared such dreams with another woman before. Does it matter?"

Anne wasn't certain how to answer. She was convinced the dreams were of vital importance, although why she could not say. She considered the matter for several seconds before replying.

"I think it may," she said, ignoring the dreams' carnal implications, and concentrating instead on the emotions they evoked in her. Passion was there, yes, but there was something else as well, something every bit as warm and pleasurable as the passion she felt in Ruairdh's arms. Comfort, she decided, tasting the word in her mind before giving a slow nod. She felt comfort with Ruairdh, and more importantly, she knew he derived comfort from her. Unsure how she felt about this realization she cast it aside for the moment.

There was one last thing she had to know. "That night," she said, unaware she had inched closer, "the night before my father died, was that you in my room?"

He shook his head violently. "No," he denied, his hands grasping her arms and pulling her against him. "I swear to you, Anne, by all that I believe in, it was not me."

Her biggest terror soothed, Anne stood on tiptoe to twine her arms about his neck. "Thank God," she murmured, and then pressed her mouth to his.

Chapter Nine

Ruairdh pulled her into his arms, his mouth taking hers with a hunger rivaling her own. Anne clung to his broad shoulders, her heart racing with a heady mixture of anticipation and fear. Everything she was experiencing was so achingly familiar and yet so terrifyingly new, her whirling senses couldn't separate fact from fantasy. She knew only that if it was real, she didn't want it to stop.

"Anne." Ruairdh tore his mouth from hers to string a necklace of burning kisses down her throat. "I want you, *mo cridhe*. I want you until I think I shall die if I do not have you." His lips returned to hers fiercely, tracing her lips with his tongue.

The brazen kiss had Anne gasping, and he took advantage of her shock to deepen the kiss even further. The brush of his tongue against hers was an intimacy Anne had never experienced, and it filled her with a wildness that made her long for more. When he lifted his head to draw in a ragged breath, she was trembling with desire.

"If this a dream, I never want to awaken," she murmured, scarcely aware she was speaking aloud. She was lost in a world of sensual wonder, and after the nightmare of the last two days, she wanted nothing more than to lose herself in its misty realms.

Ruairdh's hands cupped her face, his touch almost rough as he forced her to look up. Her eyes fluttered open, the breath lodging in her throat at the raw emotion glittering in his eyes.

" 'Tis no' a dream," he said, his voice harsh as he gazed down at her. " 'Tis real. And the consequences if we continue are real as well. If you don't want those consequences, for the love of God, tell me now while I've the control to stop. Tell me, Anne, and you've my word I will do as you say."

The graphic demand shattered the pretty illusion Anne was clinging to, forcing her to make a decision she never thought to make. It should be easy, she thought, her gaze locking with Ruairdh's. A lifetime's morality dictated there could be but one choice, and to choose any other way would be folly beyond measuring. There could be but one choice, and in the end, there was.

"I don't want you to stop," she said, knowing that with those few words she was forever altering her future. "Stay with me, Ruairdh."

A muscle flexed in his lean jaw, but he made no other move. "If I stay, we will make love."

His words proved his honor to her more than anything else could have done, and she smiled softly.

"Stay," she repeated, and turned her head to press a fleeting kiss to his hand.

He drew in his breath on a hiss of sound, and then he was sweeping her up in his arms and carrying her from the room.

"Ruairdh!" She gave a startled gasp, taking care to keep her voice low. "What are you doing?"

"Taking you to my room," he replied, walking briskly down the hall. "For all she's drunk enough brandy to fell a sailor, I'll not risk having Mrs. Collier waking up and remembering her duties at an inopportune moment. We'd never revive her from the faint."

Anne hadn't imagined she could laugh at such a time, but that was what she did as he carried her down the corridor and up the winding stairs to a set of wide, ornately carved oak doors. Still holding her, he shouldered the doors open, striding arrogantly into the room and setting her down in the center of the massive chamber.

"Mind you stay here," he warned gruffly, pressing a quick kiss to her lips before striding away to close and bar the doors.

That done, he knelt before the fire, taking care to see that it was well stoked before turning to light several of the candles scattered about the room. Anne watched him through wide eyes, the enormity of what she was about to do making her tremble in uncertainty. She was discovering it was one thing to decide to abandon all respectability and give herself to a man who was not her husband, and quite another to actually carry that decision out. She swallowed uneasily as Ruairdh approached her, a sensual gleam in his eyes.

"I wish I had some champagne to offer you, *an-*

nsachd," he murmured, his slow, masculine smile setting her pulse racing anew.

Anne's resolve wavered as she took a hesitant step back. "I—I don't require any champagne," she stammered, and then flushed, feeling hopelessly naive.

"Do you not?" he asked, pausing in front of her to gently place his hand on her neck. "You'd be less nervous, I'm thinking, with a glass or two in you to settle your nerves." He bent his head and kissed her again, before drawing back to give her another smile.

" 'Tis still not too late, you know," he told her softly. "I will take you back to your rooms if you have changed your mind."

Anne hesitated, weighing her natural fears against the wild pleasure she remembered from her dreams. It was unlikely she would ever marry, she told herself, facing her bleak and barren future with searing honesty. Did she truly want to live out the rest of her life without ever knowing in real life those wondrous emotions from her dreams?

"I haven't changed my mind," she told him with what dignity she could muster. "But that doesn't mean I can't be a trifle nervous. I've never done this sort of thing before."

His lips curved in a devilish grin, making him look unexpectedly boyish. "Of course you have, *leannan*," he drawled, running a finger down her nose. "Remember the dreams?"

Her cheeks heated in embarrassment. "That is hardly the same thing," she said, trembling at the memory of the more passionate of those visions.

"No," he agreed, his hands sliding up to begin plucking the pins from her hair. "This will be even better—another thing you've my word on."

Anne could think of no proper response, nervously biting her lip as Ruairdh continued undoing her bun. When her hair was free and tumbling about her shoulders, he next turned his attention to her gown.

"So many buttons and hooks you have, my love," he teased, turning her around to begin unfastening them. "It must take your maid forever to be closing them all."

He continued talking as he unfastened her gown, his prosaic chatter oddly soothing. He had comments aplenty about her hoop skirts and petticoats as well, making her smile even as he carefully removed her clothing. She wondered if he meant to completely disrobe her, and soon had her answer when he stopped, leaving her clad in her chemise and pantalets.

"You are so beautiful, Anne," he whispered, his heated gaze sliding over her in a caress she could almost feel. "More beautiful even than in my dreams; I ache for you."

Anne trembled at his words. "And I ache for you," she replied, shyly laying her hands on his chest. Being all but nude while he was still fully clothed left her feeling at something of a disadvantage, and she was determined to remedy the situation as quickly as possible. With his help she soon divested him of his evening jacket and waistcoat, but when it came to removing his starched white shirt her courage deserted her, and she cast him a helpless look.

"Don't stop, sweetest," he implored, capturing her hands and pressing them against his chest. "I want to feel your hands on me."

His hoarse plea swept away the last of her reticence, and she slipped her hands inside the open front of his shirt to caress the hair-dusted flesh she remembered from her dreams. The heat of it seared her palms, and when her fingers found his masculine nipples she was unable to resist caressing them.

His response was immediate. With a raw oath he released her, tugging his shirt over his head and tossing it carelessly onto the floor. He swept her up into his arms, kissing her passionately as he carried her over to the waiting bed. After laying her on the velvet-and-satin spread he stepped back, his gaze never leaving her as he quickly shed the rest of his clothing.

Anne's eyes widened at the sight of his aroused masculine body, the warm honey in her veins suddenly cooling. She ran a nervous tongue over her lips, but before she could give voice to her fears he was joining her on the bed.

"How perfect you are, my love," he murmured, brushing his mouth lightly over hers. "The first time I laid eyes upon you, I thought you the most beautiful woman I had ever seen."

Anne had a somewhat different memory of that meeting. "You were rude," she reminded him, her lips curving under his. "You cursed at me, and then ordered me from the castle."

"Only because I wanted you so desperately," he replied, shifting until she was tucked partially beneath him. "My decisions were already made, *leannan*, and you were a complication I could ill afford. Of course I cursed you."

Anne wasn't certain she liked being called a complication, but it was becoming increasingly difficult to think. Ruairdh's lips were sliding lower to press teasing kisses against the hollow of her throat, while his fingers toyed with the ribbons closing the front of her chemise. Half-formed memories were merging with reality, and the pleasure she felt was almost more than she could bear. When his tongue flicked across a lace-covered nipple she gave a soft gasp.

"Do you like that, Anne?" he demanded, his deep voice rough with desire. "Do you like my mouth on you? Tell me."

"Yes," she admitted, terrified he would stop if she did not respond. "Yes, I like it."

"Good." He unlaced the front of her chemise and slipped his hand inside to stroke her breast. "Then perhaps you will like this as well." And he ducked his head, closing his lips over her nipple and drawing it into his mouth.

Anne squeezed her eyes shut, biting her lip to hold back a cry of desire. Not even the wildest of her dreams prepared her for such ecstasy, and she gave herself up to the exquisite magic. Ruairdh continued suckling at her nipple, using his fingers to tease and torment her other breast until she was writhing in delirium.

"Ruairdh," she pleaded, not knowing what she was pleading for. "Please, please."

"I will please you, *aingeal*," he vowed, using his teeth and tongue with devastating thoroughness. "I will please you until you are mad with it."

Anne tossed her head and moaned softly, speech beyond her. She couldn't have imagined she could ever feel such closeness to another person, and she knew she would never know it with anyone else again. When he moved completely over her, parting her legs with his, she was more than ready for him.

"This last step we take changes everything," he said, his fingers reaching down to tease her feminine softness. "It will bind us with chains that can never be broken. Do you understand that, Anne?"

Caught on the sharp edge of desire, Anne could only nod. Her heart was racing, and everything inside of her was drawing into a tight ball of need. She sensed something calling to her, and she was eager to follow wherever it led.

"Anne?" Ruairdh nudged her with the tip of his manhood. "Do you understand?"

Anne moaned at the intimate touch, and managed another nod. "Yes," she said in a gasp, raising her hips in search of more. "Yes, Ruairdh, I understand."

He gave her a deep, hungry kiss, sliding his hands down to her thighs. Holding her gaze, he lifted her legs until they were wrapped about his own. "There will be some pain, my love," he told her, his eyes shadowed with regret, "but it will quickly be gone." And he rocked his hips, sliding deep within her with a single thrust.

Anne gave another gasp, not from the hot flash of pain, but from the indescribable sense of completeness she felt. It was beyond all imagining, and when he began to move inside of her, the intensity of it was shattering. She sobbed in pleasure, her legs tightening about his as she moved with him in the sweetest of dances.

"Anne!" he cried out her name, his thrusts increasing

in power and speed. "Yes, *mo cridhe!* Yes!"

The excitement building in Anne rose ever higher as Ruairdh made wild love to her. She was so hot she feared she would burst into flame, and she couldn't seem to get enough air in her lungs however hard she tried. It was the most wondrous experience of her life, and she prayed she would survive the power of it all. Then the pleasure inside of her exploded, hurling her over the edge and into oblivion. But even as she was falling she felt him pull from her, his muscular body shuddering as he emptied himself onto the bed beside her.

He was damned to an eternity in hell, but the heaven he had just found might well be worth the price.

Ruairdh lay beside Anne, his chest rising and falling as he struggled for breath. A fine layer of sweat coated him, and the sweet languor he had all but forgotten left his body feeling wonderfully replete. If only his mind and heart could be equally content, he brooded, drawing his finger down Anne's bare arm.

He'd never intended to go to her rooms. He had told himself that if he had any feelings for her at all he would stay as far away from her as he could. Ruin and scandal would be a poor way to repay her, considering all she'd already lost because of him, and yet when the time had come for him to retire, he'd found himself standing outside her door with no memory of having walked there.

He would have liked to lay the blame for it on the Shadowing, but he refused to play the coward. His family's curse had nothing to do with his need for Anne, and he thanked God for it. Had he been taken by the

Shadowing, he would never have possessed the control to withdraw from Anne as he had. The consequences if he had not filled him with sick terror. He might have broken his vow never to make love to a woman again, but he was determined to keep the most important of his vows: there would be no child, no heir to reap his horrific inheritance.

Thinking of his inheritance made him think of the heated dreams he and Anne shared. Since realizing the incredible truth he'd given them a great deal of thought, and the more he considered them the more convinced he became they were not part of the Shadowing. However improper the dreams might have been there was something about them, some element of rightness that made him certain they had naught to do with the evil threat hanging over him. They gave him a sense of peace, and that was what made him believe they had far more to do with salvation than damnation. Perhaps it was heaven's way of granting him a respite, he decided, smiling at the thought.

"Ruairdh?" Anne stirred beside him, pressing a shy kiss to his chest. "Are you awake?"

"Aye, *leannan*," he said, shaking off his black thoughts and ducking his head to press a tender kiss to her lips. He studied her flushed face for several seconds before speaking.

"I did not cause you pain, did I?" he asked, lifting a golden curl from her cheek and tucking it behind her ear. "I do not think I could bear it if I had."

She shook her head, her lips curving in a dazed smile. "You did not," she assured him, her voice husky with spent passion. "It was quite the most wonderful thing I have ever experienced. Thank you."

He blinked in surprise, and then grinned as he realized she was already half-asleep. "You are welcome, *mo cridhe*," he assured her wryly. "The pleasure was mine."

"Mmmm." She cuddled closer, draping her arm about his middle. He thought she was drifting off, when she sat up with a sudden cry.

Ruairdh reacted instinctively, catching Anne by the waist and tucking her beneath him, shielding her with his body. "What is it?" he demanded, his gaze searching the thick shadows for some sign of danger.

"I . . . It is nothing," she stammered, and he glanced down to see her rosy-cheeked in distress. "I just realized I dare not stay here. What if your valet should discover us?"

Realizing there was nothing more amiss than a sudden attack of maidenly distress, Ruairdh allowed himself to relax. "Then he should turn around and leave," he replied, amazed and delighted to feel his body hardening again. "Richard is a smart lad who values his position too much to wag his tongue when he should not. Besides"—he nipped her chin—"I locked the door. Remember?"

"Oh." Her cheeks grew rosier. "I'd forgotten. But I still think I should go. If one of the guests should see me—"

He silenced her with a kiss, and when he raised his head they were both breathing heavily. "Stay, Anne," he said, his voice both a plea and a command as he slipped inside her again. "Do not leave me to face the darkness alone. I will see you safely to your rooms." And he began making love to her with a passion so tinged with desperation it was hard to separate one emotion from the other.

The rest of the night passed in a sensual blur. Ruairdh made love to Anne again and again, unable to sate his desire for her. But however hot his passion, he was always careful to satisfy her first, and never to let himself reach culmination inside of her. Finally they both slept, and he savored the sweet feel of her in his arms.

Light was peeking through the partially opened drapes when Ruairdh stirred sleepily awake early the next morning. Anne still slumbered beside him, and in the soft light of a Scottish dawn, he drank in the sight of her.

Her beautiful hair lay in a tangle about her shoulders, and he remembered how soft it felt in his hands, and the sweet smell of it when he'd buried his face in the golden waves. Her eyes were closed now, hidden by her thick lashes, but he had no trouble remembering their color. When she'd been shy or uncertain as she'd touched him they'd been the gray of a winter fog, and when she'd moved with him in wild abandon they'd gleamed like the purest silver. His body hardened at the thought, but he stoically ignored his arousal. His sharpened senses told him the household was already stirring, and if they had any hopes of avoiding scandal, they would have to move now. He lifted her hair and kissed her creamy shoulder.

"Wake up, Annie," he crooned, giving her a gentle shake. "Wake up. 'Tis morning."

She started awake, and he saw both awareness and

embarrassment flare in her crystal-colored eyes before she glanced away.

"What time is it?" she asked, holding the bedclothes to her chest to hide her nakedness as she moved away from him.

"Early," he answered, fighting a sudden attack of possessiveness that had him wanting to claim her again. "But with so many guests expected, the servants are already up and moving about. We'll need to be quick, if you've no wish to be seen."

She colored and then paled in distress, and he was instantly ashamed of his callous behavior. Silently calling himself every foul name he could think of, he rose from the bed and walked over to grab a dressing gown from the wardrobe.

"Don't bother with your clothing, *leannan*," he said, gently helping her into the thick robe. "I'm no lady's maid, and breakfast will have come and gone before I'd manage to get half those hooks fastened. To say nothing of lacing that cursed corset." He added this last as a jest, hoping to win a smile from her; instead she looked perilously close to tears. Hiding his own fears and regrets, he slipped his hand beneath her chin and tilted her face up to meet his gaze.

" 'Tis a little late to be embarrassed, Anne," he said softly. "What's done is done. And if you're still fretting about anyone seeing us, you needn't worry. The way we are going, there will be no eyes to spy upon us."

Her cheeks grew even rosier. "It's not that, precisely," she murmured, her gray gaze full of chagrin as she kept her eyes locked firmly on his face. "It is just that I was wondering if you would be so kind as to cover yourself. You surely don't mean to escort me back to my rooms like that." She waved her hand helplessly.

Ruairdh glanced down, his concern vanishing as understanding dawned. He gave a low chuckle, the sense of humor he'd all but forgotten he possessed returning as he raised his eyes to meet her self-conscious gaze.

"Do no' fash yourself, *mo ghradh*," he said, his lips curving in a boyish grin. "I mean to take you back through one of the secret passageways. The cold from the stones will solve the problem for us both, I promise you. Now come; 'tis time we were tucking you into your bed before Mrs. Collier awakens and sounds the alarm."

Three hours later Anne was sitting across the breakfast table from Ruairdh, doing her best not to look in his direction. His demeanor was without fault, and he was as cool and proper as any host faced with a houseful of guests. Looking at him now, calmly responding to one of Mr. Cavendish's rambling questions, she could hardly believe he was the same man who had made such wild and thorough love to her throughout the night. If it hadn't been for the lingering soreness she was suffering, she could almost believe the entire episode had been but another of her fanciful dreams. The thought had her hiding a secretive smile.

Until last night she'd thought the things in her dreams too wonderful to be real, but Ruairdh had showed her how very wrong she'd been. The lovemaking he'd shared with her had given her a glimpse of heaven she could never have imagined, and however wrong it might be, she would always be grateful to him for it. She also wondered if he would be willing to share it with her again, and felt her cheeks heating at such wanton thoughts.

"Miss Garthwicke?" Mrs. Collier gave her a gentle nudge with her elbow, and Anne glanced up to find the other woman regarding her with an expression of alarm.

"Are you all right, my dear?" she asked, her piercing voice drawing the attention of those seated closest to them. "Your color is dreadfully high; I do hope you are not catching a fever. Did you sleep well last night?"

Anne's color rose even higher. "As a matter of fact, I slept quite well, Mrs. Collier, thank you," she said, painfully aware of Ruairdh's amused glance resting on her. "As for my color, it is just rather warm in here; that is all."

"Warm?" Mrs. Lorring gave her an incredulous look. "You must indeed be feverish, my dear, to call this place warm. It is positively freezing in here." And she gave a delicate shudder, casting Ruairdh a pointed look.

It was ignored. "Would you like me to send for the doctor, Miss Garthwicke?" he asked Anne, every inch the dutiful host. "I would not wish you to take ill."

Anne almost blushed. She knew her temperature had nothing to do with being sick and everything to do with Ruairdh. She certainly didn't need a doctor prodding her. "There is no need to bother the good doctor, Mr. MacCairn," she said, her fingers clenching about her fork as she struggled to emulate his calm demeanor. "I am sure it is nothing."

"Well, mind you lie down this afternoon, just in

case," Mrs. Collier advised, shifting cautiously away from Anne. "And if you start sneezing, I am sure you will understand if I ask you to keep your distance from me. A woman of my delicate constitution cannot risk exposure to a diseased person."

The idea that a few well-timed sniffles would be enough to send her chaperon packing was sweetly tempting, but Anne managed to resist. However annoying Mrs. Collier might be, Anne knew she was all that was standing between her and scandal, and she wasn't ready to dispense with her services just yet. But that didn't mean she couldn't indulge in a harmless bit of fun, she decided, and coughed discreetly behind her napkin.

From his position at the head of the table Ruairdh raised an eyebrow, his eyes dancing with amusement as he lifted his cup of tea to her in a mocking toast. Anne glanced quickly away, shyly pleased with the moment of silent understanding. It was every bit as intimate as the lovemaking they had shared, and the memory of it sent a lingering glow of pleasure radiating through her chest.

The pleasure lasted until after breakfast, when Anne slipped away from the others to begin making her way to the armory. It was her first visit since her father's death, but she knew she could no longer postpone the inevitable. Although Ruairdh hadn't been so cruel as to order her from the castle, she knew it was impossible for her to remain. Where she would go and what she would do she did not know, but she refused to regret what had happened last night. In the years to come, it would be one of the few happy memories she would take from this place.

After unlocking the door, Anne set her brace of candles on the worktable and glanced curiously about her. Given the events of the last two days she'd expected there to be some change, but instead everything was just as she'd left it. Her father's tools were laid out neatly, making it look as if he'd soon return, and the knowledge that he would not brought a fresh flood of tears to her eyes. She picked up his magnifying glass, cradling it against her cheek as she wept for the father she had loved despite his many faults.

When she'd finished crying she set the glass back on the table and got to work. Her father prided himself on his ability to satisfy an employer's demands, and she was determined to finish what she could until it was time for her to leave. The weapons collection was of first importance, she decided, sitting on her stool and pulling on the gloves her father always insisted they wear. Weaponry was her father's forte, and therefore her own, and she wanted no whisper of censure attached to his last assignment.

She was finishing her examination of a small fifteenth-century dirk when a flash of light had her glancing up. The battle sword which had intrigued her since her first day in the armory—the sword she had taken to her room for further examination—now rested point down on the stone table beside a brace of candles. The sight of it had the dirk falling from her suddenly nerveless hands. Even as she was telling herself it couldn't be, she was rising from her stool and hurrying over to pick up the weapon.

It *was* the same sword, she marveled, running a gloved finger over the engravings. A servant must have found it in her chamber and brought it back, she decided, turning the sword so the naked edge of the blade caught the candlelight and sent it dancing. It was the only rational explanation. She started to set the sword back down when a sudden wave of dizziness washed over her. The room spun about her, and just as she feared she would faint, the whirling abruptly stopped, causing her to stagger. The sword clattered to the stone as she gripped the ledge, gasping for breath. When she was certain she could move without collapsing she turned cautiously around, a scream rising in her throat at the sight of a man standing not two feet from her.

The man wore the rough robe of a monk, his features partially obscured by the cowl covering his head. He didn't move, didn't speak, and yet an aura of such malevolence rose from him, Anne took an involuntary step back.

"This isn't happening," she said, trying to still the wild pounding of her heart. "I do not believe in ghosts."

An evil chuckle rose from the hooded figure. "Do you not, English *siúrsach*," he mocked, raising his hand to his cowl. "Mayhap this will convince you." And he pushed the hood back, revealing his features to her terrified gaze.

A gasp of horror escaped Anne's lips as she recognized the face of the man from her nightmares. His hair and eyes were black, and a smile of cruel cunning curled his lips as he returned her stare.

"You are shocked," he said with a harsh laugh, "and yet you spread your legs for that spawn of a demon."

Beneath her terror and disbelief, anger stirred. "Ruairdh isn't evil, nor is he the spawn of a demon," she denied, wondering if grief had sent her tumbling over the edge of insanity. She had to be mad, she decided, to stand here and argue semantics with a ghost.

"Is he not?" the figure demanded challengingly. "What of the dreams, woman? Can a mortal steal into dreams? Can a mortal make you burn with his unnatural touch?" He smiled as Anne flinched. "Just so. The lover you welcome into your bed is a devil, with a devil's curse hanging over him, and you court hell with him if you remain. Leave now; it is your only chance of salvation."

Anne's nerves tingled in warning, and she didn't need the acute senses that had plagued her all her life to know he was lying. "I won't discuss Ruairdh with you," she told the specter, even as she began inching back from him. "You aren't real."

Another smile touched the man's lips as he glided closer. "I am real enough. Ask your lover of me, and mark well his answers."

Anne retreated until she could feel the cool metal of the door handle beneath her fingers. "But who are you?" she demanded, her eyes never leaving him as she fumbled to open the door.

The black eyes gleamed with triumph. "His fate," he said, "and if you do not heed my words and leave at once, I will be yours. Tell him, *Sasunnach*. Tell him. The prize is mine."

He started laughing, and Anne whirled around to escape the room, his evil laughter echoing after her as she ran for the main part of the castle and Ruairdh.

Chapter Ten

"I do not understand," Ruairdh said, glaring furiously at his solicitor. "You assured me Mr. Pelham agreed to my price."

"Yes, Mr. MacCairn, and so he did," George Hughes stammered, his cheeks reddening in embarrassment, "but that agreement was contingent upon the castle and its contents being authenticated by Mr. Garthwicke. I . . . I thought you understood this?" he added, regarding Ruairdh with anxious blue eyes.

"Aye, I understood it well enough," Ruairdh replied, his jaw clenching as he struggled to rein in his temper. He'd feared just such a development, but that didn't mean he had to greet the news in silence. "But that doesn't change the fact that Garthwicke lies dead and is of little use to anyone now. Did you no' explain that to the man?" In his anxiety, his Scottish accent was stronger than usual.

Mr. Hughes bobbed his head. "Of course I did," he assured Ruairdh, "and he was most upset. He asked that I personally deliver his condolences to Miss Garthwicke. Have you her direction? I should like to call upon her before the funeral."

The fool's assumption that he would toss a woman who had just lost her father out into the cold added to Ruairdh's anger. *The devil take the prudish English*, he thought savagely. Since when did propriety take the place of common sense and decency? "Miss Garthwicke remains in the castle," he informed the other man in clipped tones, "with Mrs. Collier, our vicar's sister, acting as her chaperon. She is resting now, but you may see her before dinner, if you wish. In Mrs. Collier's presence, of course." And he fixed the younger man with a cold stare meant to intimidate.

Mr. Hughes cleared his throat and began shuffling his papers. "Of course," he said, his gaze not meeting Ruairdh's. "Now, as to Mr. Pelham, I fear you may have misunderstood me. He is not withdrawing his offer, precisely; he is merely requesting that any payment be delayed until such time as the castle can be verified to his satisfaction. It shouldn't take longer than a month, perhaps two, to find someone acceptable to you both. I have a list of acceptable applicants with me; perhaps we can review them later this afternoon?"

And if I don't have a month or two? Ruairdh wondered, bitterness rising in him. He was about to give voice to those words when the door flew open and Anne dashed in, her gray eyes wide in a face that was almost white.

When she saw him sitting in front of the fireplace, she turned to him in visible relief.

"Ruairdh!" she cried, hurrying toward him with outstretched hands. "Ruairdh, the most awful thing has just happened!"

"Anne!"

"Miss Garthwicke?"

He and Mr. Hughes leaped to their feet as one, and when she saw the solicitor, Anne stumbled to an uncertain halt.

"Oh." She blinked, her pale complexion pinkening as she gazed at him. "I beg your pardon—Mr. Hughes, is it not?" she asked, her bloodless lips lifting in a trembling smile. "I didn't know you were here. Pray accept my apologies; I did not mean to interrupt." And she began backing out.

Ruairdh reached out and caught her hand in his, jerking when he felt the icy chill of her fingers. Ignoring the other man's presence he pulled Anne closer, wrapping her firmly in his arms before turning back to Hughes.

"Angley will see you to your rooms, Mr. Hughes," he said, infusing the hard edge of command into the words. "Good day."

"But Mr. MacCairn—" the solicitor began protesting, and then stopped when Ruairdh's eyes narrowed in temper. "Of course, as you say," he said, gathering up his papers and stuffing them haphazardly back into his pouch. "Good day, sir, Miss Garthwicke." And he skittered out of the room.

"What is it, *mo cridhe?*" Ruairdh asked the moment they were alone. "Why are you so pale? And you are shaking," he added in alarm, pulling her trembling body against his own. "Who has upset you? Give me his name at once!"

To his horror she gave a high laugh, edged with hysteria. "I don't know," she said, clinging tightly to him. "He never gave me his name. Perhaps in the afterlife they aren't as nice in their notions as are we."

Ruairdh stiffened warily. "The afterlife, *annsachd?*" he asked, his senses sharpening. He would have liked to believe she was overcome with nerves, but he knew her too well for that. Something had clearly upset her, and he wondered if that something had to do with the events of the past few days.

She gave another laugh, but this one sounded more like her usual self. She started pulling away, and much as he longed to keep holding her, he reluctantly let her go. She moved out of his arms and walked over to stand in front of the window.

"I'm sorry," she said after a few moments, her gaze fixed on the dark clouds bringing in yet another storm. "I'm making no sense, I know, but this is the first time I have ever been threatened by a ghost, and I don't know where to start."

He was glad her gaze was elsewhere so she couldn't see his expression. "Start at the beginning," he told her quietly. "That is usually best. What happened?"

"I went down to the armory to finish some work Father had started," she began, her voice cool and controlled as she recited the events. "I was examining a dirk when I saw the sword, and then suddenly he was there."

"The ghost?" Ruairdh asked, fighting to remain as

calm as Anne. In the first centuries after the curse had been set upon his family, the monk's ghost had often been glimpsed, but no one had seen it for more than three centuries, as far as he knew. Why was the spirit walking now? Was it because he was the last of his line?

"Yes." Anne gave a jerky nod, still gazing out the window. "He . . . he was dressed in a monk's robe, and when he pushed back his cowl, I recognized him. He was the man in my room that night."

Ruairdh's hands clenched into fists. "You are certain?"

She cast him a wry glance over her shoulder. "I am not acquainted with so many ghosts I am likely to confuse one with the other," she said, her lips curving in a half smile. "It was he."

"Did he speak?"

She nodded again and turned back to the window. "He called you the devil's spawn. He also said you were a devil with a devil's curse hanging over you, and that if I wished to avoid your fate, I should depart at once."

"What else?" he asked, gritting his teeth at the thought that the unholy creature had dared to threaten Anne.

"He said the same thing he said in my room that night: 'The prize is mine.' What does it mean?" And she turned to face him, her chin tilted in an air of challenge.

Ruairdh gave a harsh laugh, his stomach twisting in bitterness. "It means he's won."

"But *who* is he?" she pressed, moving closer. "Why should he threaten you?" She stopped until she was mere inches from him, her gray eyes troubled as she searched his face. "Has it anything to do with the Shadowing?"

Ruairdh's head jerked back in shock. "What do you know of that?" he demanded hoarsely.

"Only that I've heard it mentioned in hushed whispers and with frightened looks," Anne said, her level gaze never wavering. "And that when I ask of it, people respond as you are responding now, with evasiveness and half-truths. Is this the curse Sir Lorring mentioned last night?"

God. He squeezed his eyes shut in pain. She was killing him by inches. "Anne—"

"No," she interrupted, taking that last step until she was close enough to lay her hand against his cheek. "No, Ruairdh. Refuse to answer, if you wish; that is your right, I suppose. But don't pat my head and send me away like a child who must be sheltered from every ill wind. Tell me the truth."

He opened his eyes, as near to tears as he had been since they'd had to lock the door of his father's cell. "And if the truth is the stuff of nightmares?" he asked, longing to touch her but fearing that his touch would somehow contaminate her. "What then? Would you still want to know it?"

She brought up her other hand until she was cradling his face in her palms. "I would want to know it even more," she said softly, her gaze never leaving his. "Because I would want to help you awaken from that nightmare. Tell me."

It was more than he could bear. Unable to resist the solace she offered, he bent his head, his lips covering hers in desperation. All of his pain, his passion, poured out of him, and he kissed her as if it were the last thing he would do on this earth. When he drew back, he was shaking with the wild need to make love to her.

"You are my curse," he whispered in a raw voice, tears stinging his eyes as he rested his forehead against hers. "When I am with you, I can forget I am not like other men. I can want what they want, ache for what they have and I will never know. You make me hope, *leannan*, and 'tis killing me."

"Ruairdh—"

"No!" This time it was he who interrupted, thrusting her away from him. "Come no closer!" he warned, holding out his hand to ward her off when she took a hesitant step forward. "I mean it, Anne. My control is all but ended, and I want you too much to be near you now. If you do not leave this room, I will take you."

He could see the blunt words both hurt and alarmed her, but he hadn't the time to be kind. The emotions were rising in him, and he feared that at any moment he would be lost. If the Shadowing took him when he was in such a state . . . He shuddered, vowing he would throw himself off the balcony before he would let the foul thing inside of him touch Anne.

"Go," he said quietly, his voice filled with defeat. "I give you my word I will answer your questions later, when I'm more certain of myself. Just leave me, Anne. If you care for me at all, leave me."

There was a moment of silence, and he worried that she meant to stay despite his harsh warning. Instead she turned and walked quietly to the door, her head bent as if in sorrow. Her fingers closed about the door handle, and just as a breath of relief was easing out of him she turned to face him, her cheeks stained with tears.

"I do care for you," she said, her voice so soft he had to strain to catch the words. "Far more than is wise. Perhaps that is *my* curse." And she slipped out of the room, closing the door behind her.

"Are you all right, Miss Garthwicke?"

Mr. Hughes stood in front of Anne, blue eyes wide with concern as he peered down at her.

Anne gazed up at him, swallowing an impatient sigh. It had been like this all afternoon. She'd returned to her rooms wanting nothing more than to be left alone to try to understand all that was happening. Instead she was forced to endure the company of well-meaning people who kept patting her hand and asking questions for which she had no answer. Even pleading a headache did no good, because the ladies instantly began hovering, poking at her and arguing amongst themselves as to which cure would prove the most effective. She finally had to pronounce herself healed to avoid being subjected to any of their home remedies. Perhaps she should have swallowed the laudanum Mrs. Collier had offered, she brooded. At least then she would have been left in peace.

"Miss Garthwicke?" Mr. Hughes's anxious words recalled her to the present, and she glanced up to find him looking frantic. "Shall I summon Mrs. Collier? Perhaps you need some smelling salts?"

"No, that is quite all right, Mr. Hughes," she said with alacrity. "And I am fine. Thank you for asking."

He looked far from convinced. "I am surprised to see you dining with us," he said, settling onto the chair beside her. "You seemed somewhat upset this afternoon. I thought you would take a tray in your room?" He managed to make the observation both a question and an accusation.

Anne managed not to wince. She'd been dreading this confrontation since the moment she'd realized he was in the room with Ruairdh. She'd hoped he would be too circumspect to mention the matter, but it would seem she had been overly optimistic. Fortunately, she was prepared.

"You must forgive my dramatics, sir," she said, lowering her eyes in mock shame. "I was packing my father's things, and when I accidentally broke his shaving mug, I—I fear I was quite overcome. My mother gave it to him, you see, and he cherished it so. Seeing it shattered all to pieces was like losing them both again." And she pulled a handkerchief from her sleeve, dabbing at her eyes and sniffing piteously.

"Poor Miss Garthwicke!" He was properly understanding. "How awful for you. I am so sorry."

"You are too kind," she said, thinking that if he were half so sorry as he claimed, he would take pity on her and leave. "Mr. MacCairn was very good to me, although I am sure I must have embarrassed him terribly. You know how unemotional these Scots can be," she added, sending him an apologetic look.

"Indeed," he agreed, although he was frowning. "I can see why you were upset, but I fail to see why he should have sent me from the room as he did. You must know it wasn't at all proper."

"Yes, something that Mr. MacCairn quickly remedied by sending for my maid," Anne continued, allowing a chiding note to steal into her voice. "I am in deep mourning, Mr. Hughes. Surely I should be allowed some small degree of latitude in such things?"

Her words had the desired effect, as he turned beet red and began stuttering his assurance that none but the cruelest of souls could find anything untoward in her behavior. He also vowed not to repeat a word to anyone of what had happened, which Anne took leave to doubt—not because she thought he would break his word, but because she had already caught the speculative glances of several of the newly arrived guests, and assumed he'd already said more than he should.

"As for Mr. MacCairn, I do agree with you that he is very much the proper gentleman," Mr. Hughes was continuing. "I have never met a finer man, or one whom I admire more. Not many in his sad condition would show such bravery, I can tell you."

The heartfelt observation had Anne's ears pricking in interest. "Sad condition?" she echoed, wondering if he was referring to the Shadowing. "What do you mean, Mr. Hughes?"

To her annoyance, he turned even redder and began glancing about them. "I beg your pardon," he said, lowering his voice to a conspiratorial whisper. "I shouldn't have said anything. Mr. MacCairn would be upset if he knew I'd violated his confidence."

"Of course," Anne answered, hoping she sounded sympathetic. "And I am certain Mr. MacCairn appreciates your discretion. You must know he has gone to some lengths to keep the matter a secret."

"Yes, I can imagine it would cause no end of gossip and speculation if it became known he was dying," he agreed, sighing. "Poor man. I wonder if it is consumption; it is dreadfully common in the Highlands, one hears."

He went on talking, but Anne didn't hear any of what he was saying. *Dying.* Her gaze went to Ruairdh, who was seated across the elegant drawing room, listening attentively to an ancient man in an equally ancient kilt. His expression was grave, as it so often was, but about him there was such an air of vitality, of life, that it seemed impossible to associate such a man with death. It couldn't be true. It mustn't be true. And yet . . .

When I am with you, I can forget I am not like other men. I can want what they want, ache for what they have and I will never know. Ruairdh's anguished words came back to haunt her, and her eyes filled with tears.

"No," she whispered, horror making her tremble. "Dear God, no."

"Miss Garthwicke?" Mr. Hughes was patting her hand. "What is it? Have you taken ill?"

Anne shook her head, but before she could reply the gong announcing dinner sounded. She saw Ruairdh offer his arm to Mrs. Lorring, and she tightened her fingers about Mr. Hughes's hand. "I would be honored if you would escort me into dinner," she said, ignoring his protestations as she rose to her feet. "I am quite famished." And then she took a step forward, leaving him no choice but to follow.

Dinner was endless, and the talk that followed even more so. Anne kept to the shadows, a glass of sherry clutched in her hand. The new arrivals, most of whom had been her father's friends for many years, wanted to talk, but in the end her blank looks and monosyllabic answers drove them away, leaving her in peace. She caught Ruairdh watching her several times, worry and speculation making him look even more austere. She wanted to run to him, throw her arms about him, and demand he tell her the truth. She wanted him to assure her he wasn't dying, and then she wanted him to kiss her. More, she admitted, with painful honesty—she wanted him to make love to her. Now.

Across the room she saw Ruairdh suddenly freeze, turning his head and meeting her gaze with a jolt of sensual power that had the breath catching in her throat. Had he read her mind? She rather thought he had, and the fact she could admit such a thing so coolly showed how much she had changed. Prior to coming to Castle MacCairn she'd viewed the possibility of the netherworld with the wary detachment of a scientist—intrigued but ultimately unconvinced.

Since coming here, however, she'd seen enough to convince the most hardened of skeptics that some dark and evil force was clearly at work. From her first glimpse of the castle when the odd affinity she bore for ancient places gave way to a strong sense of recognition, her senses had witnessed so much she could scarcely believe all that was happening. Perhaps that was why she found it so easy to accept her and Ruairdh's shared dreams, she decided. They were simply part and parcel of all that she had experienced since crossing the cobblestones of the courtyard.

"Miss Garthwicke." Ruairdh was standing before her, as if summoned by her thoughts, his penetrating green eyes holding hers. "Would you like to retire to your rooms? It has been a long day for you."

Anne could feel herself flushing and prayed the other guests would put it down to embarrassment. "Yes, yes, it has," she said, setting her untouched glass of wine to one side. "Thank you, Mr. MacCairn; I shall see you in the morning."

"Not at all." He helped her to her feet, his touch burning her. If he felt it too, he gave no indication, summoning Mrs. Collier with no more than a lift of his eyebrow. "If you would be so kind, ma'am," he suggested. "I am sure Miss Garthwicke would welcome your assistance."

The older woman bustled forward at once, slipping a firm arm about Anne and guiding her from the room. At first Anne wondered why Ruairdh should send the older woman with her when it would surely make a clandestine visit to her room that much more difficult. Then she realized he was only being cautious, and very clever. No one would suspect him of anything untoward if they'd seen him insist her chaperon accompany her to bed.

Anne suffered through both Jennie's and Mrs. Collier's ministrations. She easily disposed of the laudanum Mrs. Collier pressed on her, and when she settled down against her pillows and began gently snoring, Jennie finally left as well. Anne lay in a fever of anticipation, wondering how long it would be before Ruairdh joined her. That had to be his intention, she was certain. She had seen the desire in his eyes and felt it in the way he touched her, and the knowledge gave her a warm sense of womanly power.

While she waited, she reviewed what she would say to him once they were alone. She would demand that he explain Mr. Hughes's extraordinary remark, that was certain, and then she would demand he tell her about the ghost she'd seen. And, most important, she wanted answers about the Shadowing. Only when she was satisfied with his answers would they make love, and she would show him with her body how very much she had come to care for him. Perhaps then he would lose the sadness she saw in his eyes. The thought filled her with soft satisfaction.

Time dragged slowly by as she waited. Even through the thickness of the door and walls she could hear the other guests moving past her door as they sought their own beds, and still Ruairdh didn't come. At one point she got up and crept into Mrs. Collier's room to make certain the older woman was safely asleep. The loud snores she heard assured her the other woman would pose no threat to their assignation. Relieved, she went back to bed, but the hours passed and still Ruairdh didn't come.

She was considering giving up and going to sleep when a sudden thought hit her. Last night Ruairdh had taken her to his rooms, and this morning hadn't he taken pains to show her the hidden passage connecting her room to his? *Idiot!* she scolded herself sternly as she threw the covers back and got out of bed. She was shrugging on her robe when she heard the creak of a door, and turned around to find Ruairdh standing in the opened door leading to the tunnel.

"I had hoped to find you asleep," he told her, looking weary. "I prayed that you would be."

This was not the loverlike greeting she had been expecting. "Why?" she asked, studying his face in the flickering light of the candle he was holding. "Because you don't want to answer my questions?"

"Perhaps," he agreed, making no move to approach her. "And perhaps there is more. I cannot marry you, Anne. I cannot give you my name and trap you in hell with me."

Anne remembered Mr. Hughes's words, and her heart rent in two. "I have not asked for marriage," she said, perilously close to tears.

"But you've a right to it," he continued, his voice lacking any inflection. "You were a virgin last night, and even though I took care to see there'd be no babe, that does not absolve me of all sin. I took an oath I would never have a son, and I was content with that oath. Now you make me want to break it. I would give my soul to see you grow big with my child, and it is the one thing I dare not risk. It dies with me, do you understand?"

His anguish and pain were so palpable, Anne felt them as if they were her own. Since he would not come to her she went to him, abandoning her pride as she ran over to throw her arms around him.

"No, no, I do not understand!" she cried, tipping back her head to gaze up at his tortured face. "What dies with you? Why can't you risk a child? Is it some sort of illness? Is that what this Shadowing is?"

" 'Tis no illness," he cried, his fingers digging into her arms as he pushed her back. " 'Tis worse than an illness, for an illness can be cured. There is no cure for me. No hope. I will die as all of my line have died before me: locked in the east tower, chained to a wall and screaming like the madman I'll have become. That is the Shadowing, *annsachd*. That is the curse that has doomed my family for five hundred years. And it dies with me. I am the last of the MacCairns. The bloody witch has won. The prize is his, and there's not a damned thing I can do to stop it."

Chapter Eleven

He had done it. Ruairdh stood his ground in weary defeat, steeling himself for the horror and revulsion Anne must surely be feeling. How could she help but be repulsed, he asked himself, considering what he had told her? He had revealed a secret no *outdwellar* had ever heard, but it was a secret he could no longer keep hidden. She had given him her innocence and more last night; the truth was the least he could offer her now.

Seconds ticked past in agonizing slowness, but still Anne did not speak. She stood there studying him in cool silence, her beautiful face showing neither terror nor the pity he dreaded.

"Tell me more about this curse," she said at last, her voice strangely calm. "Who placed it upon your family, and more important, why?"

At first Ruairdh was too bemused to answer. He'd

prepared himself for hysterics and damnation, and her quiet request for information left him at a loss. It took him a few moments before he could answer.

"As to the who, he was a monk from a nearby monastery who renounced his faith and embraced Satan and all his powers," he said, watching her cautiously. "It was his ghost you saw earlier. And it is his presence that haunts the east wing so powerfully, especially the tower. 'Tis said he practiced the foulest form of the black arts, even to sacrificing innocent babes to the demons he conjured. When the Church learned of his crimes he was seized by the witch-hunters and brought here to await trial."

"Why here?"

"The dungeons," he answered simply. "He was kept chained there until the Church could send a tribunal to hear the case against him. He was judged a heretic, and suffered a heretic's fate: they burned him at the stake, there in the courtyard."

Other than flinching, she gave no outward sign of emotion. "Why should he curse your family, then?" she asked after a few moments. "It was the Church who tried and executed him."

He stared at her as if it were she who was mad. "The devil cannot curse God," he said, considerably shocked. "For God is stronger. But we are mortal, and therefore vulnerable to his power. And because 'twas the laird of the MacCairns who helped capture him, and it was at Castle MacCairn he was held to await his death. When he was lashed to the stake he called upon Satan, not to deliver him, but to curse us all. He damned all the

MacCairn men to die in madness, and then laughed, 'tis told, as the flames consumed him."

Another silence followed as Anne digested his words. "And has nothing been done to break this curse?" she asked, sounding faintly disapproving.

The fact that she could find fault with his family for all they had endured infuriated Ruairdh. "*Everything* was done that could be done!" he snapped back, defending his clan with all the ferocity of a Highlander. "We prayed, we fought in the Crusades, we journeyed to every shrine in Christendom seeking salvation from the Church we helped defend, and in the end it did no good. From that day to this all lairds of my clan have fallen victim to the witch's curse, dying as he said they would—as madmen. That is why I am to be the last. It is the only way."

"But—"

"Anne." He closed the distance between them to embrace her once more. "I did not come to you this night for a debate. I came to tell you the truth, and because I could not stay away from you, however hard I tried." He smiled sadly, and traced her lips with his finger. "You frighten me, *annsachd.*"

His stark confession made her eyes open wide. "I frighten you?" she repeated. "Why?"

"Because I want you," he said, replacing his finger with his mouth as he gently kissed her. "Because I need you. Because if you put your hand in mine and say you'll come with me, I've no' the strength to let you go." He held his breath, waiting for her response, and praying he had the strength to abide by her choice.

He hadn't long to wait.

Gazing into his eyes, she moved closer to him, her breasts brushing against his chest as she lifted her arms to encircle his neck. Their mouths met, held, and she returned his kiss with warm, womanly passion before drawing back again. Still holding his gaze, she took his hand in hers, her voice strong as she spoke the words offering him salvation, offering him some respite in the face of his terrible fate.

"I will come with you."

For that night and the next, Ruairdh immersed himself in Anne's sweetness and in her shy sensuality. She was all he could have dreamed of in a lover, in a wife, and making love to her was as painful as it was wondrous. Each time he held her he vowed it would be the last; then he would start kissing her, and he would be lost.

But however lost he was, however enthralled he might be in the lovemaking, he always stopped before climaxing, spending himself instead on the sheets. He knew Anne was too innocent to comprehend the significance of his actions, and he thanked God for it. He didn't want to spoil their all-too-brief times together worrying over the consequences of their passion.

Another thing troubling him was what would become of Anne once she left the castle. Although she'd never directly mentioned the matter, he'd learned enough to know that she and her father had relied on the income they earned in order to survive. With her father now dead, how would she live? He'd tried broaching the subject with her a number of times; but she remained annoyingly elusive, telling him only that he was not to worry. Well, he did worry, damn it. He worried enough that he even tried using the heightened powers the Shadowing had given him, cautiously probing her mind for any hint of her plans. That she was aware of the probing was evident by the mental slap she had given him, followed later that evening by a stern lecture on the impropriety of such behavior.

As for the Shadowing itself, he adamantly refused to discuss it again. He'd already told Anne all he dared, and to tell her more would be to tell her things he hadn't even told Angley. Her father's death had been hard enough for her to bear; he refused to burden her with the knowledge of his death as well. It was for the best, he told himself, and closed his mind to any pangs of remorse.

The day of the funeral dawned cool and gray, the rains and mists clinging to the valleys below the cairn. More than thirty guests were billeted in the castle, and many more besides filled the few rooms to be had in the nearby villages. News of Anne's father's death had caused a stir both in Edinburgh and London, and the entire antiquarian society seemed bent on attending his funeral. For a while it was even whispered that the queen's consort would be in attendance, but fortunately the weather and the long distance to travel changed His Highness's mind.

Ruairdh was more relieved than he dared admit. He hadn't experienced any further attacks of the Shadowing in the past two days, but he knew better than to think the danger was past. The last thing he needed was to be overtaken while a member of the royal family was in residence. Although from what he had heard of that lot, a touch of madness would scarce be noticed.

An hour before the funeral was to start, he retired to his study to await Mr. Hughes. The solicitor was returning to London with the first wave of guests, and he had several items of business he wanted the younger man to attend to for him. He'd just settled behind his desk when there was a tap at the door, and Mr. Hughes cautiously entered the room.

"Good morning, Mr. MacCairn," he said, offering Ruairdh a polite bow. "You wished to see me?"

The solicitor's diffidence amused Ruairdh as it always did, but beneath the amusement he felt the warning stir of malevolent power.

"Come in, Mr. Hughes," he said, ignoring the sibilant whispers in his mind. "I have been studying these names you left me," he continued, after Hughes had taken a seat in front of his desk. "I've circled the ones I find acceptable. I wish you to contact each of them, and the one who says he can be here within the week shall have the position."

"The week?" the solicitor repeated, frowning as he accepted the piece of paper from Ruairdh. "But Mr. MacCairn, it will take at least that long for me to contact these gentlemen, and another week more for them to answer back. And what if they aren't free? Both Mr. Brewton and Mr. Merringvale are affiliated with the British Museum. They will need permission from their superiors before accepting your offer."

"Then strike them from the list," Ruairdh retorted, wondering how the useless fool even managed to dress himself. "That leaves only Mr. Fielding and Mr. Thomas. Surely it shouldn't take you a week to contact them?" He lifted an eyebrow derisively.

"No," Hughes agreed, looking uncertain. "I suppose it should not. But still—"

"A week, Mr. Hughes," Ruairdh interrupted, deciding he'd suffered the fool all he intended. "A sennight at the most. That is all the time I can give you, and pray to God I have it to give."

Mr. Hughes paled at once. "Of course, Mr. MacCairn," he said, biting his lip in distress. "I am sorry. I-I had quite forgotten about . . . about your illness. I shall leave after the services."

"Wait," Ruairdh said when the other man made to rise. "Before you go, there is something else I wish to discuss with you."

"Yes, sir?" Hughes looked at him expectantly.

Ruairdh hesitated. The idea to leave Anne something in his will had occurred to him shortly after her father's death, but knowing her pride he had been reluctant to discuss the matter with her. Now it seemed the perfect answer to both their problems.

"I wish to provide for Miss Garthwicke," he said firmly, a feeling of relief washing over him. "I feel very badly that her father died while here, and I wish to make it up to her."

Mr. Hughes beamed his approval. "Of course, Mr. MacCairn; a small request should be more than acceptable. How much do you wish to give her? One hundred pounds? Two hundred?"

Ruairdh winced at the paltry sum. "I was thinking perhaps a third of the estate," he said, calculating the figures in his head. If Mr. Pelham paid the amount he was asking, there should be enough left over to keep Anne in comfort for the rest of her life.

"A third?" Hughes gasped in horror. "But that could be well over ten thousand pounds! You cannot leave her that great a sum!"

"Why the devil not?" Ruairdh demanded, scowling. "The money is mine to give, is it not? 'Tis not as if I have any heirs to quibble over every penny."

"The gossip, Mr. MacCairn, the gossip!" Mr. Hughes exclaimed, clearly scandalized. "It is understandable that you would want to leave her some small amount of money to compensate her for the death of her father, but to leave her so much . . ." He shook his head. "You must see it will not do."

Anger boiled through Ruairdh's blood as he leaped to his feet. "To hell with what others say, the bloody hypocrites!" he raged, his eyes flashing in fury. " 'Tis not their place to judge her."

"Their place or not, they *will* judge her," Mr. Hughes replied, his voice surprisingly firm, "and if you leave her that kind of money, that judgment will be harsh indeed. If you have any affection for Miss Garthwicke at all, I beg you to reconsider. If you make her your heiress, people will whisper she is your mistress. They are whispering it now," he added impatiently, when Ruairdh opened his mouth as if to protest.

Ruairdh's head jerked back. "Who?" he demanded gutturally. "Who dares whisper such foul lies about Anne? Give me their names so that I can demand satisfaction."

"It was no one of any importance, sir," the other man said, looking decidedly ill at ease. "And to be frank, it is mainly the ladies who were talking. You cannot harm a lady . . . can you?" He looked as if he fully expected Ruairdh to say yes.

But even with the dangerous voice in his head crowding out his more rational thoughts, Ruairdh wasn't so lost to propriety as that. "No," he admitted grudgingly, "I cannot. But," he added, "I can tell them another word from them, and I shall ruin their husbands. That should still their vicious tongues."

"Yes," Hughes agreed, "while they have cause to fear you. But after you are gone, it will be a different matter entirely."

Knowing the younger man was right did little to soothe Ruairdh's temper. "There must be something I can do to see she wants for nothing," he said, shoving an impatient hand through his hair as he tried to think of some way he could provide for Anne without ruining her in the attempt.

"You could make private arrangements with the executor of your will, I should suppose," Hughes replied after careful consideration. "Something unofficial, you understand, so there will be no record. Of course," he said, tapping his chin thoughtfully, "you will have to rely on this man's honesty to do as he promises. But at least you'll have done all you could."

Ruairdh bristled at the implied insult. "I trust Angley with my life," he told Hughes crisply. "I am trusting him with my clan."

"To be sure," Hughes replied, holding up his hand in a placating gesture, "but as you know, I have not been entirely pleased in your choice of executor. Mr. Angley is a fine and honorable man, that I will grant you, but he is also well past sixty. What if he should die shortly after you, or he dies first and you haven't time to amend your will? Who would see to your clan and Miss Garthwicke then?"

Ruairdh muttered a Gaelic imprecation beneath his breath. He had no answer for that. Unless . . . He gave Hughes a sharp look.

"Can a woman be an executor?"

"In some cases, yes," Hughes answered, meeting Ruairdh's gaze levelly. "In which case she would be called an executrix, but I fear that is still no answer. Naming Miss Garthwicke as your executrix will cause as big a scandal as if you named her your heiress. It cannot be done. Unless—"

"Unless what?" Ruairdh prompted, even though he strongly suspected what the answer would be.

"Unless," Mr. Hughes concluded, his expression bleak, "she was your wife."

"A lovely service, my dear, a lovely service."

The ancient man who had been her father's first partner gave Anne a gentle smile, his watery blue eyes regarding her with kindness. "Your father would have been quite pleased, I am sure."

"Thank you, Mr. Graham, I am so very glad you could come," Anne replied, summoning an answering smile for the old gentleman's benefit. She'd invited him simply out of form, and had been genuinely surprised when he'd accepted. But then, he was one of the few people in the world whom her father had treated with any degree of partiality and respect. Certainly he had spoken of him with far more fondness than he had ever spoken of her. She felt a shaft of pain at the thought.

He loved you, annsachd, in his way. The low, familiar voice sounded in her mind, and she glanced up to find Ruairdh watching her. Even though he was across the room from her, she could feel the warm weight of his hand on the small of her back, and it disconcerted her as much as did the murmur of his voice.

"Have I upset you?" Mr. Graham gave her hand a paternal squeeze. "Forgive me, my dear. But at my great age one sees death more as an old friend than an enemy. I trust you are not offended?"

"No, of course not, Mr. Graham. How could I be?" Anne replied soothingly, wishing she knew what it was he'd said. She gave Ruairdh a warning look before turning her attention back to the man at her side.

"I lost my father when I was less than six years old," Mr. Graham continued. "The French wars, you know. For years I had forgotten what he looked like, but now I can see him quite clearly. That is the way of it, you see. The dead are always with us."

Anne gave an involuntary shudder, thinking of the ghost of the evil monk. She started to reply when Mrs. Collier came scurrying over to join them. She was accompanied by several of her friends from the village, and the avaricious expressions on their faces had Anne bracing herself in wariness.

"There you are, Miss Garthwicke!" the older woman said, as if she'd been searching for Anne all over the castle.

"How are you feeling?" one of the women asked, her dark eyes bright with speculation as she studied Anne. "Dear Mrs. Collier told us you hardly ate anything at breakfast. You mustn't fall into a decline, you know."

"I shall eat later, Miss MacMillian. I thank you for your concern," Anne replied, thinking how nice it would have been if the other woman *had* been genuinely concerned about her, instead of angling for some juicy bit of gossip.

"But where will you go from here?" A plump blonde with catlike green eyes demanded, crowding closer. "Charlotte has already announced she will be returning to her brother's home, and you can hardly remain here without her. The scandal, you know."

"Yes"—the other woman smirked—"the scandal."

Anne regarded them all coldly, wondering what they would do if she tossed her cup of tea at them and told them to go to the devil. She allowed herself to imagine doing just that, before giving them a polite smile.

"If you ladies will excuse me," she murmured, ignoring their outraged gasps as she turned and walked away.

She spent the next hour moving from group to group, receiving condolences and deflecting questions about her plans for the future. Anne wished she had news to give them, but the truth was, she had no notion of what lay ahead. The idea of leaving the castle and Ruairdh filled her with such despair that she couldn't bear to think of it, even though she knew she would soon have no other choice. The funeral was ending, and once the last guest left she would have no reason to remain. Fresh tears burned her eyes, and she was blinking them back when a man appeared in front of her. It took her a few seconds to place him, and when she did, she was far from pleased.

"Mr. Beechton," she said, eyeing the village magistrate with veiled dislike. "Thank you for coming."

Instead of mouthing the empty platitudes she'd been hearing for the last hour, he leaned toward her, casting a furtive look about them before speaking.

"A word with you, Miss Garthwicke, if I may," he said, his voice low and urgent. "It is most important, I assure you."

The dull headache Anne had been ignoring gave her a vicious jab, and she resisted the urge to rub her throbbing temples. "Certainly, sir," she said, too weary to feign politeness. "What is it?"

He cast another nervous look about them. "Not here," he said, and then nodded toward the open French doors leading to the terrace. "There." And he scurried away, not looking back.

Disinclined as she was to follow, Anne did just that, telling herself she would give him two minutes and no more. She walked out onto the stone terrace, shivering as the cool, rain-scented mist enveloped her.

"Very well, Mr. Beechton, I am here," she said, wishing she'd thought to bring her shawl. "What is it you have to say, and why did you feel it necessary to drag me away from my father's funeral in order to say it?"

"It is about Mr. MacCairn," he said, looking both defiant and ill at ease. "You've been here only a short while, so you are likely unaware of the stories, but I feel I would be remiss in my duties as magistrate did I not warn you."

Anne gave him a considering look, recalling that Ruairdh had mentioned the man's animosity toward him. "You're referring to the curse, I gather?" she asked, deciding it was best to pretend disinterest.

"You know of it?" He looked stunned, as if such a possibility hadn't crossed his mind.

"Of course," she replied. "My father heard of it before we arrived, but naturally, being a man of science, he rejected such talk as nonsense." The smile she sent him was deliberately cutting.

To her surprise he didn't take offense; instead, he looked more nervous than ever. "I once thought it no more than nonsense," he said, beginning to pace uneasily. "But now I am not so certain. There is something about this place. Something evil. Something *alive.*" He whirled around to face her, his eyes burning as with a fever. "You must feel it, too," he said, his words an accusation. "You do, don't you?"

Because Anne wasn't certain what he was after, she waited a moment before answering. "I have felt the age of the place, and the history that clings to the stones," she prevaricated. "But I have felt those same things in other places as well. Old buildings have that air about them. That doesn't make them evil."

"But it's more than that!" he insisted, his eyes wild. "Evil walks these halls, Miss Garthwicke. It has for over five hundred years. And it was that evil that killed your father."

Anne took a cautious step away from him. "My father fell. That is all there is to it."

"Yes." Mr. Beechton moved toward her. "He fell. But have you never asked yourself *why* he fell?" His hand shot out and grabbed her arm, staying her when she would have retreated farther. "Haven't you wondered what made him go up stairs so unsafe even a child would have known to avoid them? Why did he go up so far? What caused him to lose his balance? What terrible thing did he see that made him fall?" His fingers closed viciously about her arm. "Who killed him, Miss Garthwicke? Who killed him?"

She struggled to free herself from his grip, annoyance turning to genuine alarm. "Mr. Beechton, stop this at once!" she protested. "You are frightening me!"

Her words had the desired effect, and she was released so abruptly she stumbled back.

"I beg your pardon," he said, sounding genuinely apologetic. "It wasn't my intention. I have no idea what came over me. I—"

"What is going on here?" Ruairdh appeared in the doorway, his flashing green eyes and clenched fists radiating fury. He turned a gaze on Mr. Beechton so murderous, the other man looked ready to leap over the edge of the terrace.

"What did you do?" The demand was issued in a soft whisper.

"Nothing!" Mr. Beechton denied, paling. "I was only offering Miss Garthwicke my condolences." When Ruairdh took a menacing step forward, the magistrate sidestepped quickly out of his path, then dashed back through the French doors.

Ruairdh ignored him, his attention centered on her. "Are you all right?" he asked, studying her with worried eyes. "Did he hurt you?"

"No," Anne denied, even though she was still trembling.

"But he frightened you." Ruairdh cupped her head in his hand and tipped her face up to his. "I could feel your fear. That is why I came in search of you." His thumb brushed over her lip. "What did he say to you?"

Anne started to answer, but then stopped. "I'm not certain," she said, recalling the conversation and the odd turn it had taken. "At first he said he wanted to warn me about the curse, but when I told him I already knew, he started talking about the castle. He called it evil."

A rueful smile touched Ruairdh's lips as he lightly touched them to hers. "He'll get no argument from me," he murmured, then drew back to study her again. "Are you certain you are all right? You're so pale, *an-nsachd.*"

His concern warmed her. "It has been an eventful day."

"Aye, it has," he agreed. "Go lie down. I'll not have you taking ill."

Her gaze went to the open door behind him. "But the guests . . ." she began weakly.

Ruairdh's eyebrows met in a furious glare. "To the devil with them," he said with a flash of heat. "They've seen what they came to see. If they say one word against you, I'll have them tossed from the castle."

Because she was genuinely exhausted and because she believed he would do just as he threatened, Anne returned to the drawing room. Several people stopped to speak with her, and almost a quarter hour passed before she was able to slip away. Jennie was waiting when she walked into her room, issuing gentle scolds as she helped her out of her clothes and into bed.

She hadn't meant to sleep, but the horrific events of the past four days—and the more pleasurable lovemaking of the last two nights—overwhelmed her, and she was asleep before she was aware of it. At first she slumbered dreamlessly, like an exhausted child, but then dreams began spinning behind her eyes, dreams that pulled her in and then under.

She was standing in front of the cheval glass, wearing an elegant gown of white satin trimmed lavishly with lace and seed pearls. It was her bridal gown, and she was waiting for her groom to join her. Then he was holding her, kissing her, sweeping her up into his arms and carrying her to the waiting bed. His touch was soft and loving, rousing her with skill and tenderness as he stroked the beautiful gown from her. His deep voice murmured words of passion as he brought her to the brink of fulfillment, and it was only when she was tumbling over the edge that he slipped easily inside her trembling body.

"Ruairdh!" She cried out his name, wrapping her legs around his surging hips. "Yes, my love. Yes!"

She awoke with a sharp cry and sat up in the bed, shuddering with pleasure and gasping desperately for breath. A quick glance about the room showed it to be late in the afternoon, and she realized with some confusion that she had been asleep for several hours. Feeling disoriented, she climbed out of bed and rang for Jennie. She was tying the sash on her robe when the young maid came hurrying in.

"Oh, good, miss, you're awake," she said, beaming sweetly at Anne. "The laird has been asking for you. He is in the tower room, and requests that you join him there."

The tower room! Anne felt her cheeks flush, and wondered if Ruairdh had just had the same dream as she. She rather hoped he had. She reached into the wardrobe for the gown she'd worn earlier that day.

"Oh, no, miss!" Jennie exclaimed, eyeing the dress in dismay. "You canna wear *that!*"

Anne glanced at the gown in confusion. "Whyever not?" she asked, wondering if she had spilled something on the skirts and ruined it.

"Because it willna do," the maid replied, taking the dress from Anne and returning it to the wardrobe. She picked through Anne's gowns for several seconds before making her selection.

"There," she said, pulling out a gown of midnight blue satin and studying it in satisfaction. "This is what you shall wear."

Anne reached out to touch the full skirts of the exquisitely styled gown. She had purchased it for a dinner party held by the prince consort to honor those who had helped organize the Grand Exhibition. It was the most expensive gown she had ever owned, and the idea of wearing it for Ruairdh her last night in the castle was sweetly tempting.

"But I am in mourning for my father," she protested, feeling herself weaken. "What will people think to see me in colors the very day of his funeral?"

" 'Tis a dark enough blue to pass for mourning," Jennie decided, hanging up the dress and brushing out the folds. "And as for what people will say, there is no one left here to say anything. The laird sent them all on their way as soon as the luncheon was ended. All except that Mrs. Collier, of course, and she'll soon be gone as well, thank heavens."

"He sent them away?" Anne repeated, amazed she could have slept through the mass exodus. "But why?"

"He didn't say, miss," Jennie said, gently pushing Anne down onto the stool in front of the dressing table. "He only told them to go, and off they went, so fast, some of them, you'd have thought the bogey was chasing them."

Anne thought of the ghost of the monk and shivered delicately. Having made the fellow's acquaintance, she could well understand why the sight of him would have sent most people fleeing.

Jennie dressed Anne's hair in an elegant chignon, cleverly fashioning several ringlets to curl about her ears and forehead. She also applied a bit of blush to her cheeks and lips, ignoring Anne's shocked protests. While Anne was arguing with her over the matter of scent, the maid opened a square, velvet-covered box she'd brought in with her, and placed a dazzling necklace of pearls and diamonds about Anne's throat.

"Where did these come from?" Anne asked, unable to resist stroking the soft pearls. They were the most beautiful pearls she had ever seen, and she knew enough of the gems to know they were likely worth a queen's ransom.

"They belonged to the laird's grandmother," Jennie replied, bending to fasten the matching bobs to her ears. "He asked that you please wear them tonight. There." She took a step back, nodding in satisfaction as she studied Anne. "You look a perfect picture. I knew you would."

Anne stared into the cheval glass, trying to reconcile her own image of herself with the reflection in the mirror. She'd always thought of herself as average, neither plain nor pretty, with dark blond hair and her mother's gray eyes. But the woman in the mirror wasn't average. The woman in the mirror with her stunning jewels and elegant gown was beautiful. She looked the sort of woman who would have a man like Ruairdh waiting for her in a room filled with softly lit candles and freshly picked flowers. Anne laid a trembling hand on the teardrop-shaped pendant hanging from the center of the necklace and drew a steadying breath.

"Thank you, Jennie," she said, sending the maid a grateful smile. "You have worked another miracle on me."

A short while later Anne stood at the bottom of the stairs leading to the tower room. Evening had fallen, and the castle was caught in the shadowy world between darkness and light. The door to the room was open, spilling its golden light out onto the stairs as if lighting the way. She was trying to gather the courage to climb those stairs when Ruairdh appeared in the doorway. He gazed down at her for several seconds before holding his hand out to her in silent command. Feeling as if she were in one of her dreams, Anne gathered up her skirts and walked slowly up the stairs to join him.

Ruairdh met Anne at the top of the stairs, capturing her hand in his and carrying it to his lips. From the first, he'd been struck by her soft beauty, but seeing her like this, dressed in shimmering satin and wearing the betrothal necklace of his clan, he thought her the most stunning woman in the world.

"How beautiful you look, *mo cridhe*," he murmured, pressing his lips to the back of her hand and savoring her sweet taste. "You make my heart stop."

A shy smile curved her lips at the ardent words. "It is the pearls," she said, her voice sounding breathless. "Thank you for letting me wear them."

Using his grip on her hand to draw her close, Ruairdh bent his head and kissed her. He was smiling when he lifted his head.

"I always thought these the most beautiful of my family's possessions," he said, slipping his hand beneath the necklace and running his thumb across the creamy pearls. "But they pale in comparison to the color and softness of your skin." He laid the necklace down, trailing a finger across the swell of her breasts before taking a step back.

"You must be hungry, *annsachd*," he said, leading her to the center of the room, where, at his orders, a table for two had been set in front of the window. "Come, let us eat."

After seating her, he began dishing up food from the silver dishes left on a nearby cupboard. "Salmon from our streams," he said, setting a plate before her. "And later we've venison from our woods. You ate some your first night here. Do you remember?"

"Indeed, I do," she agreed, sending him a mischievous look through her lashes. "I also recall you were appallingly rude to me, and determined to send me as far from here as possible."

"Only because I wanted you from the moment I saw you, as I have already said," he replied, filling her glass with some of the chilled champagne he had also ordered. He had laid his plans as carefully as a clan chieftain plotting an attack, and he meant for everything to be perfect. He would set the trap so cleverly she'd never see it until he had her so ensnared there would be no escape. And once he had her caught he would overwhelm her with superior force, guaranteeing her surrender. He'd even arranged an ambush, in case she proved stubborn. With her safety and that of his clan at stake, he would leave nothing to chance.

"Where is Mrs. Collier?" Anne asked, glass in her hand as she glanced curiously about the candlelit room. "Will she not be joining us?"

"I pray not," he answered feelingly, lifting his own glass to his lips for a careful sip. "I'd rather the witch himself join us than that kimmering harpy. She's eating in her room, and helping herself to my whiskey, I've no doubt. I'll send a cask of it home with her for her and her brother. He'll have need of it, poor man."

They continued eating while Ruairdh wooed her with careful words and calculated gestures. A touch of her hand as he offered her a dish, a slow smile as he complimented her beauty in the candlelight. He could sense her softening, and was readying himself for the final assault when she gave a wistful sigh.

"It is so beautiful here," she murmured, glancing once more about the intimately arranged chamber. "I will miss it when I am gone."

Here was the opening he had been angling for, and he slipped quickly into it. "Anne," he said, setting his glass aside and reaching out to take her hand in his. "About your leaving—"

She pulled her hand from his and glanced away. "I have been thinking," she said, avoiding his gaze, "and I've decided to go to Bath. There are any number of ladies' academies in the town; I am certain I won't have any trouble securing a position."

Triumph was within his grasp, and he reached out with both hands to grab it. He took her hands in his. "I don't want you to leave, Anne," he said, squeezing her fingers gently, compelling her to look at him. "I want you to remain here with me."

Her gray eyes met his, full of sadness and hope, and looking into their silvery depths Ruairdh knew he couldn't go through with his scheme. He dropped her hands, pushing himself away from the table with a muttered oath. He paced the room, aware all the time of those smoke-colored eyes watching him. Finally he stopped in front of the fireplace, staring down into the flames with bitter eyes and a heavy heart.

"I had it all planned, you see," he said, rubbing his neck wearily. "Each word. Each gesture. I was going to be so cool and clever as I led you the way I wanted you to go. It would be as *I* wished it to be. I would have control. For once in my damned life, I would have control." He sighed and cast her a resigned look over his shoulder. "I might have known you would destroy those plans as you have destroyed all the others."

Anne didn't move, sitting so still she might have been carved from stone. "What is it you are saying?" she asked, her soft voice so cool they might have been discussing the weather.

Her aloofness angered him, and he whirled around to face her. "I am saying that I brought you up here, arranged all this"—he waved his hand, encompassing the room—"because I meant to seduce you into marrying me."

She paled, and he knew a moment of savage relief that she wasn't as sanguine as she pretended. "But you told me you couldn't marry me," she whispered, her voice trembling. "That because of the curse you dared not."

Something inside of Ruairdh shifted and settled, and a feeling of cautious hope stole through him. "And now it is because of the curse that I know I was wrong," he said, turning to face her. "I don't know how much time I've left before the Shadowing takes me, but I do know I cannot go until I am certain you'll be safe. And then there is my clan to think of. As their laird I am responsible for their care, and 'tis not a duty I take lightly. I've given this matter much thought, and I've decided there is but one way I can accomplish both of these tasks." His eyes met hers, and he spoke the words of his heart, and not the pretty, practiced speech he had rehearsed. "Marry me, Anne. Please."

Chapter Twelve

Silence greeted his offer—silence so deep, and so terrifying, Ruairdh thought his heart would stop. His whole life was dangling by an unraveling thread, and once again he was helpless to stop it.

"Anne?" he prodded, taking a cautious step toward her. "Did you no' hear what I said?"

Her solemn eyes studied him. "I heard."

"And?" he demanded, wondering what was ailing her. Perhaps his proposal hadn't been the most romantic ever uttered, he admitted with a flicker of panic. But given the situation between them, he hadn't thought she would want honeyed words and empty promises.

"You might do me the courtesy of answering," he continued, burying his fear beneath a show of irritation. "From the way you're staring, one would think I am already chained in the east tower. I've not yet been taken, if that is why you do not speak. I know what I am saying, and I mean every word of it."

That won a response from her. "I am sure you do," she responded, temper adding a soft bloom of color to her cheeks. "You have always meant precisely what you say. That is not the issue."

"Then what is?" He fisted his hands on his hips, feeling considerably aggrieved. "Why do you not answer me?"

"Because I don't know what to say!"

Her shouted words had Ruairdh blinking in surprise. It gave him pause, and he took a step back from his emotions to try again.

"I wanted honesty between us," he said simply, taking care to keep his distance. "I could have lied. I could have told you I loved you, and promised you an eternity of happiness, but I care for you too much to deceive you. And in the end, what good would it have done? You'd never have believed me."

"Perhaps," she agreed, her voice sounding firmer, more like her usual tones. "But that doesn't mean I like having an offer tossed in my face without any warning. You startled me, Ruairdh. And you frightened me."

"Frightened you?" he demanded, stunned. "How?"

She shook her head. "That is not important," she said, meeting his gaze. "I want you to tell me again why you want to marry me."

He was uncertain how to answer. "It is as I have already said," he answered, after taking a moment to marshal his thoughts. "I care for you, and I want to have a care of you. I want to know you will be provided for when I am gone. Unfortunately there is no way I can do so without ruining your good name, and that I will not do. The only way I can be certain you will be safe is if I marry you."

"And your clan?"

His clan. Ruairdh closed his eyes. Clan MacCairn had once been one of the wealthiest and most powerful clans in this part of Scotland. But the Shadowing had eroded that power, and centuries of warfare with England and others had drained the wealth. Now there were less than two hundred people who comprised his clan, and they lived in the village and nearby cairn. In the last ten years he had more than tripled his inheritance, and that and the money he would raise by selling the castle and its contents would mean he could do one last duty. With the money left for their protection, none of his clan need fear being removed, as so many others had since greedy landowners hungry for profits to be had from the raising of sheep began clearing out the crofters from their land.

"I am their laird," he said quietly, infusing the word with quiet pride. "How can I leave them defenseless? How long would they last before being driven from their homes? If I had an heir to follow me, he would be the new laird and would protect them. But I have no heir."

To his surprise he could see tears gleaming in her eyes. "And so you would marry me for them?"

"Aye." He wouldn't lie. "I've made Angley my executor, and there is no one I trust more. But as that dolt of a solicitor reminded me, he is far from a young man. If he dies soon after me and before arrangements can be made, the clan will still be at risk."

He went to her finally, taking her hands and drawing her into his arms. "I know you too well to think you would wed me for gain," he murmured, brushing his lips over the curve of her cheek. "But I think you would do so if it would help others. You are so honorable, so good. There is no one else I would rather charge with the welfare of my people. I trust you."

Her arms tightened about his neck, and she pressed her face to his neck. He could feel the wetness of her tears, and it humbled him. He pulled her closer, sliding his lips down to her mouth and kissing her with the passion that exploded in his veins.

"Marry me, Anne," he implored, lifting his mouth from hers and gazing fiercely down into her eyes. "Let me die knowing you and my clan will survive without me. Give me that much."

"Don't talk of dying!" she implored, rising on her toes to kiss him passionately. "I cannot bear it!"

"It is the truth!" he cried, because in his heart it was so. "I've little time left to me, and I want to spend that time with you. For the love of God, Anne, will you marry me?"

Her eyes and cheeks were wet with tears as she faced him, but she had never looked more lovely or courageous. "Yes," she said, her voice breaking with emotion. "Yes, Ruairdh, I shall marry you."

Ruairdh felt his control snap as he gathered her in his arms, sealing their vows with a fiery kiss. Anne's lips were soft and giving beneath his own, and he eagerly pressed them apart to seek the honey deep inside. She answered shyly, and the brush of her tongue against his sent him plunging over an invisible ledge. His body hardened in vicious need, and he swept her up and carried her over to the silk-draped settee.

"Anne." His voice was low and urgent as he laid her down on the soft cushions. "I want you more than I have ever wanted you. As if this is the first time. As if it will be the last."

"Ruairdh!" She called out his name with the breathless wonder that never failed to stir him, her cheeks delicately flushed with desire.

Their other times together had given him a lover's knowledge of her, and he used every bit of that knowledge to his advantage. He removed the clothing from her body article by article, lingering over each inch of her flesh as it was slowly exposed. He knew her breasts to be especially sensitive, and after teasing them with his tongue he drew the nipples deep into his mouth, licking and sucking them until she was gasping in delight. His lips followed his hands as he rolled down her soft silk stockings, and then they made the return journey up the inside of her thighs until his mouth was poised over her womanly folds. He savored the exotic spice of her, and then lowered his head.

"Ruairdh?" He heard the fear and confusion in Anne's voice as he brushed his mouth over her. "What . . . what are you doing?"

"Loving you, *leannan*," he replied, his tongue flicking out for a taste of her. "You must tell me if you like it."

"I-I don't know," she stammered, her fingers lacing through his hair and holding him in place. "It's . . . I . . . Oh, Ruairdh, yes! Yes!"

He loved her completely, using his lips and teeth and tongue to torment and pleasure her until she was arching off the cushions, her voice husky as she sobbed out her release. Only when he was certain of her satisfaction did he step back, pulling off his own clothes before returning to her.

"Before you were my lover," he said, his gaze holding hers as his hands slid down to cup her buttocks, lifting her until the tip of his manhood was nudging against her entry. "Tonight you become my bride." And he plunged deep inside of her.

His first thrust sent her into another spasm, and he had to grit his teeth to keep from following her. She was hotter than she had ever been, and the milking shudders of her inner body were almost more than he could bear. He paused a moment and then started to move, his hips rocking as he slowly and relentlessly brought her back to the peak. He would thrust hard and fast until they were both gasping for air, and then he would draw back before thrusting even deeper, until he couldn't tell where he ended and she began. It was as if he wanted to experience a lifetime of loving in this one night, and it was only when he felt his own completion approaching that he knew he had to stop. Thrusting frantically one last time he pulled out, crying out in agonized protest as his body shuddered and emptied itself against the silk.

"Ruairdh!" He heard Anne's sweet gasp, and took dark pleasure in knowing he had satisfied her yet again. The thought pleased him enough that he allowed himself to drowse, resting his head against Anne's breast as he waited for his heart to slow its wild pounding. Within moments he was drifting into sleep, until the sound of a footstep outside the chamber had his eyes flying open.

"Ruairdh!" Anne gave his shoulder a frantic push. "There is someone out there!"

The handle rattled a few seconds before a familiar voice called out. "Laird? I am come, as you bade me."

Relaxing, Ruairdh dropped his head and kissed the curve of Anne's breast. "Go away," he called out, taking care to speak Gaelic. "There is no need for reinforcements. She has said yes."

"Are ye sure?" the steward called back in the same language. "I've the woman with me to bear witness if need be."

Ruairdh laughed, feeling a lightness of heart he'd never known in the whole of his life. "Yes, I am certain," he said, this time in English. "Go away, Angley. Now."

There was a pause and then a muttered, "As you say, laird." The sound of a struggle followed.

"What do you think you are doing?" A woman's querulous voice could be clearly heard. "Stop! Put me down at once! Oh! Oh! I shall faint! Help! Help!" And the voice faded as the footsteps echoed echoed down the stairs.

Anne twisted beneath him to gaze at the door. "Was that Mrs. Collier?" she asked, turning back to give Ruairdh a look of wide-eyed astonishment. "Good heavens, what was Mr. Angley doing to her?"

Her movements made it plain to Ruairdh that his body had recuperative powers that were nothing short of amazing. "I think we are best off not knowing, *annsachd*," he said, wrapping his arms about her and deftly reversing their positions. "Now"—he grinned up at her—"where were we?"

Anne spent the next week adjusting to her change in circumstances. With Ruairdh at her side they broke the news of their engagement to the servants, and she was gratified by the approval they accorded her as their new mistress. Approval from the village was longer in coming, and as the days went by and none of her new neighbors came to call, Anne decided it was time to take matters into her own hands. Donning her best day dress and cape, she went into the study to confront Ruairdh.

"What is it, *annsachd?*" he asked, not looking up from the papers he was reading.

"I thought I would ride into the village," she said, hiding her uncertainty behind an air of brisk efficiency. "Do you think I might use the carriage?"

That got his attention and he looked up, his brows meeting in a disapproving scowl. "The village?" he repeated. "Why should you wish to go there?"

"Because I have never been," she answered calmly. "Now that I am to be the new mistress here I thought it might be prudent to introduce myself to the local shopkeepers, and—"

"Do not bother," he interrupted, his tone as cold and as aloof as his expression. "They've nothing to interest you. If there is something you're needing we can send to London or Edinburgh for it." And he glanced back down again, his actions making it plain that he considered the matter closed.

Anne hesitated. Her first response was to withdraw,

but she sternly repressed it. Ruairdh had told her he expected her to take care of the clan, and that was precisely what she intended to do.

"I am afraid I must disagree," she said, standing her ground with cool conviction. "Granted, I am not a member of the aristocracy, but I've been in enough grand homes to know how things are done. The manor house always patronizes the local shops. It is expected."

His green eyes flashed a dark warning. "In England perhaps," he informed her curtly. "But you're in Scotland now."

Anne raised an eyebrow in polite inquiry. "Are you saying Scottish shops are inferior to those found in England?"

"I am saying no such thing!" he shot back, his voice filled with exasperation. "Blast it, Anne! I've no' the time to go prancing into the village just now, and you'll not go alone."

"I won't be alone. Mrs. Collier shall ride with me."

Ruairdh rose to his feet, letting his opinion of the older woman be known in a few pithy words. He charged over to the window, staring down into the courtyard before turning back to face her.

"I don't want you to go," he said, rubbing the back of his neck as he met her gaze. "Let that be the end of it."

He sounded so weary Anne almost relented, but she felt the matter was too important for her to back away from her duty. "I cannot," she answered quietly, her heart aching at the torment on his face. "You said you wanted me to have a care for your clan when you are gone. How can I do that if I am a stranger to them?"

"Anne—"

"Ruairdh." She stepped forward, gently laying her finger against his lips. "I am not defying you out of pettiness. If there is a reason you don't wish me to go to the village, then say so. I promise I shall listen."

He was silent for several moments, his face gaunt with emotion. "It has been a week and more since I have been troubled by the Shadowing," he said at last, his gaze studiously avoiding hers. "It is because of you; I am sure of it. If you leave, I am afraid . . ."

"You are afraid it will return," she replied, nodding in understanding. "There, you see?" She rose on tiptoe to brush a light kiss across his mouth. "You had only to explain it to me."

"Then you will stay?" he asked, his eyes burning down into hers as he grasped her about the waist. "You'll not leave me?"

"I will stay," she promised, smiling softly. "But," she added, drawing back when he bent his head to kiss her, "I still think I should ride into the village. And since you don't want me to ride alone, *and* you don't want me to leave you alone in the castle, the best solution is for you to come with me."

His lips curved in an answering smile. "What a clever conniver you are, *mo cridhe*," he murmured, quickly stealing a kiss. "Very well, we shall go tomorrow, after I have had a chance to clear away some of my work. I need to see the vicar, and going there makes as much sense as his coming here. Speaking of the vicar, where is that plague of a sister of his?"

Anne hid a smile at the suspicious demand. Since their engagement had been announced Mrs. Collier had grown even more vigilant in her chaperoning duties, apparently determined that no hint of scandal should touch upon them. She'd even taken to sleeping in Anne's dressing room, which made slipping away for a bit of lovemaking even more difficult . . . and exciting.

"She is in the drawing room waiting for me," she replied, thinking of the smug glee on the other woman's face when she'd mentioned going into the village. "She'll be disappointed to learn we shan't be going. I believe she was looking forward to the chance to parade me in front of her cronies."

"She may parade you tomorrow," Ruairdh declared, giving her a husbandly kiss on the forehead. "In the meanwhile, I would like you to ask Angley to take you about the newer portions of the castle. I would take you myself, but I need to get these papers signed and off to Mr. Hughes as soon as possible."

Anne swallowed her disappointment. As her fiancé it was Ruairdh's duty to acquaint her with her new home, and she'd been waiting for him to show her the castle and its many fascinating secrets. That he wouldn't stung her pride, but she decided not to be childish. She'd already been living in the castle for several weeks, and since theirs was hardly the traditional engagement, she couldn't expect Ruairdh to act the besotted bridegroom.

After breaking the news to Mrs. Collier, Anne went in search of Mr. Angley. She found the steward hard at work in his tiny study off the kitchens, and when he saw her standing in the doorway, he struggled to his feet.

"No, please do not get up, Mr. Angley," she said, smiling as she waved him back into his seat. "I can see you are quite busy, and I promise not to keep you very long."

"Of course, *baintghearnas*," the steward replied, lowering himself to his chair and slanting her a questioning look. "Is there something you wanted?"

Baintghearnas. Anne wondered how to spell that. "What does that mean?" she asked, making a mental note to add it to the dictionary she was compiling. She'd taken to writing down each new word of Gaelic she heard in the hopes of one day mastering the language. If she was going to be the lady of the clan, it seemed prudent she should speak their tongue as well.

"Ladyship," Angley provided. "For when you wed the laird, it's our lady you will be. Unless you mean to return to England?" Sharp blue eyes studied her challengingly.

Because she'd been expecting such a question, Anne refused to take umbrage. "I will remain here," she told him softly. "I've given Ruairdh my word."

The older man relaxed against his chair. "Aye, and it eases the lad's mind to know it," he said, nodding his approval. "The MacCairns have all had a heavy burden to bear, but being the last, his is the heaviest of all. You know that, do you, lass?"

"I know it," Anne replied, thinking of the many conversations she and Ruairdh had had since they had become engaged. Then she thought of the one thing Ruairdh steadfastly refused to discuss.

"Mr. Angley, about the Shadowing—"

"Wheest! Dinna mention it aloud!" the older man exclaimed, leaping from his chair and glancing furtively about him. "Do you want to bring the devil down on us all?"

Anne bit back an oath of annoyance. "Then how else am I to learn of it?" she demanded crossly.

"You'll learn what you need to know soon enough," the steward shot back in dark tones. "If that was the only reason why you've come, then you might as well be away. I'll not break my allegiance to the laird."

Anne was tempted to point out that, as the future lady of the clan, that allegiance should now transfer to her, but she accepted that it would be a waste of her time. "Ruairdh asked that you show me about the castle," she said, hoping he would refuse. She'd had enough of dour Scots for one afternoon.

"As if you've not already seen every stone and brick of it," Angley muttered, pushing himself to his feet once again. "Let us be off, then. I've a wedding to plan, and less than a week in which to plan it."

Tempted as she was to go the opposite way, Anne swallowed her temper and followed him. She quickly learned that looking at the castle through the eyes of the chatelaine was vastly different than looking at the castle through the eyes of an antiquarian assigned to assess the monetary value of the heirlooms. Everything she saw resonated with age and tradition, and she wondered anew how Ruairdh could bear to sell so much as a piece of it. She said as much to Angley, and he gave a snort of agreement.

"And so I've asked him, but he'll say only 'tis to be done," he said, sounding reluctantly admiring. "And he's the right of it, I suppose. Old stones and fine traditions will not keep us from starving in the time ahead."

They continued the tour through the older part of the castle, although Anne noted he was careful to stay away from the east wing. Whether out of superstition or respect for her feelings, Anne didn't know; she was only grateful to be spared the pain of going there. Considering what had happened at the base of the staircase, she didn't care if she ever set foot in the place again. They were making their way back to the newer wing when Anne realized how close they were to the armory, and impulsively asked to see it.

"And why should you be going there?" Angley asked, even as he changed direction at her bidding. "You should know the place well enough, I'm thinking."

Anne thought of the sword she'd left behind when she'd fled from the ghost. "I need to retrieve my father's tools and a few other things. It will only take a few minutes."

"As you wish," Angley muttered in his aggrieved fashion. "Only mind you are quick about it. I've no desire to make the *spiorad*'s acquaintance."

The mention of the ghost had Anne shivering, and her courage nearly wavered. There'd been no further incidents, but the mere memory of the malevolent spirit was enough to give her pause. If he appeared again, she wasn't certain her nerves could bear the shock. At least she wasn't alone, she decided, sending the grumbling steward a grateful look. Given his sour nature and tendency to scold, he'd likely send the ghost fleeing in fright.

The door to the armory was locked, and Anne waited in mounting anxiety as Angley dug through his thick ring of keys until he found the proper key and opened it. Anne took a moment to gather her courage and then hurried inside, glancing about her uneasily. To her relief the room seemed almost ordinary, and there was nothing in the air that made her sense the ghost's presence. Feeling vastly reassured, she hurried over to the worktable and retrieved the sword and her father's box of tools.

"That's what you're wanting?" Angley demanded, indicating the sword with a scowl. "Is it an attack you're expecting, that you need to cart that about?"

"I merely wish to finish studying it," Anne replied, handing him the tools. "Old weaponry is a special interest of mine."

"And a good thing, too," he replied, leading her from the armory and carefully locking the door behind them. "You'll not be letting that thieving *Sasunnach* steal the pennies from our very pockets. If you're done here, 'tis time we were starting back."

God, but he was tired. Ruairdh stretched his neck to work out the painful kinks that had formed in the hours he'd spent hunched over the castle's ledgers. He hated such work, but with time growing short he wanted to have all in readiness for Anne. They would be married at the end of the week, and he prayed he could hold out until then.

He'd lied to Anne about the waning power of the Shadowing over the past week, he admitted, closing the books and locking them safely away. The Shadowing hadn't taken him—that much was true—but it was always there, pressing closer with each passing day. He beat it back again and again, but the struggle was weakening him, and he feared it was only a matter of time before he was overtaken, perhaps for good. The possibility was horrifying, but more horrifying still was his mounting fear that he would be taken while he was making love to Anne.

The very thought made him shake in terror, but despite his terror he could not keep away from her. He knew he should; he fought each day to master his need of her, and lost the fight each night when she slipped into his arms and began kissing him. Another form of madness? he wondered, shaking his head sadly. He had more than his share, it would seem.

He found Mrs. Collier in the drawing room, and when he asked about Anne he was distressed to learn she was in her rooms.

"Is she ill?" he demanded, furious that he had not been notified.

"She didn't say," Mrs. Collier replied with a sniff. "She said only that she would be in her room until dinner, and I was not to disturb her. She had a huge sword with her, and I presume she is examining it."

Ruairdh turned to leave, but Mrs. Collier stopped him. "You aren't thinking of going to her rooms, I trust?" she asked, studying him in tight-lipped disapproval.

He stopped at the door. "And if I am?" he asked quietly, his temper stirring to dangerous life.

"Then I must tell you it is not proper," she continued in prim tones. "This engagement of yours has caused quite enough scandal as it is. I cannot allow you to provoke further talk."

He returned to stand in front of her, making no effort to mask his displeasure. "How will they talk if they do not know what has happened?" he challenged. "And how will they know what has happened unless you tell them?"

Mrs. Collier bristled in indignation. "Really, Mr. MacCairn," she sputtered, "I must protest! I am not a gossip!"

Ruairdh gave her a hard-edged smile. "For your sake and that of your brother, I would hope not," he said. "The position he holds is mine to give, and mine to take away. Remember that."

An expression of fear and resentment flashed across the older woman's face, but since fear was the stronger of the emotions, Ruairdh was content. In his triumph, he decided to be generous.

"I am only going to peek in on Anne and make certain she is all right," he said, although he felt he owed the older woman no explanation. "I have no more desire than you to have her good name destroyed." He watched her for several seconds until he was certain she understood, and then inclined his head in gracious condescension.

"We shall see you at dinner, Mrs. Collier. A pleasant afternoon to you." He left the room, pausing outside the door and using his preternatural abilities to spy upon her. As he watched he saw her fumble in her knitting bag, reaching for the flask of brandy she kept hidden from all. She unscrewed the top and took a hasty swig, sighing in relief as the potent brandy flowed through her veins. When she lifted the flask to her lips for another sip Ruairdh fastidiously withdrew, leaving her to drink in privacy.

The door to Anne's room was closed when he arrived, and after a brief hesitation he pushed it open and stepped into the room. A cheerful fire was blazing in the grate, shedding a warm, golden light over Anne. She was dozing in the overstuffed chair, the sword laid across her lap. The sight of his beautiful angel sleeping so peacefully while clutching one of the most deadly weapons in the castle struck him as incongruous, and he walked over to kneel beside her.

"Wake up, Anne," he commanded, brushing a gentle kiss over her cheek. "Wake up, *mo cridhe.*"

She gave a soft sigh, her lashes fluttering as she opened her eyes. "Ruairdh," she said, her lips curving up as he pressed a teasing kiss upon them. She returned it before drawing back to give him a languid smile. "What is it you wanted?" she asked.

He gave her a roguish wink, desire stirring inside him. "You can ask that, *annsachd*, after the past few nights?"

"Ruairdh!" She flushed prettily and pushed at his shoulder. "You know that is not what I meant. And mind yourself; what if Mrs. Collier were to walk in on us?"

Ruairdh gave an indulgent chuckle. "There's not much chance of that, my sweet. She is in the drawing room swilling brandy like a lord. She drinks, you know. I am most shocked."

"As if anything could shock you," Anne replied, shifting on the chair. The movement shifted the sword on her lap, and she had to grab at it to keep it from sliding to the floor. Ruairdh glanced down at the weapon in mild interest.

"What have you there?"

"The sword I was telling you about," Anne said, carefully picking up the sword by its curved hilt. "I believe I may have identified the source of the markings." She tilted the sword to show him.

"Be careful, Anne," he warned, alarmed at the way the blade was gleaming in the firelight. "The edges are sharp. You'll cut yourself." And his fingers closed around the hilt.

A roar filled his ears, like the sea in a gale, and he felt himself being swept away. He saw Anne's face, heard her musical voice as she explained the engraving on the sword, but it was as if there were a wall of glass separating them. He threw himself against the barrier, pounding at it with his fists as he screamed at her to run. But even as he called out his frantic warning he already knew he was too late: the Shadowing was upon him.

"Not Templar but akin to them," Anne concluded, sounding pleased. "I think it may be a form of heraldry associated with the Masons, but I can't be certain until I've had more time to study and compare." She glanced up then, and through the glass he saw the excitement on her face fade into confusion. "Ruairdh? Is something wrong?"

"Wrong?" The voice emerged from his lips in a mocking purr. "What could be wrong, *annsachd*, when I am about to have you?"

No! Ruairdh shrieked out his agony in a howl of fury. This was his worst nightmare come to life, and he flung himself against the glass with renewed desperation.

"I think it's not only Mrs. Collier who has been drinking," Anne said, giving the creature that wore his face a reproving look. "You know you should not say such things to me. Now kindly let me up. I need to change for dinner." She started to sit up, only to have the creature push her back down.

"Ruairdh!" She glared up at him, more vexed than frightened. "Stop that! What in heaven's name is wrong with you?"

Ruairdh thanked God for her temper. If she distracted the beast just enough, he still had a chance. He stepped back from the clear walls of his cage fighting his panic and trying to think. The other times when he had been aware of the Shadowing, he had managed to push the madness from his mind. All he had to do was remember what he had done and repeat it.

"Lift your skirts, *Sasunnach*." The creature was holding Anne down, and Ruairdh was disgusted to feel his sexual excitement as well as his evil glee. "Give me what you have given him. It is my right."

"Ruairdh! I said stop!" There was alarm in Anne's voice, and she began struggling in earnest. Her fear shattered Ruairdh's heart, but he couldn't let it affect him. He could sense the other one's annoyance, and for a brief moment the wall was down. Ruairdh leaped through it with a shout of fury.

"No!" He screamed it aloud, jumping up from Anne and staggering back. He was too close to the fireplace, and his heel caught the edge of the carpet. Off balance and unable to gain control of himself, he stumbled and came crashing to the ground. His head hit the side of an andiron, and he felt a flash of white-hot pain before the blackness claimed him.

Chapter Thirteen

Anne stared down at Ruairdh in horror before scrambling to her feet. "Ruairdh!" she cried, her anger with him forgotten as she rushed to kneel beside him. "Oh my God, Ruairdh! Are you all right?" She laid shaking fingers against his head, and was sickened when they came back stained crimson with his blood. She leaped to her feet and ran to the door, throwing it open and calling out in desperation, "Help me! Someone come at once! Help!"

She ran back to Ruairdh, and was dabbing at the blood flowing from his head when Angley came scurrying into the room.

"Laird!" he cried out, and hurried over to join Anne.

"He fell," she said, fighting tears and panic at how pale and still he was. "He hit his head, and there is so much blood I cannot stop it." She raised her eyes to study the older man fearfully. "Is he . . . is he alive?"

"Aye, for the moment," Angley said, his voice quavering as he placed his fingers against Ruairdh's neck. "God be thanked for that thick head of his. He'd be dead otherwise."

Several other servants crowded into the room, and at Angley's clipped orders four of the younger footman picked Ruairdh up and carried him from the room. Anne ran after them, paying Mrs. Collier no mind when she tried to stop her.

"Aren't you going to send for the doctor?" she asked, after Ruairdh had been summarily stripped of his clothes, dressed in a nightshirt, and stuffed into bed.

"Only if we must," Angley said, gently wiping blood from Ruairdh's head. " 'Tis a clean wound, and we can take better care of him than that half-blind fool in the village ever could." He spared Anne a quick look, his bushy white brows set in a scowl.

" 'Tis better you return to your rooms, Miss Garthwicke. He is not yet your husband, and 'tis not proper you should be here."

Anne ignored him. "To the devil with propriety," she announced, settling on the chair beside Ruairdh's bed and folding her arms across her chest. "I am staying here until he awakens."

Angley's gaze sharpened, and then to Anne's astonishment he gave her a surprisingly sweet smile. "As you say, *baintghearnas*," he said, inclining his head to her in courteous respect. "Only mind you keep well out of my way. I've no' the time to deal with you."

The next half hour seemed to stretch endlessly for Anne. Ruairdh lay still as death; only the steady rising and falling of his chest assured her he was alive. Soon he began growing restive, his head moving on the pillow as if he were fighting his way back to consciousness. Finally his thick lashes fluttered and then lifted, and he blinked heavy, pain-filled eyes.

"Angley," he asked in a thick voice. "Where am I?"

"In your rooms, laird," Angley said, and Anne's interest stirred at his question. He asked not what had happened, but *where* he was. "You fell and hit your head, or so the lass has said."

Ruairdh slowly turned his head, his gaze seeking her out. "Anne?"

"I am here, Ruairdh," she said, leaning forward to cover his hand with hers. "Rest easy; you've lost a great deal of blood."

Ruairdh studied her for a brief moment, and then turned his attention to Angley. A quick exchange in Gaelic followed, and then he closed his eyes and drifted back to sleep without speaking to Anne again.

"I don't suppose you'd care to tell me what he said?" she asked after pulling the covers over Ruairdh's shoulders to protect him against the pervasive chill brought on by the night.

"No, I would not," Angley declared, and then relented. "He was only reassuring himself you were well," he said, turning back to gaze at the man lying on the bed. "He feared seeing him hurt as your father was hurt would upset you."

Anne gave a quick jerk of embarrassed surprise. Until this moment she hadn't given her father a single thought; all her thoughts and concerns had been centered solely on Ruairdh.

"He should worry more about himself," she said, her gaze following Angley's. "He is going to have a dreadful headache when he awakens. Is there nothing we can give him?"

Angley looked thoughtful for a moment. "I'll have a word with Mrs. Doughal," he said, rising to his feet. "She has a fine hand with herbs and the like." He excused himself, slipping from the room and leaving Anne alone with Ruairdh.

He returned in less than ten minutes, carrying a steaming pot smelling faintly of peppermint. "She had it steeped and waiting for me," he said, setting the tray carefully on the bedside table.

Anne gave the pot a suspicious sniff. "What is in it?"

"Mint and willow bark for the pain, and clover to help mend his wound," Angley provided. "You're to give it to him when he wakens."

"*I* am to give it to him?" Anne repeated, surprised Angley would willingly give up his watch. "Where will you be?"

"Tending to everything else," the older man replied in his brusque manner. "The lad doesn't need both of us standing guard over him, and since you'll not leave, I'd best be away." He gave her shoulder a companionable pat, and slipped from the room.

After he'd gone Anne pulled her chair closer to the bed, taking Ruairdh's hand in hers and leaning forward to watch him anxiously. She thought he was sleeping more easily; his breathing was deeper and more natural, and she breathed her own sigh of relief. With her fear temporarily assuaged, she settled back to simply study him. It wasn't often she was granted the luxury of looking upon him while he was resting, and she drank her fill of him.

He was undoubtedly one of the handsomest men she had ever seen, with a raw, masculine power that made every other man she had met seem pale and effete. His face, with its high cheekbones, wide forehead, and strong jaw, was almost beautiful—a description she knew would embarrass Ruairdh if she were so foolish as to tell him. She smiled, her gaze sliding down to rest on Ruairdh's lips parted slightly in sleep. Unable to resist their allure, she leaned over and pressed her mouth to his.

As if he'd been waiting for only that, Ruairdh began stirring, his lips responding to hers even before his green eyes flickered open.

"Anne?" He breathed her name as softly as a prayer.

"Yes." She reached out and brushed back hair from his forehead. "How are you feeling?"

"Like the roof of the grand hall has landed on my head," he grumbled, wincing as he glanced about the room. "Where is Angley?"

"I've no idea," Anne replied with a chuckle. "He said you didn't need both of us watching you, and off he went."

"That sounds like Angley," Ruairdh said, a smile tugging at his mouth as he cautiously sat up in the bed.

Anne leaned forward to help him, stuffing pillows behind his head before retrieving the pot from the table. "Before he left he brought this from Mrs. Doughal," she said, pouring out a cup of the tea and handing it to him. "She said I was to give it to you as soon as you were awake, and that you were to drink all of it."

Ruairdh accepted the brew with a grumble, sipping it with obvious reluctance. "It tastes better than I remember," he said, finishing the tea before handing the cup back to Anne.

"Are you hungry? I could ring for dinner," she offered, aware of a sudden desire to avoid the confrontation she knew was unavoidable.

"No, thank you, *annsachd*," he said, his expression solemn as their gazes met. "Tell me what happened. All of it."

Now that the moment had come, Anne didn't know where to start. "I'm not certain what happened," she began, forcing herself to remain objective, as her father had taught her. "You came into my room and we were talking, and then suddenly you weren't you anymore." She flushed, thinking how ridiculous that sounded.

"What do you mean?"

Anne took a moment to gather her impressions of those terrifying seconds in her study. "I mean," she said, choosing each word carefully, "that for a moment, for a very brief moment, you were not Ruairdh. It was as if you had become someone else. Someone I did not know. Someone evil.

"And this isn't the first time I have seen it happen," she added, recalling at least two other times when he had changed without warning. She gave him a sharp look as sudden understanding dawned. "Is this the Shadowing, the madness controlling you?"

He looked stunned, and then resigned. "Yes," he said heavily. "It is."

Anne nodded, understanding at least part of the reason behind Ruairdh's anguish. *How horrible,* she thought, *to live with the knowledge of that terrible loss of self hanging over you.* She frowned as a new thought occurred to her.

"Why do you call it that?" she asked curiously. "You have never said."

Now it was Ruairdh who seemed to search for words. "That is what it has always been called," he said, looking uncomfortable. "It is a shadow that that has hung over all of the men in my family, following us wherever we go, always there, waiting to devour us. Sometimes we are strong enough and can fight it, other times, like now, we are helpless against it and are taken however hard we struggle." He shook his head angrily.

"What does it matter what it's called?" he demanded, his eyes flashing with temper. "It is death; that is all you need to know."

"I am trying to understand it," Anne replied, her mind racing as she thought and measured. "I was raised to study, to observe, and to record my data before reaching a conclusion."

"And what conclusion have you reached?"

"I am still reviewing the matter," she replied, a sense of excitement stirring inside of her. Since her father's death she had been drifting, lost in a miasma of grief and guilt. Now she felt a surge of energy, of purpose. Ruairdh seemed resigned to his fate, but that didn't mean she had to follow suit.

"Why must you dissect it like this?" Ruairdh demanded, his voice low and full of anguish. "Why is it so important that you understand it? What difference can it make?"

"All the difference in the world," she replied, feeling in control for the first time since her father's death. "Because if I understand it, then perhaps I can find a way to cure it."

He looked at her as if she'd just announced her intention to fly to the moon. "Cure it?" he repeated. "That is impossible."

"Perhaps," she acknowledged, not wanting to give him false hope, "but we'll never know until we try, will we?"

"It's not possible," Ruairdh repeated, grinding out the words between clenched teeth. "I know, Anne. I *know*."

"Do you?" Anne asked. "I have been thinking, and it seems to me that if a spell was cast, then a spell can be broken. All we have to do is discover how."

"Don't you think that's been tried?" he exclaimed, his hand snaking out to grab her wrist and give it a gentle shake. "My family has endured the Shadowing for five hundred years. There is nothing we've not done to rid ourselves of this curse, and all for naught. Nothing can break the curse. Nothing." His voice broke on the last word.

"We can't give up hope." Anne covered his hand with her own, holding him to her with mounting desperation. "This is the age of science, Ruairdh, of reason. What was considered impossible a hundred years ago is a matter of course today. I am not saying we will succeed in our quest, but we can try. We can try."

His eyes, full of despair and the acceptance of his

own death, met hers. "Why?" he asked wearily. "Why do you care so much?"

Anne's heart began to beat painfully, and her mind shied away from a truth she was not yet ready to face. "Because I care about you," she prevaricated. "And I'm not willing to simply sit back and watch you die. I will fight for you, Ruairdh, do you hear me?" She met his gaze with a fierceness that surprised even her. "I will fight for you."

I will fight for you.

The words echoed in Ruairdh's head as he went down to breakfast the following morning. They'd haunted him during the night, alternately soothing and terrifying him. He couldn't remember any time in his life when anyone had said such a thing to him, and he wasn't pleased to be hearing it now. With the end closing in, he couldn't allow his resolve to waver. He would do what he must, as he had always done.

The fact he'd been taken despite his best efforts terrified him more than all the horrors he'd yet experienced. He'd hoped and prayed his earlier victories meant he had more time with Anne, but now he realized how truly evil the Shadowing was. It made a man hope, he thought bitterly, and then it destroyed that hope in as cruel a way as possible. The time he had with Anne was growing smaller with each passing day, and if he couldn't trust himself to fight and win when the Shadowing threatened, then that time was smaller still.

The footman standing by the door snapped to attention as Ruairdh walked into the morning room. Breakfast was spread out in chafing dishes on the sideboard, and after helping himself to some eggs and crisp bacon, he took his seat at the head of the table.

"Mrs. Collier," he said, giving the suspicious woman a cool nod. "Will you be joining us on our visit to town?"

"Do you mean we are still going?" she asked, giving a disdainful sniff. "I thought you were recovering from your *accident*."

Ruairdh raised an eyebrow at the accusation in her words. "I see no reason why Anne should be deprived of her treat because of my clumsiness," he said mildly, nodding to the footman to fill his cup with hot coffee. "Will you be joining us or not?"

He felt the battle being waged inside her. Much as she would like to refuse his offer in a fine show of moral outrage, she couldn't resist the chance to be seen in his carriage. "I will accompany you," she said imperiously, the need to win the envy of her friends easily overcoming her scruples. "Although as an engaged couple you can certainly ride in an open carriage without inviting gossip, I should prefer not to take that risk. There has already been quite enough cause for talk as it is."

Ruairdh took a sip of coffee. "Indeed?" he inquired politely. "And what cause might that be?"

Mrs. Collier's face turned red, and she turned her attention to the food heaped on her plate. Ruairdh watched her until he was satisfied she would say no more, and then tucked eagerly into his own food. He hadn't eaten since yesterday afternoon, and he was quite famished. He couldn't remember the last time he'd been this hungry, and he ate greedily, savoring the taste of the food as he hadn't done in years. He was working his way through his second plate of eggs when Anne walked into the room.

"Mrs. Collier, sir," she said, nodding to each in turn before spooning some of the eggs onto her plate and joining them.

Ruairdh studied the portions on her plate and scowled. "That is not enough to keep a bird alive, *mo cridhe*," he scolded in gentle disapproval. "You must eat more, or you will become ill."

Anne gave him a cool look, her chin lifting in pretty disdain. "And you should have remained in bed to rest, or you will make yourself ill," she informed him in lofty accents. "If you will return to bed, I will eat more."

Ruairdh stared at her in surprise, and then gave a low chuckle. "Touché, my dear," he said, bending his head in mock submission. "You may consider me chastised. Pray accept my apologies."

Her lips twitched at his words, but she did not respond. Instead she turned to Mrs. Collier.

"It is very kind of you to offer to show me about the village, Mrs. Collier," she said, taking delicate nibbles of her breakfast. "I am most anxious to see it."

"There really isn't that much to see, I am afraid," Mrs. Collier answered with a sigh. "It's a poor, rough place, to be truthful, but as more English settle in the area the quality of life improves. We are talking of starting a musical society. You'll want to join, of course," she added, in the tone of one conferring a great honor.

Anne paused before taking another bite and shot the

older woman an interested glance. "What sort of music?" she asked. "Scottish music?"

"Oh, my heavens, no!" Mrs. Collier exclaimed with a shudder. "I am referring to *real* music, not those dreadful bagpipes."

Ruairdh bristled in instant umbrage, but before he could tear a strip off the cursed woman, Anne spoke.

"I see," she said, continuing to eat her meal. "You don't approve of Scottish music, I gather?"

Mrs. Collier's lips twisted in a derisive smirk. "Hardly, my dear. I can think of no one in our society who would."

"Then I can only presume you have never had the honor of meeting Her Majesty," Anne said, her gray eyes all innocence as she smiled at Mrs. Collier. "She adores all things Scottish, and I fear she would find your opinions"—she paused delicately—"displeasing."

Mrs. Collier's eyes widened. "You have met the queen?"

"At a dinner held before the opening of the Exhibition," Anne said, so casually one would think she dined with royalty every day. "She had a piper for the event, as I recall."

"Indeed," Mrs. Collier said, looking stunned. "Indeed."

She remained blessedly silent through the rest of the meal, occasionally shooting Anne quizzical glances and then muttering to herself. When they had finished eating she excused herself to fetch her bonnet and cape, leaving Anne and Ruairdh alone.

"You can be a devil, I see, when it suits you," he said, leaning back in his chair and grinning at her. "I would be ashamed of you, were I not so proud. You vanquished the enemy so cleverly, *annsachd*, she's not even aware she's defeated."

She feigned indignation. "I am sure I have no notion what you may mean, sir," she said, lifting her nose into the air. "Every word I told Mrs. Collier is the truth."

"I didn't say it wasn't," he said, chuckling softly. "I am saying you will make an excellent champion for my people. It is good to know I shall be leaving them in such capable hands."

He spoke the words in jest, to make her laugh, but instead an oddly determined look stole across her face. He remembered her vow to fight for him and reached out for her, first with his mind and then with his hand. "Anne, we must talk," he began, reaching across the table to link his fingers with hers.

She pulled free of his grasp and stood up. "Yes," she said, studying him with cool disapproval, "we must. But if you will excuse me, I believe I shall also go and fetch my cloak. Mrs. Collier and I will meet you in the great hall."

Ruairdh said nothing, his jaw clenching in anger as he watched her walk away. *The devil take the cursed woman*, he fumed silently. Couldn't she understand the rare compliment he was paying her? His people were everything to him; that he was entrusting her with their care should be more than ample proof of the esteem in which he held her. Of how much he—He killed the thought with an angry growl, refusing to think it even in his own mind. If the monster of madness stalking him were to suspect what Anne meant to him, he would be truly lost. For her sake—for his own—he must never think such things again.

Because the sun was shining after so many days of rain and gloom, Ruairdh ordered the brougham his father had had custom-designed to be brought out. The bright yellow and black paint sparkled like new, and even Mrs. Collier seemed impressed as he helped her up into the high-sprung carriage. She chattered like a magpie during the entire ride down the road and into the village, annoying Ruairdh by pointing out things to Anne he wanted to point out, and showing her things he had been aching to show her. Of course, the older woman offered a constant stream of criticisms along with her comments, and he took some comfort in knowing that Anne was more annoyed than entertained. Perhaps once they were wed he would take her about, he decided, a wolfish smile touching his lips at the thought of the isolated glens and meadows he could show her. The notion had decided possibilities.

In the village his light mood soon vanished as he became aware of his people's emotions, beating at him like the fluttering of bird's wings. He could feel their hope, their despair, as they watched him drive past. He also sensed their relief that he was taking a bride, and hopefully providing them with a laird who would care for them as he had done. Even though it was deceit of the first order, he decided to let them keep that hope, knowing they would need it to sustain them. They would realize the truth soon enough, when he was gone.

The Reverend Felix Gordon was as quiet and even-tempered as his sister was loud and quarrelsome. He was waiting with the necessary papers when Ruairdh arrived, and in his calm, efficient manner cleared the way for Ruairdh and Anne to be wed the following week.

"You'll be wanting the wedding at Castle MacCairn, I presume?" he asked, studying Ruairdh over the top of his spectacles. "To accommodate all your guests?"

"I want it at MacCairn, aye," Ruairdh agreed, thinking of the small, intimate chapel where members of his family had been wed and buried for half a millennium. "But more for tradition's sake than convenience. And there will be no guests, other than the servants. I've just rid myself of a houseful of those parasites; I'll not be calling them back scarce a week later."

A wry smile of understanding touched Mr. Gordon's lips. "It was Benjamin Franklin, I believe, who observed that guests, like fish, begin to reek after three days. It is a sentiment with which I can readily concur."

Now it was Ruairdh who smiled in understanding. Had Mrs. Collier been his sister, he would have locked the bothersome creature in the dungeon and been finished with her. They spent the next half hour briefly discussing his tenants and their needs, and the younger man's knowledge and kindness impressed Ruairdh. He would tell Anne to seek his counsel should she have need, he decided, and was annoyed at the jealous anger that followed.

When he was finished with his appointment he walked out into the parsonage's tiny parlor, glancing about him in annoyance when he saw no sign of Anne.

"Where is Miss Garthwicke?" he demanded of the

tiny, beak-nosed woman who acted as Mr. Gordon's housekeeper.

"Gone away wi' that *briosag*, and praise be for it," the older woman informed him tartly. "Tea and oatcakes is no' fine enough for her, and so 'tis off to the inn they've gone."

Ruairdh thanked the woman for her help and started for the door, pausing when the elderly housekeeper called out to him.

"Yes?" he asked, casting her an inquiring look over his shoulder.

"Yer bride's a bonny lass, laird," she said, offering him a broken-toothed smile. "May she be of comfort to you in the times ahead, and may she give the clan many strong sons."

Ruairdh gave the housekeeper his curt thanks, and took his leave. He walked briskly through the cobblestoned streets, his grim expression enough to keep those who would speak to him at a safe distance. The old woman's blessing rang closer to a curse, as an image of Anne, sweetly rounded with his child, rose up to taunt him. Such a prospect was his vision of heaven—and hell—and he vowed to take better care to ensure that it did not come about. The method he had been using to prevent Anne from carrying his baby was better than nothing, but if he meant to keep making love to Anne, stronger measures would be needed. When next he wrote Mr. Hughes, he decided, he would instruct the younger man to bring him some French sheaths from London. The knowledge that such a request would mortify the earnest solicitor beyond enduring did much to lighten Ruairdh's dark mood, and he was almost smiling as he walked into the inn.

Almost at once his gaze fell upon Anne and Mrs. Collier sitting at a table in front of the fire. The innkeeper rushed forward to greet him, but Ruairdh waved him away, his interest fixed on Anne. She glanced up at his approach, a soft smile of welcome curving her lips as he stopped at their table.

"*Mo cridhe*," he said, taking her hand in his and raising it to his lips. "Have you been enjoying your walk about our village?"

"I have, sir," she replied, her gray eyes bright as they met his. "It is as lovely as I thought it would be."

Mrs. Collier gave a disagreeable titter. "You are too generous with your praise, my dear, to call a disagreeable collection of rough huts and shops 'lovely.' Either that, or you have seen precious little of the world."

Ruairdh's eyes narrowed in fury, but before he could respond, Anne was already speaking.

"As it happens, I have traveled extensively with my father, and I assure you I have never seen any village half so lovely," she said, her voice so cool ice all but formed on each word. "However," she added, sending the other woman a cutting smile as she raised her cup of tea to her lips, "perhaps it is just as well it is not to your liking. Then you shan't miss it once you return to your own home."

Ruairdh suppressed a grin at the expression on Mrs. Collier's plump face. She looked as if a toad or something equally as vile had just hopped into her mouth. Her fingers tightened about her teacup as she took a noisy sip.

"But how is my dear brother, Mr. MacCairn?" she

asked, turning to Ruairdh. "Did he speak of me?"

"That he did," he answered, recalling the vicar's amusing quote. He also realized the older woman had handed him the perfect excuse to dispose of her company, and he was quick to make use of it.

"Speaking of your brother, you'll be wanting to visit with him, I am sure. Will two hours' time be sufficient?" he asked, making what was actually an order sound more like a polite inquiry.

Mrs. Collier's lips grew even thinner. "That would be fine, Mr. MacCairn," she said stiffly, and then said no more.

"Really, Ruairdh, that was too bad of you," Anne scolded, slipping her gloved hand into the crook of Ruairdh's arm as they walked down the village's winding High Street. "You were very cruel to poor Mrs. Collier."

"I, *annsachd?*" he asked, feigning ignorance. "I am not the one who gutted her so neatly and so publicly. I was but giving her the chance to quit the field with some scrap of pride to call her own."

"Nonsense," Anne returned, chuckling. "You wanted to be rid of her, and well you know it. But," she added, giving his arm a teasing squeeze, "as I was also eager for her absence, I shan't quibble with you." She sighed in contentment as they continued on their journey.

"This really is a beautiful place, Ruairdh," she told him, glancing at the small houses with their whitewashed bricks and neatly thatched roofs. "Tell me about it."

To her pleasure he did just that, pointing out various

houses and shops, and making her laugh with tales of the people who lived there. The air of chilly reserve and brooding power that so often clung to him dissipated like fog beneath the midday sun, and she was once again blessed with a tantalizing glimpse of the man beneath the facade. The man he might have been, she thought, had it not been for the Shadowing.

They reached the edge of the village and were about to turn around, when a man dressed in the rough clothing of a crofter approached them.

"Yer pardon, laird," he said, taking off his cap and bowing to Ruairdh, "but I would speak wi' ye. 'Tis a matter of great importance." His gaze slid uneasily to Anne, and she took his meaning at once.

"Go with him, Ruairdh," she said. "I shall be fine on my own."

"Are you certain?" He gazed down at her, his green eyes troubled. "I don't like the idea of leaving you alone."

"What could befall me in so tiny a village?" she asked, and then, sensing the crofter's desperation, she gave Ruairdh a gentle push. "Go," she repeated. "I shall meet you back at the parsonage."

He gave her a searching look, and then raised her hand to his lips for another kiss. "Mind you go directly there," he ordered sternly. "I will join you when I can."

After watching him walk away, Anne turned and began making her way back. A few of the villagers gave her odd looks, but no one approached her, and she continued on her way unmolested. She was a street away from the church when she almost bumped into a man who suddenly blocked her path.

"Miss Garthwicke!" Mr. Beechton exclaimed, his air of surprise ringing suspiciously false. "Where is Mrs. Collier?"

"At the parsonage, where I am now bound," she replied, amazed at the magistrate's audacity. She would have thought, after the awkwardness of their last meeting, that he would have been too embarrassed to approach her without invitation.

"I will accompany you," he said, falling into step beside her. "You shouldn't be walking about without proper escort."

His persistence had her gritting her teeth, but she was too well mannered to make a scene. Which didn't mean she intended to let his high-handed behavior pass without comment, she decided proudly.

"You surprise me, Mr. Beechton," she said, sending him a challenging look from beneath her lashes. "Are you saying it's not safe? That hardly speaks well of your efforts as magistrate."

He bristled in umbrage. "I have done my best," he said, his lips thinning in anger. "But there is only so much I can do with a bunch of ignorant Scots. And in any case, I didn't mean to imply you were in any physical danger. The villagers here are too lazy to break the law, and they know better than to do so in my jurisdiction. At least, some of them know it." He slid her a speculative look that had Anne feeling decidedly unclean.

"Felicitations are in order, I hear," he continued. "The village is abuzz with news of the laird's engagement."

Anne wondered how best to respond to the insinuation in his tone, and decided it was wise to feign ignorance.

"Thank you."

"I must say I was surprised to hear of it," he continued, seeming oblivious to her cold response. "When we spoke at your father's service, you made no mention that you were contemplating such a thing."

"That is because Mr. MacCairn hadn't yet made his feelings known to me. He proposed after the service," Anne replied. She could see the gabled roof of the parsonage and increased her pace, anxious to reach its dubious sanctuary.

"That is rather odd, don't you think?" Mr. Beechton demanded, pulling her to a halt. "Not many men would offer for a woman at her father's funeral."

"As I was planning to leave the next day, I suppose Mr. MacCairn wished to speak to me before I left the area," Anne said stiffly, wondering why she was answering his increasingly impertinent questions. They were almost to the parsonage; a few more steps and she would be rid of her irksome escort.

"Are you certain you are doing the right thing?" he demanded, his fingers tightening with surprising power. "You'll forgive me, but there is that old saying, 'Marry in haste, repent at leisure.' Have you given it any thought?"

Enough was enough. Anne pulled free of his grip, her eyes flashing as she faced him. "You forget yourself, Mr. Beechton," she said, consciously imitating Ruairdh at his autocratic best. "Your company is no longer desired. Good day." She turned to leave, only to have him grab her arm and pull her back against him.

"Listen to me!" he said, his voice desperate as his hands closed on her shoulders. "You laughed when I told you he was cursed, but it's not a laughing matter. MacCairn is doomed to die a madman, and if you marry him, you doom yourself with him! He's not a man like other men. You risk your immortal soul if you enter into this ill-advised union."

The narrow street wasn't crowded, but neither was it deserted, and Anne was painfully aware of the attention centered on them. Since avoiding a scene was now impossible, she said a mental good-bye to propriety, bringing up her hands and shoving against his chest with enough force to send him staggering back several steps.

"This is not your affair, and I will thank you to keep out of it," she snapped, making no effort to lower her voice. "You may be the magistrate here, but that doesn't give you leave to involve yourself in things that are none of your concern. Stay away from me." And with that she turned and walked away, turning a deaf ear to the threats he shouted after her.

Chapter Fourteen

Any hopes Anne harbored of keeping the confrontation with Mr. Beechton secret vanished the moment they arrived back at the castle. They were going into the drawing room for tea when Ruairdh dismissed Mrs. Collier with such finality that for once the older woman offered no argument. She seemed relieved to be gone, shooting Anne an apologetic look before scurrying away from the aura of deadly fury emanating from the castle's laird. The moment they were alone, Ruairdh turned to Anne.

"Well, *leannan?*" he demanded, folding his arms across his chest and regarding her with cold displeasure. "Are you going to tell me what happened in the village, or are you going to force me to learn it on my own? I warn you: one way or the other, I will have the truth of it."

Anne scowled at him, as much out of annoyance at his imperious behavior as from a genuine desire for prevarication. She'd known it was likely he would learn of what happened, but she had hoped for at least some time in which to concoct an acceptable explanation for Mr. Beechton's behavior. Since that had been denied her, she decided a carefully edited version of the truth would have to suffice. She just hoped her words wouldn't bring about one of his disturbing episodes. She wished she could better pinpoint what triggered his fits of madness.

"It was that tiresome Mr. Beechton," she said, playing up her impatience. "Really, it is time someone was doing something about the wretch. If he weren't the magistrate, I daresay he would have been locked away as a public nuisance by now."

Ruairdh's expression grew even darker. "What did he do?"

"Made a fool of himself on High Street," Anne said, trying to imagine what Ruairdh might have already heard. "That was bad enough, but for some reason I shall never understand, he saw fit to involve me in his charade. It is obvious he is sulking over his failure to make trouble because of Father's death, and is trying to wreak whatever havoc he can."

Ruairdh regarded her in silence. "That doesn't answer my question," he said, the very mildness of his tone an indication of his fury. "What did he do?"

She should have known he wouldn't be so compliant. Anne thought for a moment before deciding to brazen it out.

"Acted out a scene straight from a silly drama," she

said, making no attempt to hide her derision. "Uttering gloom and portents like one of the witches in *Macbeth*; saying you were cursed, and if I married you I would be cursed with you."

Ruairdh's arms dropped to his sides. "He said that?"

"Well, for heaven's sake, Ruairdh!" she exclaimed, deciding it was now time to transfer some of her impatience to him. "It's not as if the entire village—or at least those of your clan—don't already know about the curse! It's common knowledge, is it not?"

He looked taken aback by her angry charge. "Aye," he said slowly. "I suppose that it is."

"There, you see?" Anne gave a decisive nod. "Mr. Beechton must have heard the talk, and decided to turn it to his own advantage. Fortunately, the only thing he succeeded in doing was making a laughingstock of himself in front of the entire village. You ought to have heard the snickers as he walked away. It will be a very long time before he can show his face again, that I can tell you."

Ruairdh stepped forward to cup her face between his hands. "You weren't frightened?" he asked, his solemn eyes searching hers.

Anne felt herself melting at his touch. "I was annoyed," she said, and because it was the truth, she smiled. "I almost boxed his ears, and I wish now that I had. The overbearing little worm."

Instead of smiling in return, as she had hoped, he looked even more dangerous. "He placed his hands upon you," he said quietly, moving his hands down to rest in the same place where Mr. Beechton's hands had rested. "I can feel his touch. Smell it upon you. And for that reason alone I could kill him."

Anne jolted at the primitive words. His words, his tone of voice, and the expression on his face were making her uneasy, and she wondered if he was about to succumb to his odd affliction.

"And give the Crown the excuse it needs to disband the clan?" she asked, determined to make him see reason. "What a fine victory that would grant him. Forget him, Ruairdh. He is not worth the bother.

"Now," she said, stepping back from him and walking over to the fireplace with a casualness she was far from feeling. "What did the crofter want with you? Can you tell me, or is it clan business?"

For a moment she didn't think her plan would succeed, but then Ruairdh moved to join her.

"If 'tis clan business, then 'tis your business as well," he said, his manner guarded but a great deal less intimidating. "As for what Leitch wanted, he was seeking my permission to go to Canada with his family. I gave it to him, along with enough gold coin to make certain they do not starve on the way."

The easy kindness he showed to everyone touched her, as did the raw anguish she could detect in his voice. "I am sorry, Ruairdh," she said, reaching out instinctively to take his hand in hers. "I can tell this hurts you. Was he a tenant?"

He shook his head. "Our smithy," he answered, brushing his thumb over the back of her hand. "You'll need to hire a new one; an estate cannot be without a blacksmith. Angley will help you."

This oblique reminder of why he was marrying her

made Anne's heart clench in pain. "Perhaps this is something you should see to yourself," she suggested, releasing his hand and turning away. "I am afraid I know precious little about such things."

"Then it's time you were learning!" The lash of his words took her by surprise. "You promised to guard my people for me; are you going to wash your hands of them at the first sign of difficulty?"

His sudden attack reminded her of those last years with her father, and she felt a stinging sense of betrayal. "Of course not," she denied, embarrassed to find herself fighting back tears. "I merely meant—"

"I am sorry, Anne," Ruairdh interrupted, gathering her to him and pressing his lips to her cheek. "I didn't mean to snap at you. I'm weary, that's all. Forgive me for my sharpness?" He drew back to gaze down at her, regret evident in his expression.

Anne studied the planes of his face, seeing hollows and shadows that hadn't been there before. She also noted his color seemed off, and her anxiety for him returned.

"You do look pale," she said, laying the back of her hand against his forehead. The cholera had raged in London the summer before, and she hadn't forgotten how quickly the victims had sickened and died. "Are you ill?"

"No." He captured her hand and gave it a soft kiss. "As I said, I am but weary. You are a demanding lover, *mo ceile*," he added, flashing her a grin that was meant to be provocative.

Anne blushed scarlet, but before she could think of an acceptable reply, Ruairdh was already turning away.

"If you will pardon me, I believe I will go up to my rooms." He walked toward the door, pausing to cast her a glance over his shoulder. "And I would be grateful, *annsachd*, if you would talk with Angley about finding a new smithy. It is very important that you acquaint yourself with your new duties as soon as possible."

Anne faced him, her nails deep into her palms as she clenched her fists. "Of course, Ruairdh," she said, forcing her lips to curve into a stiff smile. "I will do whatever I can to help. Shall I see you at dinner, then?"

"Yes," he said, turning away. "Good-bye, Anne."

Anne waited until he was gone before collapsing on the settee. Her heart was racing, but her mind was oddly still as she sat staring blindly in front of her. She loved him, she realized, her entire body shaking as she faced the enormity of her feelings for Ruairdh. She'd been lying to herself to think it was only desire, or pity, or even something so halfhearted as friendship. She loved him. The admission brought a warm glow of happiness to her heart.

But as quickly as the joy came, it was tempered by a crushing sorrow. Ruairdh was dying. The knowledge brought a shaft of excruciating pain to her heart, and the agony of it was almost more than she could bear. The thought of losing Ruairdh just as she had found him seemed monstrous, and more monstrous still was knowing there was nothing she could do. Or was there? She froze, the tears on her cheeks drying as a thought suddenly struck her.

What on earth was the matter with her? she wondered angrily, leaping to her feet to pace the room. Why was she sitting here wringing her hands like some silly girl when she should be turning her mind to finding some way of saving Ruairdh? She had told him this was the age of reason, yet where was her reason? If Ruairdh had been suffering from some earthly affliction, wouldn't she do all within her power to cure him? Why should it be any different because the Shadowing was not of this world?

"You can't have him, do you hear me?" she charged, hurling her challenge at the unseen foe she sensed lurking in the darkness.

"He is mine, and I'll see you damned to the hell you belong in before I'll let you take him!"

Heavy silence greeted her words, but beneath the silence Anne thought she could hear mocking laughter and feel a gloating sense of triumph emanating from the stones. The evil was strong, that much she acknowledged, but it wasn't invincible. There was a way to defeat it; there had to be, and she would find it. But first there was a small matter to which she had to attend. Squaring her shoulders, she turned and walked out of the drawing room, her mind whirling with plans for the coming battle.

Ruairdh lay in bed, his jaw clenching as his aroused body burned for release. It was almost midnight, the time of night he usually went to Anne's bed, but after the day's events it was a pleasure he dared not take. The Shadowing was racing toward him like one of those great steam engines, and he was helpless to stop it. He still planned to marry Anne, but until then he was determined to keep his distance from her. Not just for his sake, he admitted, but for hers. He no longer trusted himself around her.

Until now the attacks had occurred only in the castle, and he'd felt it would be safe to go into the village. Everything had proceeded better than he'd dared hope, and then he'd felt Anne's panic and realized she was in some sort of danger. He'd thrust a handful of money into Leitch's hands and dashed off, a black mist of fury filling his mind. His heightened senses had not allowed him to see where she was, only to feel her emotions. It had been pure torture. He'd thought her to be at the parsonage and had gone there, intent upon destroying whoever had dared harm her. Discovering she hadn't yet arrived had the demons in him roaring, and he shuddered to think what might have happened if she hadn't arrived at that moment.

He was brooding over the possibilities when he heard the hidden door swing open, and he rolled over to stare as Anne glided silently into his room. She was wearing one of her prim robes of soft blue cotton, her glorious blond hair cascading about her shoulders in shimmering waves. When she saw him staring at her she set her burning taper on the wardrobe and cast him a languid glance.

"Good, you are awake," she said, removing her robe to reveal a nightgown of lace-trimmed lawn. "I feared you had fallen asleep."

She began walking toward him, and had almost reached his bed before Ruairdh managed to find his tongue.

"Anne, what are you doing here?" he demanded, trying to think beyond the wild desire that flared up to consume him. "Go back to your rooms before Mrs. Collier sees you!"

"Rot," she replied decisively, her gray eyes languorous in the flickering light of the candles. "We are to be married in two days' time, and I doubt if even Mrs. Collier would dare disapprove. Besides"—her lips curved into a siren's smile—"it's not as if I haven't shared your bed before now. What difference does it make?"

"More difference than you may suppose!" he snapped, clutching his bedclothes to his chest and feeling foolish. He made one last grab for sanity. "Anne, you hussy, you canna come in here!"

"I love you."

He felt as if the wooden canopy of his bed had just struck him on the head. He stared at her blankly.

"What?"

"I love you," she repeated, seeming oblivious to his stunned stare as she continued gliding toward his bed.

Her simple declaration shattered him, robbing him of the ability to think. "Anne, *annsachd*, you don't know what you're saying," he said, feeling as if his heart were breaking.

"Don't I?" She stopped beside his bed, holding his gaze. "I've thought about this a great deal, and I've decided I would never have given myself to you unless I loved you."

He wondered how many more shocks a poor man was expected to endure in one evening. "Anne—"

"Hush." She leaned down and brushed her finger over his lips. "You don't have to say anything," she whispered, sliding into bed with him. "Only know that

I love you." She kissed him softly. "I love you, Ruairdh MacCairn. I love you."

Ruairdh gathered Anne in his arms and pressed her to his heart. Tears burned his eyes and words of love burned his throat, but he choked both back with a strength born of desperation. Anne's love was a glorious miracle he'd never allowed himself to wish for, and he would carry the wonder of it with him to his death. He deftly tucked her beneath him, holding her head between his hands as he stared down into her eyes.

"*Mo cridhe*, my heart," he translated, his voice guttural with the force of his emotions. "*Mo ceile*, my wife." He kissed her softly and then drew back, his gaze holding hers. "The church will bind us in a few days' time, but I bind us now. With my body I thee worship, Anne MacCairn. For now, for always."

He made love to her fiercely, showing her with each caress, each kiss, the love he dared not offer her. His body became his words, and he offered it to her without reserve, for the first time holding nothing of himself back. She responded with the wild delight that had enchanted him from start, wrapping her legs about his hips as he moved purposefully over her.

"Ruairdh!" Her eyes were closed, her creamy cheeks washed with hectic color as she shuddered beneath him. "I love you!"

Now it was he who shuddered, clenching his teeth to hold back his own declaration. He slid into her welcoming warmth, his control dissolving when her sweet flesh clamped around his. He thrust into her greedily, losing himself as he brought them both to the edge of fulfillment and then beyond. When she cried out in completion his voice joined hers, his body shaking as he found his release inside of her.

He drifted in lazy contentment for long minutes, savoring the feel of her cuddled against his side. When he felt her stirring, he slid his hand into her tangled curls and ruffled them with tender affection.

"Well, *annsachd*," he teased, brushing a finger across her swollen lips, "you've had your wanton way with me. What now?"

Her arm tightened about his waist, and she pressed a light kiss to his sweat-dampened chest. "I want to know about the Shadowing," she said calmly, shocking him into silence.

"And if you're thinking of trying to intimidate me, or changing the subject, you may think again," she added, raising her head to send him a fierce scowl. "I love you, and I am to be your wife. I have a right to know."

The arguments he'd been about to utter died, and he stared at her in resigned acceptance. "What is it you wish to know?" he asked.

She moved closer until her breasts were pillowed on his chest. "To begin, why do you remain in the castle?" she asked, seeming oblivious of her nudity or the effect it was having upon him. "If it's so dangerous, why don't you leave? That should break the curse, shouldn't it?"

Her question quelled his ardor. "Aye, if it was the stones and the mortar that were damned," he muttered, feeling a grudging respect for her sharp intelligence. "But they are not; the men in my family are. I told you we have done all we could to fight this thing, and leaving the castle's been tried more times than I can tell you. It does no good. A MacCairn can be in India, and still he is taken. My great-grandfather went to America to avoid it, but in the end the Shadowing called him home to meet his fate."

She was silent for several seconds before speaking again. "How do you know so much about what was done and what was not?" she asked curiously. "Are there records?"

Ruairdh thought of the dozens of volumes lining the shelves of his study, and of the tales of horror they contained. "Aye," he said, frowning. "But they are private—for the laird's eyes only."

Her chin came up in defiance. "And I am soon to be the laird's wife, am I not?" she reminded him, her gray eyes challenging. "That gives me the right to examine them."

He nodded, reluctantly conceding the point. "What is it you hope to learn?" he asked, curious.

"I won't know until I have had a chance to study them."

Her honest reply soothed him more than an elaborate answer would have done. "It can be arranged, I suppose," he said slowly, and then frowned as a sudden thought occurred to him. "But mind you read them up here or in the study," he warned, glaring down at her. "I don't want you going into that hellish armory again."

She gave a brief nod. "As you wish," she said, and then paused, her brows gathering in thought.

"What else is it you wish, *leannan?*" he asked, reaching up to rub between her brows. "When you are thinking deeply about something, you get a line right here."

She made no attempt to deny his charge. "Do you

have any of this priest's belongings? A journal, perhaps, or a crucifix?"

Ruairdh drew back in surprise. "How am I to know?" he asked in bewilderment. "It was five hundred years ago, Anne. If he left anything behind him, 'tis certain to be dust by now. Why do you ask?" he added, giving her a wary look.

She laid her head on his shoulder. "I thought it might contain clues to the spell he cast, and how we might counter it. There must be something we can do. I did promise to fight for you, you know."

"I know," he replied, feeling his body stirring to life. He lifted her up, grinning at her as he slowly lowered her onto his straining erection. "Shall I thank you for it, *mo cridhe?*"

Her eyelashes fluttered shut. "If you insist," she murmured, sighing in pleasure as he began thrusting with slow deliberation.

"Oh, I do, sweetest. I do," he said, and proceeded to show her, making love to her again and again until they were both too exhausted to move.

It was only later, as he was drifting off to sleep, that he suddenly remembered the first time he had made love to her tonight. He'd been so aroused, so determined to share her pleasure, that he'd forgotten his usual caution. When he'd felt his completion approaching he'd kept making love to Anne, unable to leave the sweet haven of her body. He hadn't stopped in time.

"Ah, God!" The words of anguish were wrenched from him as the full magnitude of his actions struck him.

Anne jerked away at the sound of his voice.

"Ruairdh?" she asked, stirring drowsily. "What is it?"

He kissed her gently. "Nothing, love," he said. "Go back to sleep."

"All right." She cuddled closer. "Love you," she mumbled, already falling back to sleep.

Ruairdh lay beside her, staring up at the ceiling with burning eyes. What had he done? he wondered, his throat aching. God in heaven, what had he done?

In the two days leading up to her wedding, Anne was too busy to give Ruairdh's promise to show her the journals more than a passing thought. There was no time for a proper trousseau to be prepared, and after discussing the matter with Mrs. Doughal, Anne chose her best day gown for her wedding dress. The modest gown of dark blue sarcenet banded at the hem and full sleeves with black velvet braid was deemed appropriate for a small, intimate wedding, and she decided to wear it with the set of sapphires she had inherited from her mother.

In between her other duties and seeing her belongings moved into Ruairdh's suite, Anne also found herself besieged with another round of callers. Several of Mrs. Collier's annoying friends arrived, and Anne was forced to endure their company. They were full of questions and innuendoes, but when she failed to respond to either they finally gave up and took their leave. Nor were they the only guests to descend upon the castle. The day before the wedding Ruairdh's solicitor, Mr. Hughes, returned from London. She expected he would spend most of his time holed up with Ruairdh, and was surprised when he sought her out.

"I have several documents requiring your signature, if you do not mind," he said, blushing and avoiding her glance. "Would after dinner be convenient for you?"

"Of course, Mr. Hughes," she replied, wondering what on earth ailed the man. He'd always seemed shy and somewhat diffident in her company, but she couldn't recall anything she might have done to make him so uneasy.

"I should like to extend my best wishes to you and Mr. MacCairn," he continued, studiously avoiding her eyes. "I am pleased to see he is marrying a sensible lady like yourself. Given the circumstances, it is for the best, I am sure."

Ruairdh had told her the story he'd spun for the other man, and she nodded. "Yes," she agreed quietly, "it is."

Anne was still pondering his odd behavior when she encountered Ruairdh outside the drawing room. Seeing her distraction, he asked her what was troubling her, and she was curious enough to tell him. He bristled at once.

"The insolent puppy!" he said, his lips thinning in temper. "Has he presumed to insult you?"

"No, of course not!" she assured him, not wanting to place the timorous solicitor in danger. "Quite the opposite, in fact. He acted afraid of me. No," she corrected, frowning as she recalled the way the other man had stammered and squirmed, "he acted as if he was embarrassed to be with me." She bent a stern look on him as a sudden thought occurred to her. "You didn't threaten him, did you?"

"I did not," he denied, scowling indignantly. "I cannot think what might have come over the lad—" He broke off and started chuckling.

She frowned at him accusingly. "Why are you laughing?"

"No reason," he said, his green eyes dancing with rare mirth.

"Ruairdh . . ."

"I will tell you tomorrow night, love," he said, giving her hand a teasing kiss. "Better, I will show you. Now come." He tucked her hand into the crook of his arm and led her toward the dining room. "It will not do to keep our guest waiting."

Following dinner, Anne joined Ruairdh and Angley in Ruairdh's study. Mr. Hughes was waiting for them, a mountain of official-looking documents piled in front of him. Anne signed them, taking care to study each one first, as Mr. Hughes instructed. Most dealt with their marriage and the various settlements, but the last document awaiting her signature was a copy of Ruairdh's will, and after reading it she raised stunned eyes to meet Ruairdh's gaze.

"You have made me your principal heir?" she asked, horrified.

"Aye," he agreed. "Did I not say I would?"

Anne glanced back at the will, her breath catching at the amount set down in careful printing. "But it is so much," she whispered, raising a trembling hand to her throat.

"And the amount will nearly double once the castle sells," Mr. Hughes said, sounding pleased. "Which reminds me, should I arrange to have the monies transferred to London? You'll be wanting to move once the castle sells."

Anne's head whirled. She'd forgotten Ruairdh's plans to sell the castle. "Perhaps that won't be necessary," she said, casting Ruairdh a pleading look. "The money here should be more than enough to take care of the clan for many years to come."

"The decision has already been made," Ruairdh said, his voice cold. "Sign the papers, Anne. 'Tis late, and you'll be wanting to be fresh for tomorrow."

His harsh tones hurt, but Anne pushed the hurt aside. She'd hoped her declaration of love would close the distance between her and Ruairdh, but it would seem she'd been foolishly optimistic. She accepted the pen Mr. Hughes offered her and silently signed her name to the bottom of the will. When she was finished, she rose to her feet to take her leave.

"If you gentlemen will excuse me," she said, gathering her shawl about her. "Mr. Angley, Mr. Hughes." She nodded at each man, and then turned to Ruairdh. "Sir." She dipped him a polite curtsy, something she'd never done. "I will see you tomorrow."

If she'd hoped he would try to stop her, she was soon disappointed. He gave her an imperious glance, inclining his head with a mocking courtesy he hadn't shown her in several weeks. Humiliation burned her cheeks, and she walked out of the room with her head held high. Her pose of quiet dignity lasted until she was up in her own rooms and she was alone.

"Arrogant, overbearing tyrant!" she muttered, pacing across the elegant carpet. "Sending me to my room as if I were an errant child!" A sound at the door had her spinning around, spoiling for a fight. Jennie stood in the doorway, her eyes wide with distress.

"I—I am here to help you prepare for bed, miss," the pretty maid stammered, wringing her hands nervously. "If you aren't tired, I can come back later." She began backing from the room.

"No, Jennie, wait," Anne called out, embarrassed at having been found indulging in a rare fit of temper. "I am sorry," she apologized, and then because Jennie was still looking wary, she scraped up a rueful smile. "I fear I am just a trifle overwrought. Bridal jitters."

The maid's expression cleared at once. "Of course, miss," she said, bustling forward. "Any lady would be nervous the night before her wedding, I am sure." She tipped her head to one side and regarded Anne skeptically. "Shall I send for Mrs. Collier?" she asked. "She said she wanted to speak with you before you retired."

The idea of facing the older woman, who doubtlessly intended lecturing her on a wife's marital duties, had Anne suppressing a shudder. "Tell her I'm already asleep," she said with alacrity. "I'll speak with her in the morning."

Jennie's eyes twinkled in understanding. "Yes, miss."

With Jennie's cheerful assistance she was soon dressed in a nightgown and tucked between the sheets. Anne asked that a candle be left burning, using the fiction that she wished to read for a little while. In truth she wanted it in case Ruairdh decided to visit her via the hidden passage. Not that she thought he would. Since the night she had told him she loved him he hadn't come to her in the night, and she was too proud to go to him. She hoped one of them would have the common sense to put aside their pride; else it would make for a most interesting wedding night. She smiled at the thought, closing her eyes as she fell into a surprisingly easy sleep.

The morning of her wedding dawned cool and clear, and as befitted a bride, Anne took her breakfast in solitary splendor in the new rooms she would have as Ruairdh's wife. She was playing with her eggs and nervously dwelling on the coming ceremony when there was a tap at the door, and Mrs. Collier came bustling in.

"I've come to help you dress, my dear," she said, sweeping a critical glance over the plain wrapper Anne had donned. "It is almost time for the ceremony."

Anne glanced at the clock on the mantel. It was scarcely nine in the morning, and the wedding wouldn't take place until noon. "That is very kind of you, ma'am," she said, trying to think of some way of refusing the other woman's assistance without hurting her feelings. "But my maid is more than capable of—"

"It would be my honor," Mrs. Collier interrupted with an imperious look. "Also it will give me the chance to speak with you. I feel I would be remiss in my duties as your chaperon if I didn't discuss the duties that your husband will expect of you."

Having already anticipated this, Anne had her refusal prepared. "I understand, Mrs. Collier," she said, smiling politely, "and I can assure you such a talk is quite unnecessary. My mother spoke with me about such things prior to her death."

"Indeed?" Mrs. Collier's brows gathered in a frown.

"It was my understanding your mother died when you were quite young."

"I was eighteen," Anne said truthfully, "and Mother wanted to make certain I knew what to expect in the event I should ever marry." This was said less truthfully. Her mother had sickened and died without warning, but she liked to think that had she lived, her mother would have told her whatever she'd needed to know.

"I see." Mrs. Collier's lips thinned. "I am superfluous, it would seem. I shall just go and see to my packing; I will be returning to my brother's house after the ceremony. Good day, Miss Garthwicke, and pray accept my best wishes on your marriage. I am sure you will have need of them." She began backing out of the room.

Anne hesitated; she preferred that the other woman leave, but good breeding dictated she say something. She surrendered to the inevitable with a sigh.

"Thank you, Mrs. Collier," she said, forcing herself to smile. "And thank you for coming to the castle to act as my chaperon. It couldn't have been easy for you to so disrupt your life."

Mrs. Collier looked surprised and then pleased. "It was rather a trial," she acknowledged, dipping her head. "But I am sure I know my Christian duty as well as the next woman."

"It was very good of you," Anne said, hoping to flatter the woman on her way. "You must come back for tea after I am married."

"I should be delighted." Mrs. Collier smiled. "Although I must confess I shall be quite relieved that I shan't be required to spend another night here. This is a dark and terrible place, and if I weren't a rational, God-fearing woman, I would swear it was haunted." And then she flushed, as if realizing she'd said too much.

"If you are settled, then, I will just be going," she said, backing again toward the door. "Good-bye, Miss Garthwicke, and may God help you." She fumbled open the door and then turned and fled, leaving Anne staring after her in uneasy astonishment.

Chapter Fifteen

It was his wedding night. Ruairdh stood in the center of Anne's bedroom, nervous as an untried lad waiting to have his first woman. More nervous, he admitted, taking a sip of champagne. He'd been seventeen his first time, and pathetically eager to taste the forbidden fruit of lovemaking. He was a man now: a man who stood to lose a great deal more than his innocence. His soul he knew to be already forfeit, and now it seemed his heart was lost as well.

He took another sip, his body hardening at the memory of Anne standing proudly at his side as she took the vows irrevocably binding her to him. He'd heard the minister's words, made the expected responses, but even as he was bowing his head in benediction he was feeling like the greatest sinner in the kingdom. Only a man truly damned would have stood before God and told such foul lies. How could he have promised to honor and cherish Anne, he wondered bitterly, when in a matter of weeks he would be leaving her as a widow?

"Ruairdh?" Anne's voice sounded from the door leading to the dressing room, and he turned, the breath lodging in his throat at the picture she made. She stood framed by candlelight in the doorway, her slender body draped in the shimmer of silver satin. He set his glass down and held out his hand.

"*A gradidh*, come to me," he murmured, his heart pounding with the rise of passion as he watched her walking slowly toward him.

"That is a new word," she observed, smiling as she slipped into his arms. "I shall have to write it down. What does it mean?"

He willingly translated. "My darling," he murmured, kissing the soft curve of her shoulder.

"And *leannan?*" She tilted her head back with a sigh.

"Much the same," he replied, opening his lips to tease her soft flesh with the tip of his tongue. "Sweetest. And you are sweet, my love. Like a fresh peach, soft and full of the sweetest juice. I adore tasting you." He playfully nipped her skin.

"What of *annsachd?*" Her hands slipped beneath the lapels of his velvet robe to slide down the plane of his stomach.

"Beloved," he said, then groaned when her fingers closed around his straining erection. "If it's a lesson in Gaelic you're after, *ceile*," he warned, passion replacing his earlier desolation, "you're going about it the wrong way."

Her lips curved in wicked pleasure. "Indeed?" she asked, her fingers trailing lightly over the sensitive head. "But there are several more words I should like to learn."

"Later," he promised, stepping back from her and stripping off his robe. "But if it's knowledge you seek, I will be happy to oblige you." He swept her up in his arms and carried her to the waiting bed.

"I cannot believe you asked Mr. Hughes to bring you those awful things," Anne said a long time later, covering her cheeks with her hands. "No wonder the poor man wouldn't look at me. How *I* shall look at him again, I am sure I will never know."

Ruairdh gave a satisfied chuckle. "I shouldn't let it trouble you," he said, rubbing her shoulder companionably. "You're the lady of the castle now, remember? It is for him to worry what you think of him, rather than the other way about."

"Perhaps." She sighed, snuggling back against his chest. "But I don't see why we need to use those things. We're married now. What does it matter if I am with child or not?"

Ruairdh froze, his lazy contentment vanishing at her grumbled question. "I am the last MacCairn," he reminded her, a chill of unease washing over him. "There can be no children. Ever. You agreed to that, Anne."

She moved away from him. "I know I did," she said quietly, wrapping the bedclothes about her body, as if suddenly aware of her nudity. "I beg your pardon; I wasn't thinking."

Ruairdh felt her withdrawal, and it enraged him. He

pulled her back into his arms, his hands gripping her shoulders. "Do you think I don't want a child?" he demanded, giving her a gentle shake. "A son? God—" He broke off, fighting tears as he faced a grief so deep, so painful, he seldom allowed himself to think of it. He drew a deep breath and gazed down into her eyes.

"If I were a man like any other man, I would give my life and more for a child," he said in a raw voice. "But how can I wish my fate upon an innocent babe?"

Tears filled her eyes as she gazed up at him. "But what if there is a child already?" she asked, raising a trembling hand to his cheek. "We've made love many times before, and this is the first time you used those sheaths. What if—"

"The other times I took care not to spill my seed in you," he said, uncertain whether he was reassuring her or himself. "Except for that one time, and I can only pray that one mistake will not doom us all."

She flinched, but did not glance away. "Doom us?" she repeated. "Would it really be so terrible as that?"

"It would be worse than hell," he answered bluntly. "You cannot know, Anne—"

"No," she interrupted, and he sensed the sudden heat of her temper. "I cannot know, because every time I have asked about this curse you have refused to tell me more than the barest of facts!

"Tell me, Ruairdh!" she demanded, her eyes silver with fury. "Explain it to me so that I will know the truth once and for all."

His own temper flashed to life. "You want to know the truth?"

"I need to know the truth," she corrected.

"As you wish." He tossed back the bedclothes and rose from the bed, pausing to snatch up his robe before stalking from the room. He returned fifteen minutes later, nursing a stubbed toe, his arms filled with leather-bound books.

"Here." He dumped them on the bed beside her. "The journals of my family. Study them as I have studied them, and then you'll understand why there will be none of my blood to follow me. Read them, Anne, and believe."

She glanced at him and then down at the volumes, her hands trembling as she picked one up. Unable to remain, he turned and walked to the door separating their rooms. He sent her an anguished glance over his shoulder.

"I should have cut my own throat before touching you," he said wearily, the full weight of his sins pressing down upon him. "I am sorry, *annsachd.* Forgive me." And he walked from the room, closing the door behind him with quiet finality.

Anne spent her wedding night not as a bride but as a scholar, poring over the books Ruairdh had brought her. At first she'd been unable to read them, her heart breaking at seeing the grim facts set down in such cold-blooded detail. Studying them became a lesson in horror, and knowing they were true made what she was reading that much more terrifying. But with so much at stake she refused to give in to weakness, and she'd called upon the skills she had learned working with her father as she forced herself to continue.

Since the journals spanned several generations, the

first thing she did was to arrange them in proper order. The earliest was written during the time of the Tudors, while the most recent had been written by Ruairdh's grandfather, William MacCairn. Each contained a thorough record of the Shadowing, from the onset of the first symptoms to the final ravings as the writer descended into madness. At first the different authors seemed oddly detached, describing the impossible in a cool, arrogant manner that reminded her of Ruairdh. But as the Shadowing took hold the notations became erratic, and cool discourse gave way to the furious ramblings of a lunatic.

Even the handwriting changed, Anne realized, her weariness forgotten as she lost herself in the thrill of discovery. Sometimes it improved, sometimes it grew worse, but it always changed, as did the language. The journals usually began in rough English interspersed with a few phrases in Gaelic and French, but toward the end they were written almost entirely in Latin. That must surely mean something, she decided, rubbing her burning eyes. The question was, what? Too exhausted to pursue the matter any further, she carefully marked her place in the last journal and tumbled into a deep and dreamless sleep.

She awoke several hours later, tired, but eager to get back to her reading. She rang for Jennie, enduring the maid's shy teasing as the younger woman helped her bathe and dress for the day. She also didn't seem in the least surprised by Anne's request to have breakfast served in her room, and the door had scarcely closed behind the maid before Anne was once more hard at work.

Retrieving the Latin dictionary her father had sometimes used, she began laboriously translating the Latin passages in each journal. It was difficult to be certain, because some of the ink had faded or flaked away from age, but it soon became apparent that in the final stages of the Shadowing, whoever wrote the entries became convinced he was the witch who originally cast the spell. There were several references to Satan, and even more to "the prize," the words filled with such a vile sense of gloating and evil, it made her feel unclean to read them.

More puzzling was one entry talking about the "anchor" and the fact that it had almost been lost. It was apparently vital to the spell, and Anne began to look for more references to it. As she searched, she noticed that the words *dog* and *lackey* kept appearing. She followed this route, her heart leaping into her throat when she finished translating a particular passage found in one of the earlier journals.

The dog follows the mighty master, thinking himself the servant of God. He will oppose the cursed and aid in his destruction, mouthing the words of the just even as he serves the unjust.

She set the book down, thinking immediately of Mr. Beechton. Was it possible the magistrate was being driven by this thing? she wondered, her brows gathering in thought. If so, it would explain his deep enmity toward Ruairdh. It also meant the ghost of the witch was even more powerful and therefore more dangerous than she had first supposed. Not a comforting thought, she decided, and picked up the diary once more.

She continued reading and making notes, filling several pages with her observations. One thing that struck her was that although it was obvious the journals had been written many centuries apart, the entries written in Latin shared several similar characteristics. The way the words were formed, the spelling, even the tone of what was written were so alike, it was almost as if the same hand had written them. But that was impossible, of course. Then she noticed something else, something that had her temper stirring to dangerous life. She checked her notes again to make certain she wasn't mistaken, and then she rang for her maid.

"Where is Mr. MacCairn?" she asked the moment Jennie stepped into the room.

"In his study, Mrs. MacCairn," Jennie replied. If she was surprised so new a bride had no idea of where her groom might be, she was too well trained to show it. "He's only just finished his breakfast after riding all morning. Would you like me to bring him a note, ma'am?"

Anne's lips thinned in anger. "There's no need," she said. "I will deliver the message to the laird myself."

Ruairdh had ridden out early in the morning, having spent a sleepless night tossing in torment. After a bruising ride across the countryside that left both him and his mount sweating and exhausted, he had turned and made his reluctant way back to the castle. He knew from questioning his staff that Anne had already risen and was taking breakfast in her room, and he knew he would have to face her sooner or later. She was certain to be upset, and doubtless full of dozens of questions.

He only hoped he could find the answers she sought without giving away more than he dared.

After a hurried breakfast he had retreated to his study to begin the day's work, and had no sooner settled behind his desk than there was a tap on his door, and Anne entered.

"Good morning, *leannan*," she said, walking boldly up to him to give him a soft kiss on his cheek.

"*Annsachd*," he returned, his expression giving no indication whether he was pleased or annoyed by her use of his language. "You didn't sleep well last night," he said, his eyes narrowing as he watched her settle in one of the chairs facing his desk. "I want you to rest this afternoon. I'll not have you making yourself ill."

"You didn't sleep well last night either, from the looks of you," she said, meeting his gaze with a raised eyebrow. "Does this mean you shall seek your bed as well?"

He glowered at her but said nothing, not about to get into a wrangle with her. What was she up to? he wondered, and leaned back in his chair to find out.

"I've finished the journals," she began, pulling a list from her pocket. "And there are several questions I should like to ask."

"What sort of questions?" he asked, his manner wary.

"The journals indicate the lairds all died at various ages," she said, peering at him over the top of the list. "Why is that?"

He gave an uncomfortable shrug. "Who is to say?" he asked, crossing one booted foot over the other. "Perhaps it has to do with when they were first taken. Some succumb to the Shadowing in their youth, others as grown men, although most are taken before their fortieth year." He shifted his gaze to meet hers. "I am thirty-five."

She gave a sudden start and then glanced back at her list. "Is this a physical disease? That is, does it kill?"

There was another silence as Ruairdh considered his reply. "Not in the way you mean, as a fever would kill," he said, choosing his words cautiously. "But it leaves us dead all the same."

"Then," she pressed, folding her hands on her lap and regarding him calmly, "having succumbed to this disease, a person doesn't immediately sicken and die? He can expect to live for many more years to come?"

"Aye," he conceded, feeling he was being led but not quite sure how or in what direction. "I suppose it is so."

"If that is so, why did you tell me that you are dying?" she asked, pouncing on him so quickly, he wasn't even aware of the ambush. "Why do you speak as if you are? If this Shadowing doesn't kill, shouldn't you have many more years of life ahead of you?"

"Life?" He gave a painful roar, his eyes flashing as he leaped to his feet. "You call it life to be chained to a wall, month after month, year after year, living in your own filth and waste like a mad dog? Is that what you call life?"

"But it doesn't have to be like that!" she cried. "I've read the journals and studied the symptoms. You're at the beginning of the process; you're still in control, and there's nothing to indicate you can't go on like this for a very long time."

"For how long?" he demanded, his hands clutching the front of the desk as he leaned toward her.

"I don't know!" she admitted, tears shimmering in her eyes. "No one does. But there has to be an answer, a way to defeat this thing; I know there is. I only need a little time to find it; that's all. A little time."

He studied her for several seconds and opened the desk drawer. He took the gun out, studying it for several seconds before extending his hand. "This is my answer," he said, opening his hand and showing Anne the pistol lying in his palm. "When the time comes, when I can no longer fight the Shadowing, I will end this curse. I will end it my way and in my time, as it should have been ended years ago." He placed the pistol back in his drawer and quietly locked it, slipping the key into the pocket of his jacket.

Anne stared at him in sickened realization. "You mean to commit suicide?" she asked, looking so stunned he feared she would faint.

"Some would call it that, aye," he admitted, his manner coldly defiant. "But as my soul is already damned, I hardly see that it matters. I've only waited this long because I wanted to make certain the clan would survive my death. The lairds might be no more, but I'll not let the MacCairns fade away as so many other clans have since Culloden." His lips twisted in a bitter smile. " 'Tis a small victory, I grant you, but 'tis a victory nonetheless."

She stared at him, so pale her silvery gray eyes looked almost black. "When?" She forced the word out.

He wouldn't meet her eyes. "Soon," he said quietly. "Very soon."

He expected pity, steeled himself for tears; the last

thing he expected was temper, liberally laced with contempt.

"I see. You're giving up, then."

His head snapped up at that. "What?"

"You are giving up," she repeated, her manner dispassionate as she met his gaze. "Surrendering the castle without so much as attempting to mount a defense. If the rest of your clan gave in so easily, I count it a wonder you have managed to survive until now."

Ruairdh shook his head, wondering if his hearing had failed him. "You are accusing me of cowardice?" he demanded, his voice shaking with fury. "You dare?"

"I dare because it is true," she shot back, not seeming in the least cowed by his temper. "You don't want to fight this thing; you'd rather take your own life than face it. What is that if not cowardice?"

Ruairdh was torn between raw fury and a burning sense of betrayal. "Damn you," he said, pain adding fuel to his anger. "Damn you, Anne, you cannot know—"

"So you keep saying," she interrupted, still the picture of cool control, "but the fact is, I now know a great deal. I know this thing has its limits, that it must have human confederates to aid it. I've no proof, but I suspect Mr. Beechton may be just such a confederate. That is why he was so opposed to you, and why he did everything within his power to frighten me away."

"He tried to frighten you?" Ruairdh was momentarily sidetracked.

"Of course." She sniffed, giving him a superior look. "It didn't work. *I* do not frighten so easily."

His brows lowered in a scowl. "Anne, I am warning you—"

"I also know the answer lies in those books," she continued as if he hadn't spoken. "We can look for the answer together, or I can look on my own, but either way I am determined to find what I seek. He shan't have you, Ruairdh. I won't allow it."

Ruairdh couldn't have been more stunned if she'd gutted him with that sword she was so fond of. In one breath she scolded him for being a coward; in the next she announced her intention to fight the forces of hell for him. Was it any wonder that he loved her? he thought, gazing at her in sheer astonishment.

"Well?" She was regarding him imperiously, her arms folded across her chest and her chin set at a pugnacious angle. "What is your answer? Are we going to fight together, or are we not?"

A dozen different responses occurred to Ruairdh, but he discarded them all. He rose from behind the desk and walked to where she was sitting, scooping her up in his arms and kissing her with all the love and passion he had kept hoarded in his heart.

"We fight, *mo ceile*," he said, grinning down at her. "We fight. But first there is something I must tell you." He smoothed an errant strand of hair back behind her ear and looked into her gray eyes. "I love you." He held his breath, waiting for her response and feeling humbled and exulted at finally having the courage to say the words aloud.

She wrapped her arms around his neck, smiling up at him smugly.

"I know," she said, returning his kiss with considerable warmth. "And it's a good thing, too. I was going to box your ears if you did not tell me. Tell me again."

Ruairdh threw back his head and roared with laughter. "I will, my demanding tyrant. In bed," he said, carrying her out of the study and past the gaping servants.

Over the next few weeks Anne spent every moment she could spare examining the journals. She was a bit dismayed to discover that there were at least a dozen other journals in addition to the ones Ruairdh had first brought her, but she quickly discovered them to be a treasure trove of information. Not every laird had kept a diary, but those who had provided her with something: sometimes a single clue, sometimes more, and with each passing day she felt she was drawing closer and closer to the answer she was so desperate to find.

All was not smooth, of course. There were two episodes when the Shadowing overtook Ruairdh, but he was always able to fight his way back. She knew these episodes frightened him as much as they frightened her, but she refused to let either of them grow discouraged. This terrible curse had taken enough of the MacCairns, she decided stubbornly; she would not let it take Ruairdh as well. She used both those incidents as an opportunity to learn even more of the Shadowing, writing down her observations and filing them carefully away with her other notes.

Three weeks after their marriage she was going over the journals again, this time using one of the magnifying glasses she and her father had used for authenticating an item's age. She was examining the handwriting toward the end of the journals, verifying with scientific calm what she had already begun to suspect with mounting disbelief. The writings in each entry didn't just appear to be identical; they were identical. The same hand had written them almost five centuries apart.

She set the magnifying glass down carefully, her hands shaking as a wave of sickening fear washed over her. The journals weren't the only things she'd studied in the past few weeks. The castle's library was filled with every manner of book on witchcraft and black magic, as earlier MacCairns had evidently sought the same answers for which she was now searching. She'd read several, and while most of what they contained could be discounted as superstitious nonsense, there was one word that had occurred over and over again. A word she had dismissed as being more foolishness: *possession.*

"Excuse me, *baintghearnas.*" The gruff voice had Anne leaping to her feet, a startled gasp tearing from her lips as she scattered papers about her like so many snowflakes. She whirled around to find Angley standing in the doorway.

"Oh, Angley, you frightened me," she said, laying a trembling hand over her wildly thudding heart.

"Ye didna do my own heart a service, mistress," the steward returned sourly, walking in the room and setting several pieces of mail on the desk. "The post has come, and the laird has asked that I bring it to you. He also asked that I give you this," he added, holding up a thick envelope. " 'Tis to that solicitor of his in London. He wants you to glance over it before sending it on."

"I'll do that, Angley; thank you," Anne said, feeling

more than slightly foolish about her earlier behavior. "And I am sorry if I frightened you. As I said, you startled me."

The elderly steward's response was a sniff. "I'm no' so thin-blooded as a *Sasunnach*, to quiver and cry at so small a thing as a lady's shrieks," he informed her with tart pride.

"Are you no' going to write that down in the small book you carry with you?" he added, when she failed to respond to his teasing. "I'd be happy to tell you its meaning."

She couldn't help but smile. "As it happens, I am already acquainted with its meaning," she said, feeling a surprising affection for the irascible man. "And I take leave to remind you that your mistress is as *Sasunnach* as they come. Mind that you remember that in the time to come, you disagreeable old Scot."

To her relief he took her words in the fond spirit in which they were intended, shooting off a string of Gaelic insults before walking away with a delighted chuckle.

After he'd gone she glanced through the mail, dismissing most of it as unimportant, before picking up the letter Ruairdh had written for Mr. Hughes. She knew he was sending the solicitor some changes to his will, and was frowning over the words when she felt a chill of recognition. She stared down at the writing, wanting to deny it, but knowing she could not. She had been studying that careful penmanship for days; she knew every loop, every firm downstroke of the pen, as well as she knew her own handwriting. It wasn't identical, thank God, but it was written by the same hand:

the hand of a priest who'd been burned as a witch five hundred years ago.

She heard the door open behind her, and thinking it was Angley returning to tease her, she paid it no mind. Then she heard the soft laughter, and turned to find Ruairdh standing in the doorway.

"So, little whore," he said smoothly, his eyes dark with malicious amusement. "You think you have won, do you?"

Although the man walking toward her with the odd, shuffling gait she had come to fear had Ruairdh's face and wore Ruairdh's clothes, Anne knew it wasn't Ruairdh she was facing. She allowed herself to absorb the horror of that before meeting the creature's malevolent gaze. "I think given time, I shall," she said, beating back her fear with measured calm.

He smiled, and it was ghastly to see the lips she loved, the lips that had loved her a hundred times and in a dozen different ways, curving in that sadistic sneer. "Then you are mistaken. I have spent a dozen lifetimes planning, waiting for this moment, and I will not be denied. The prize is nearly mine, English bitch, and you will hand it to me."

"And if I refuse?" she asked, ignoring her own terror in her determination to learn everything she could of the creature inhabiting Ruairdh's body. "What can you do about it? Have Mr. Beechton arrest me?"

Ruairdh's body gave a convulsive jerk. "Clever bitch, aren't you?" the creature said, his words slurring. "But as it happens, I've no need of that useless fool. You will give me what I want, because you'll have no choice. Remember what I told you, whore of MacCairn: love defeats life. Tell your lover that, and tell him this as well," and without warning he grabbed Anne, his icy hands tearing at her clothes.

Fighting him was easy, because she knew that deep inside Ruairdh was fighting his own battle as well. His hands were rough, brutal, and she could hear the sound of ripping cloth as she fought her way out of his foul embrace. She tore free, prepared to flee if necessary, but already she could see the darkness receding from Ruairdh's eyes. He shook his head, staggering slightly, and she stepped forward to catch him by his shoulders and help ease him to the ground.

"Anne?" He gazed up at her in sleepy puzzlement. "What is wrong?"

"Ruairdh?" She ran her hands over his chest and his face, checking him for any sign of injury. "Are you all right? Did he hurt you?"

"Who, *annsachd?*" He sounded more confused than usual, his voice thick and the words uncertain. "Has who hurt me?"

"The priest," Anne said, too upset to measure her words. "He was just here."

Ruairdh pulled back, and she could see the moment he was himself again. "What? The ghost, do you mean?" he demanded, pulling her close to him, and protecting her with the shield of his body.

"No, the priest. He was here, in you. He was you, or rather, you were him," Anne said, knowing she was babbling but helpless to stop. "Ruairdh, that's what the Shadowing is. Not madness, but something worse, something far worse. The Shadowing is possession."

"What are you rambling on about?" Ruairdh gazed

down at her in genuine alarm. "Anne, you're not making any sense!"

"Yes, I am," she said, wanting to laugh and cry all at the same time, because she had solved the mystery at last. "I am making perfect sense. I don't know how or why, but the priest's spirit has somehow found a way to exist beyond death. It is able to come into your body and slowly force your spirit out. Your own soul naturally fights, and that is what causes the symptoms of madness. It is the struggle of your will against his. Do you see?" She stared at him, pleading for him to understand.

"Aye," he said slowly, "I can see it, and as you say, it makes sense. Perhaps that is why sometimes I can fight him and sometimes I cannot, why sometimes I am not conscious of my actions during the Shadowing and other times I remember. It is because he is weaker at such times, but I still do not see why—Mother of God!" He broke off, staring at her in horror. "Anne! What has happened to you?"

"What?" Confused, Anne glanced down at herself, blushing when she saw the ruin of her bodice. The neat buttons had been ripped apart and the neckline gaped open, revealing a trio of bright red marks across the swell of her breasts.

"I did that?" he demanded, his voice shaking as he reached out and stroked a trembling finger above one of the angry scratches. "I hurt you?"

"No!" she cried, sickened that he could think that of himself. "No, it wasn't you! It was him, Ruairdh."

Ruairdh ignored her, his expression filled with self-loathing and fury. "I laid hands on you?"

"Ruairdh, no!" she said, cupping his face between her palms. "Listen to me," she said, and gave him a tiny shake to emphasize her words. "Listen," she repeated, her voice slow and deliberate. "It wasn't you, Ruairdh. It was him."

Ruairdh stared at her through cold, unreadable eyes. "Did he touch you?"

Anne took his meaning, and was relieved to assure him on this point. "No," she said quietly. "He only wanted to hurt you through me. Don't let him, Ruairdh."

"God!" The word was torn from his soul, and he rose to his feet and walked across to his desk. He stood behind it for several seconds, looking so shattered it broke her heart to watch him. She was trying to think of something to say to ease his pain, when his gaze met hers.

"Anne, look at me," he said, his voice lacking its usual power. "Sometimes when the Shadowing is upon me I can see what is happening, and God help me, I can remember every hellish moment of it. But other times I've no memory, no knowledge of what happened, and those times are coming faster, and more often. It is winning, Anne, and that is why I want you to promise me something," he said, his expression solemn as he studied her. "I want your word, right now, that you will do as I ask. Promise me that."

"Ruairdh—"

"Your word, Anne," he interrupted. "Please. This is the last thing I shall ever ask of you."

When he put it like that, there was no way she could

refuse. "I promise," she said, wiping tears from her cheeks.

He took the gun out of his desk and held it out to her. "Take this," he ordered. "Carry it with you always. If the time comes when I try to hurt you and I cannot stop myself, I want you to use this. I want you to stop me."

Anne stared at him in sick understanding as she realized what he was really asking. "No, no, Ruairdh," she pleaded, her legs trembling beneath her. "Please don't ask this of me! I love you!"

"And I love you, my heart," he replied, his anguish evident. "That is why I must ask what I do. I cannot hurt you, Anne; I won't. If you don't keep your promise to me, then you leave me no choice. I will take the gun and do what must be done myself—now, this very night. I'll protect you, Anne, even if it means my life."

Beneath the pain and the terror, resentment stirred inside Anne. "And that is the choice you are giving me?" she cried, furious he could ask such a thing of her. "I can lose you tonight or kill you later? What sort of choice is that for me?"

It was the tears she saw in his eyes that killed her temper before it could ever fully come to life. "The only one I can give you, my love. Now you see why I should have walked away from you," he added, his lips trembling in a bitter smile.

Anne stared at the gun in revulsion. "Ruairdh, I don't know if I can do what you want. I love you so much, I would rather die than—"

"No!" he shouted, and hurried around the desk to her. "No, if you love me, you will live! Promise me that, Anne!" he begged, staring down into her eyes with a wild desperation that surpassed anything she had ever known. "Promise me that you will embrace life so my soul can know some measure of peace. Don't deny me that if you love me, Anne. I beg of you."

Anne could only stare at him, trapped by her love and the love he professed for her. There was nothing she could do, nothing she could say. Broken by grief and by love, she silently took the gun from him, tears blinding her as she walked away from him.

The next week passed in agonizing slowness for Anne. She continued her research, driven by the knowledge that she wasn't fighting only the vicious spirit of the priest, but the promise Ruairdh had wrenched from her as well. The incidents of the Shadowing grew more frequent, and she and Ruairdh withdrew into their suite of rooms, allowing only Angley to come near them. She seldom slept, fearing Ruairdh would be taken while she was asleep, and that she would awaken to find herself with no choice but to carry out her promise to him.

Ruairdh helped her as much as he could, but she sensed he was doing so only to appease her. In his hollow green eyes she could see he had already accepted his death, and that he was waiting for it with a grim courage she couldn't begin to fathom. The books yielded more information on the anchor, and she now realized it was the key to breaking the curse. The anchor was somehow what enabled the priest to move between the realm of the dead and that of the living. If she found it and destroyed it, then she could destroy his means of power. The only problem was that she had no idea where to search for it, or even what it could be. The castle was so huge it would take months, even years to search, and she was coming to the realization that they didn't have that much time left.

It was almost dawn before she went to bed, and later than that when she finally managed to fall into a fitful sleep. In her dream she could see her father, sitting at his worktable and working over something. She kept trying to see what it was but he kept shooing her away, refusing to show her until she was maddened with curiosity. She pleaded with him as she would never have done in real life, and finally he relented, stepping back to give her an unobstructed view of the sword lying on the worktable. It was the sword that she had tried identifying, and in the morning sun the engraved figures seemed to come to life, shining so brightly it all but blinded her. *The sword . . .*

"The sword!" She sat up with a sharp cry, her hair tumbling about her shoulders. She pushed it back impatiently, her heart racing with excitement as she leaped from the bed.

"Of course!" she cried, furious with herself for being so blind. She should have known at once that it was involved! Hadn't Ruairdh's touching it triggered in him one of the worst episodes she had witnessed? Castigating herself for being every kind of fool, she hurried over to the wardrobe, where she had hidden the weapon away after seeing the effect it had had on Ruairdh. She dragged it out and then quickly changed, so excited she didn't bother waiting for Jennie to come to her. She was glad Ruairdh had risen early, so she could avoid his questions.

Dressing by herself took a great deal longer than she would have liked, and she managed it only after deciding to dispense with her corset. While she pinned up her hair, her mind raced with the problem of what she should do with the sword. It had to be destroyed—that much was a certainty—but precisely how did one destroy over a yard of finely tempered steel? She could toss it over the balustrade, she supposed, or throw it into the loch, like Excalibur, but neither of those options held enough certainty for her. She wanted it completely destroyed; it was the only way Ruairdh would be safe.

After careful consideration she decided to take it to Angley, certain the clever Scot would devise some way of disposing of the wretched thing once and for all. Pleased with her plan she hurried down the hall, doing her best to keep the sword hidden from any curious eyes. She was so intent on what she was doing that she paid no attention to where she was going, and was almost knocked off her feet when she ran full-tilt into Ruairdh.

"Be careful, *annsachd*, I almost knocked you down," he scolded gently, then tilted his head to one side as he studied her. "What have you there?"

"Nothing," she replied, keeping the sword tucked behind her skirts. "I just need to speak with Angley for a moment. If you will excuse me, I—"

"No." He reached easily around her. "What is it you are hiding? A sword? You need to have a care; it is sharp and you will hurt yourself. Give it to me."

"Ruairdh, no!" she cried, desperately wrestling with him. "Don't touch it!"

But it was already too late; his fingers closed about the sword's hilt, and almost at once his eyes darkened, and the waves of cold wafting from him had her stumbling back in revulsion. She stared at him, unable to believe how quickly he had been overtaken by the Shadowing. It was a testament to just how powerful the sword was. Hiding her deepest fear, she forced herself to meet his gaze.

"Not so clever as you thought, eh, whore?" he jeered, swinging the sword in the manner of one who had been well trained in its use.

Anne began backing toward the study, praying she could make it inside so she could lock the door. "I'm not afraid of you," she lied, inching away. "Ruairdh won't let you harm me."

His dark eyes mocked her. "Ruairdh's not here, *Sasunnach*," he said, advancing toward her. "He is gone. I rule now. I rule as I was meant to rule until they handed me over to the witch-hunters.

"Five hundred years," he said, his hand clenching around the sword's hilt. "Five hundred! But it was worth it, by Satan's mighty power; it was worth it in the end. The prize is mine, just as I said it would be."

Anne could feel the door handle beneath her fingers. "I'll stop you," she vowed, shoving the door open. "I'll find some way of stopping you. I promise it!" And then she fell into the room, slamming the door shut behind her.

He swung it open with such force he knocked her almost into the middle of the floor. "You'll stop me?" He laughed, gloating as she scrambled to her feet. "A mere woman?" He smiled with such icy menace she almost swooned. "You couldn't even save your father, you pathetic creature."

"My father?" Anne's fear was replaced by shock.

"Of course." He smiled derisively. "The old fool. He gazed but once upon me and became so a'feared I didn't even have to touch him. He tumbled down those stairs all on his own, and would have made a fine bit of trouble for the laird had you not stepped in to absolve him of all blame. You have been a nuisance ever since. It will be a pleasure taking your life." He twirled the sword again, this time wrapping both hands around the hilt. An evil grin twisted his features. "Thank you for the sword, my sweet," he said. "It will make this so much easier."

Anne leaped away from him as the blade of the sword whistled over her head. She tried to run, but he blocked every avenue of escape, slashing with the deadly weapon until she had no choice but to retreat against the wall. She could feel the cold stones at her back, and knew there was nowhere else to hide. Death wearing her husband's face advanced on her, and her hands fumbled as she drew out the gun Ruairdh had given her and trained it on him.

"Stand back!" she warned, aiming the pistol at his chest. "Your body is mortal. If I kill it, what will you have gained?"

"Everything." He laughed, continuing toward her. "Everything."

His answer puzzled her, but when she saw him raising the sword high above his head to deliver the killing blow, she squeezed her eyes shut. "Ruairdh, I am sorry," she whispered in agony, and slowly began to pull the trigger.

Love shall defeat life.

The words echoed in Anne's head and she paused, wondering what they meant. She cautiously opened one eye, watching the creature standing in front of her. He was grinning, his dark eyes shining not with fear or anger, but with triumph. She lowered the gun to her side.

"You coward," she said, facing him coolly. "I won't do your killing for you. If you want Ruairdh dead, then you kill him."

The creature's face assumed such a look of comic outrage that Anne almost laughed. "What?" he sputtered, clearly stunned. "Are ye daft, *bean-cuthaich?* Kill me! Kill me or, by Satan, I shall kill you!" He slashed the sword inches above her head.

"No!" Anne stood her ground, fighting for Ruairdh's soul as well as her own life.

"Then so be it." He raised the sword again, and in his eyes Anne saw her death. "Die, whore. Dic."

She looked into the demon's eyes. "I love you, Ruairdh. I always shall."

He took another step forward; then he started swaying, his entire body quivering as if in a fever. "No," he said, shaking his head from side to side. "No!" he repeated, roaring out in rage, "by Almighty God, no!" And he whirled, slamming the sword into the wall, snapping the blade in half, just above the foible, and shattering the weapon into pieces. Ruairdh collapsed onto the floor beside it.

At once a great roar of wind filled the study, tearing

the drapes from the windows and sending the tapestries flying. A terrible scream echoed through the room and out into the hall, and the smell of burning flesh filled the air with its putrid stench. The scream rose to an unholy wail and then stopped, and blessed silence filled the room.

Anne raced to where Ruairdh was doubled over on the floor, holding his arm against himself.

"Ruairdh!" She knelt at his side, trying to see his face. "Darling, are you all right?"

"My arm," he said at last, his breath hissing though clenched teeth. "I think I broke my damned arm." He cautiously made a fist, cursing violently at the pain. Finally he turned his head, his eyes brilliant green in his ashen face.

"Anne?"

"What there is left of me," she said, summoning up a smile for his benefit. "You just tried to cut my head off, you know."

He grew even more ashen, grabbing her and pulling her against him. "Anne! God, are you hurt?" he demanded.

"No, no, I am fine." She laughed, pulling back to gaze at him. "How are you? That's what's important. How do you feel?"

He was silent for several moments as he considered her question. "Empty," he said cautiously, testing the word. "Free." He gave her a stunned look as realization set in. "It's gone, Anne. The Shadowing. It's gone."

"Yes, I know, the sword—"

"It's gone!" He all but screamed the words, holding her in his arms as he leaped to his feet to whirl her around in a giddy circle. "Praise God, it is gone!"

"Be careful of your arm!" She called out the warning with a merry laugh, her eyes filling with tears at his joy.

"To hell with my arm!" he said, his face alight with happiness as he beamed down at her. "It hurts like the bloody devil, and I don't give a bloody damn. I'm free, Anne. I'm free."

"I know." Tears wended their way down her cheeks. "The curse is broken. You broke it when you shattered the sword."

He shook his head, laying a finger on her lips. "No, *annsachd*," he corrected. "You broke it with your love and your courage. I love you."

She smiled as happiness threatened to overwhelm her. "And I love you."

They were kissing, oblivious to the people who crowded in around them, shouting questions and demanding answers. Reluctantly they drew apart, but Ruairdh was careful to keep her tucked against him as he shared their joyous news with the household. The maids began to sob, and Mrs. Doughal wept copiously into her apron; even Angley, to Anne's utter amazement, began to cry, his pale blue eyes bright with moisture. Almost at once it was decided that they would host a grand dinner to celebrate. Ever the dutiful laird, Ruairdh granted them leave to do it, and then carried Anne off to their rooms for a private celebration.

Later that night, when they were cuddled in bed, Anne's heart swelled with love as she smiled languidly up at Ruairdh.

"I've just thought of something," she murmured,

pressing a kiss over his rapidly beating heart.

"What *mo ceile?*" he asked, teasing the bare flesh of her bottom with skillful fingers. "Talk fast; I am no' in a mood for one of your scholarly chats."

"Then you shan't receive one." She gave a masculine nipple a playful lick and then gazed back up at him. "What I was going to say is that now that the Shadowing is no longer an issue, there is no reason why you can't give me a child; isn't that so?"

His hand stopped moving, and his body responded at once to the suggestion. "Aye," he agreed, his voice suspiciously hoarse. "No reason at all."

"Good." She smiled beatifically at him, moving over him in unmistakable demand. "Then kindly dispense with those wretched sheaths. I want only you tonight—all of you. Is that quite clear?"

He grinned. "Aye, love, it is," he said, holding her in place as he slid easily inside of her. "And it's all of me you shall have." And he began making love to her with desperate want and frenzied need, the sound of their passion and later their laughter floating out the open window and ringing about the cobblestones of the courtyard.